JennKL

Originally from Houston, Texas, **GWENDOLYN WOMACK** studied theater at the University of Alaska, Fairbanks. She holds an MFA in Directing Theatre, Video and Cinema from California Institute of the Arts. Her first novel, *The Memory Painter,* was an RWA PRISM Award winner in the Time Travel/Steampunk category and a finalist for Best First Novel. She now resides in Los Angeles with her husband and her son.

gwendolynwomack.com

ALSO BY GWENDOLYN WOMACK

The Memory Painter

The Fortune Teller

GWENDOLYN WOMACK

PICADOR / NEW YORK

THE FORTUNE TELLER. Copyright © 2017 by Gwendolyn Womack. All rights reserved. Printed in the United States of America. For information, address Picador, 175 Fifth Avenue, New York, N.Y. 10010.

picadorusa.com • picadorbookroom.tumblr.com
twitter.com/picadorusa • facebook.com/picadorusa

Picador® is a U.S. registered trademark and is used by Macmillan Publishing Group, LLC, under license from Pan Books Limited.

For book club information, please visit facebook.com/picadorbookclub or e-mail marketing@picadorusa.com.

Designed by Jonathan Bennett

Library of Congress Cataloging-in-Publication Data

Names: Womack, Gwendolyn, 1970– author.
Title: The fortune teller : a novel / Gwendolyn Womack.
Description: First edition. | New York : Picador, 2017.
Identifiers: LCCN 2016058286 (print) | LCCN 2017004551 (e-book) |
    ISBN 9781250099778 (trade paperback) | ISBN 9781250099785 (e-book)
Subjects: | BISAC: FICTION / Romance / Suspense. | FICTION /
    Visionary & Metaphysical. | GSAFD: Mystery fiction. | Suspense fiction. |
    Occult fiction.
Classification: LCC PS3623.O597327 F67 2017 (print) | LCC PS3623.O597327
    (e-book) | DDC 813'.6—dc23
LC record available at https://lccn.loc.gov/2016058286

Our books may be purchased in bulk for promotional, educational, or business use. Please contact your local bookseller or the Macmillan Corporate and Premium Sales Department at 1-800-221-7945, extension 5442, or by e-mail at MacmillanSpecialMarkets@macmillan.com.

First Edition: June 2017

10 9 8 7 6 5 4 3 2 1

For Kurando and Kenzo

Some future acts are so inevitable they have been written on the Wall of the World. Like a scribe's words carved in stone on a temple doorway, nothing we can do will change the story.

~THE ORACLE OF WADJET

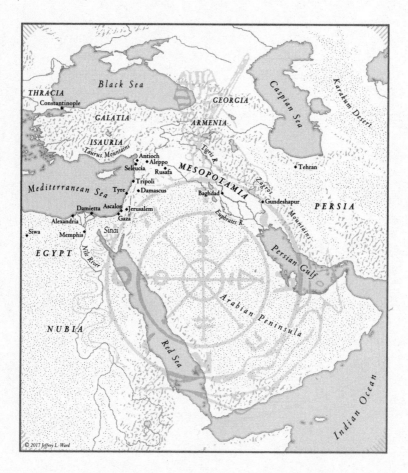

THRACIA
Constantinople
Black Sea
GEORGIA
Caspian Sea
Karakum Desert
GALATIA
ARMENIA
ISAURIA
Taurus Mountains
Antioch
Aleppo
Tigris R.
Seleucia
Rusafa
MESOPOTAMIA
Tehran
Tripoli
Zagros
Mediterranean Sea
Tyre
Damascus
Baghdad
Gundeshapur
PERSIA
Mountains
Damietta
Ascalon
Jerusalem
Euphrates R.
Alexandria
Gaza
Siwa
Memphis
Sinai
Persian Gulf
EGYPT
Nile River
Arabian Peninsula
NUBIA
Red Sea
Indian Ocean

© 2017 Jeffrey L. Ward

The Fool

The fireplace stood like a sentry in the room. Embers crackled and popped behind the grate, breaking the silence, and a log fell forward in a rain of sparks.

The flames bent and bloomed, spreading out their warmth, but Marcel could feel only coldness. His heart slowed and beat out of time, making each breath more difficult to take.

The glass of cognac slipped from his hand and tumbled across the carpet.

Unable to call out from his chair in the study, he looked toward the door and gripped his arm. The muscles of his heart closed tightly like a fist and squeezed until his body began to tremor.

Panic consumed him as his mind rode the pain to its pinnacle. He needed to tell Theo he had found her. He needed to tell Theo what to do—to warn him the manuscript was no longer safe.

He slid from his chair and tried to crawl to the phone at his desk. With a gasp, he rolled to his side and stared up at the framed photographs on the wall. His family looked down on him like angels.

Had he failed them?

His wife gazed at him with eyes full of peace. She had already made this journey. Three years ago he had watched her die—three long years. She would be waiting for him on the other side.

The certainty calmed him.

Relinquishing his last hold on life, his eyes glazed over and settled back onto the fire. His spirit departed like a thousand collapsing stars, leaving all his thoughts, all his secrets to burn away like paper.

The Magician

Semele was struck with déjà vu when she read Marcel Bossard's commemorative piece in *Art Conservator,* and the feeling wouldn't let her go.

She had never met Marcel Bossard personally, but she knew all about him. She knew his collection's history, the works that made up the collection, and over the years she'd tracked his pieces as they were donated or sold internationally.

Marcel had collected for the love of preserving history's fragile remnants. Now Semele was en route to his estate in Switzerland to place his treasures in the hands of people who could preserve them just as well.

On the plane ride from New York, she read countless articles and tributes she'd gathered over the past weeks. Only twenty individuals in the world had private collections like Marcel Bossard's, galleries that could be mistaken for rare manuscript museums, and his death last month had garnered a lot of media attention.

In the Manuscript Society's quarterly journal, there was an extensive piece on him titled "Marcel Bossard: A Personal History." It described him as the "last of the great collectors," a "Man of Letters," and "the epitome of grace and culture."

Fine Books & Collections magazine put him on the cover and included a four-page biographical piece celebrating his life. The photographer had taken a picture of him in his study at his château near Montreux. Marcel stood tall and elegant, a striking figure in a three-piece suit. An antique pocket watch dangled from his waist, and he held a bowler hat in his hand. His sandy brown hair and old-fashioned mustache made him look straight out of a saloon, and the mischievous laughter lurking in his eyes said he knew it.

From what Semele could gather, Marcel was a private man and quite eccentric. He was born into the family that owned Bossard & Vogle, one of Switzerland's oldest and most prestigious private banks dating back to the eighteenth century. He had remained at its helm until his death.

When the president of Semele's firm chose her to appraise and dismantle the Bossard Collection, her mouth had dropped open—not with surprise that she was going, but because she'd always hoped that one day she would. There were only a handful of appraisers qualified to oversee his collection, and Semele had spent years striving to be one of them.

From the moment Mikhail gave her the assignment to boarding the flight to Geneva, she could barely work or eat or sleep from the excitement. She couldn't help feeling that her whole career, everything she had worked toward, had been for this moment. The honor and responsibility was staggering.

Her anticipation heightened when the Bossards' driver met her at the airport and drove her straight to Marcel's château instead of her hotel. As they turned up the long drive and climbed the tree-lined slope toward a manor house, she caught herself biting her thumbnail and dropped her hand back into her lap. The estate looked like a Renaissance castle perched high on a hill.

In a few minutes she would be meeting her client, Marcel's only child, Theo Bossard. She didn't know much about him except that he was Marcel's only living relative and the heir to his estate. Theo had requested his father's entire collection be disbanded, not wanting to keep even one piece, a directive Semele found hard to fathom.

The driver parked and hurried to escort her from the car. She smoothed her hair and skirt when she stepped out, glad she had instinctively dressed for the meeting. Her vintage ribbed-knit dress and pillbox black jacket looked elegant yet comfortable. It would have to do.

The estate attorney, a stylish Swiss woman in her late forties, answered the door.

"Ms. Cavnow, so good of you to come," the woman said, clasping both of Semele's hands as if she were a friend.

"Thank you. The honor's mine." Semele stepped inside, momentarily feeling like Alice in the Looking Glass transported to a different world. It wasn't the grandeur that was unsettling so much as the feeling that she had been there before, as though she had buried a time capsule and suddenly rediscovered it.

Her feet felt like they were floating as she crossed the foyer; the black-and-white Art Deco marble drew her eyes. The entry hall was downright operatic and had more square footage than her apartment back in Brooklyn. It rose three stories high with a spiraling staircase that announced itself on a high C from the front door.

She crossed the hall and walked under a carved archway to the living room, where she was greeted with a breathtaking view. A wall of glass windows framed the distant Alps, and sofas divided the room geometrically. The space reminded her of a cozy ski lodge with its earth tones and leather—there was even a roaring fire in the stone fireplace.

Theo Bossard stood in front of the mantel. He was staring at the fire with his back to the door.

When Semele entered he turned around. She stopped walking, struck by the force of him. She fought to push the sensation away—the same déjà vu she'd had on the plane ride, only now it was stronger.

The feeling that they had met—would meet—vibrated at her core. Somehow she already knew this moment, down to the last detail: Theo, in his cashmere sweater; the way he stood; the way he emanated poise; his black hair and amber eyes, which added to the austere air surrounding him.

When their gazes met, she tugged at her jacket, self-consciously pulling it around her. "My condolences on your father's passing," she offered, finding her voice.

Theo inclined his head, seeming to see straight through her carefully crafted persona, the expert manuscript appraiser, only thirty-two, remarkably young for her achievements. She dressed in high-fashion vintage, wore only mascara and lipstick, and sported a sleek Ziegfeld bob that looked straight from the twenties.

Theo Bossard should have been charmed, been charming—given her a smile, a handshake, a welcoming gesture—but instead he looked at her with an unsettling seriousness, as if he had something important to say. The whole encounter left her unbalanced.

"Thank you, Semele," he murmured in a voice so soft she barely heard him at all. Then he said nothing more the entire meeting.

If their introduction seemed odd, the attorney was happy to fill the silence. She launched into a monologue about the expectations of the estate, though she had already discussed the details with Semele over the phone.

"We've reserved you a room at the Grand Hôtel Suisse Majestic, right across from Lake Geneva," the attorney explained. "The family driver will pick you up in the mornings; the château's chef can prepare your meals. . . ."

Semele could barely focus on what the woman was saying—she was too distracted by Theo. He was trailing several steps behind, keeping his gaze on her the entire time. Never had she been so unnerved by someone.

They headed to the room that housed the collection. Marcel Bossard had a special gallery situated off the main library, cloistered off from the rest of the estate.

Semele stepped inside and momentarily held her breath.

The enormous wood-paneled room contained every scroll, book, manuscript, and codex of the collection. A high-tech system controlled the temperature, humidity, and lighting, and all the works were locked away in electronic glass cases.

The attorney handed Semele several keys along with the codes to deactivate the security system, so she could come and go as needed.

"Four times a year a conservator from Geneva's Rath Museum comes to inspect the works for any damage and readjust the temperature settings," the woman explained, giving Semele a crisp nod. "Marcel took every precaution to protect his investment."

"Very impressive." Semele agreed.

She glanced at Theo and gave him an encouraging smile that he didn't reciprocate. He continued staring at her with unwavering intensity. She cleared her throat and turned away, deciding it would be best to ignore him.

～

When Semele arrived at the château the next day, she was filled with jittery nerves at the thought of seeing Theo again. Eager for a distraction, she spent long hours holed up in the gallery, appraising each piece and deciding its fate.

Most of the Bossard collection spanned from around A.D. 300 to the end of the Renaissance. She also cataloged twenty significant works from Classical Antiquity.

The collection included gospel books illuminated with pictures so stunning they looked like stained glass brought to life, scrolls of parchment detailing Roman battles, letters written by St. Augustine in A.D. 412, and a pristine collection of Greek manuscripts on botany, zoology, astrology, and astronomy from about A.D. 350. There was also a Bible embellished in twenty-four-karat gold from Constantinople, but the most jaw-dropping piece was an original *Recuyell of the Historyes of Troye* from the 1400s, the first book ever printed in the English language. Only eighteen copies existed.

Semele was already looking ahead to the work she would need

to do once she got back home. This was going to be the auction of the year, if not the decade. Her firm would hold a sale in New York for the most valuable pieces, and she would create smaller collections to donate to a select list of libraries and museums. The three weeks she had in Switzerland were barely enough time to sort everything out.

Each afternoon Theo would step into the gallery and ask, "Everything going well, Semele?" to which she would answer, "Quite well, thank you."

They would then stare at each other for a suspended moment, the air charged between them. Theo would eventually give her a slight nod and leave.

In her hotel room she would think about that day's encounter, reading more into their almost-conversations—the way he studied her, how he said her name—with each passing day. Then she would force herself to dismiss it all and try to sleep. She would lie restless in bed until she drifted off, unable to stop herself from imagining their next meeting.

In the morning, she found herself taking extra care with her appearance, to the point where every stroke of mascara felt like a guilty thought. She chose siren-red lipstick instead of her typical soft sienna, and wore her lavender angora sweater more times than not, knowing its feminine lines flattered her figure. She would turn from side to side in the mirror with critical precision, until the act of dressing for that single exchange with Theo began to feel like an infidelity to her boyfriend, Bren, back home.

Maybe she had acted the same way when getting ready for her first string of dates with Bren, but she couldn't remember her appearance ever having mattered this much. That's what bothered her the most. She wanted Theo to find her attractive.

Every day she tried not to look at the clock and wonder when he would stop by. She tried reasoning with herself. The château, its romanticism, and its eccentric owner were simply clouding her judgment. She enjoyed a good gothic novel as much as the next person, but that was not her real life.

⌣

One day Theo stayed longer. He looked as if he was about to leave, but instead he stopped at the door and turned back to her, his hands in the pockets of his slacks.

"You know, I met your father once," he said.

Semele stared at him, speechless. That was the last thing she thought he would say.

Theo must have sensed her confusion. "At one of the World Book summits years ago," he clarified. "He was keynote speaker for the International Federation of Library Associations. I had just begun working with UNESCO."

Semele had no idea Theo was connected to UNESCO. "What kind of work were you doing for them?" she asked.

"I head one of the subcommittees that assesses nominations for the Memory of the World Register."

She couldn't have been more surprised if he had told her he was an astronaut and had landed on the moon.

Her father had been a curator at Yale's Beinecke Rare Book & Manuscript Library, and she knew all about UNESCO's global conservation programs, including MOW nominations. Memory of the World was an international initiative to preserve archives and library collections that transcended the boundaries of culture. Being listed on the register was just as impressive as getting a National Historic Site designation and ensured that those works would survive.

"He gave a wonderful speech about the history of the world's libraries and their effects on different time periods." Theo gave her his first real smile.

Semele couldn't help giving a faint smile back. She could just imagine her father talking about his favorite subject. How every second a book somewhere in the world disappeared, destroyed by the divine hand of time for any number of reasons—natural disasters, worms, insects, rats, humans. Even the acid in paper worked against a book's survival. It drove him mad.

"Well," Theo said, looking uncomfortable, "please give him my best."

Semele only nodded, unable to explain that her father had passed away earlier this year. The loss still gripped her like it was yesterday. She and Theo had more in common than he knew. That he had met her father made her look at him differently.

When she went back to the hotel that night, she decided to google Theo. What she discovered surprised her even more.

Theo owned a computer software company that specialized in storing high-value information. His client list included Fortune 500 companies and government institutions. They were also working with the Japanese IT specialists who were archiving the Vatican's library—over 82,000 manuscripts and 41 million pages.

She read every news article and press release she could find, both impressed and intimidated at the same time. Talk about out of her league—the pope was his client.

In one interview he discussed the vital need for engineering long-term digital preservation, explaining that the digital world had its own set of threats and needed to be safeguarded, or one day, digital archives would vanish too. Files were no different from papyrus or parchment.

Semele devoured every word. Astounded by how similar their philosophies were, her attraction to him only became more real and unsettling. She liked it better when she had assumed he was just an eccentric heir.

Now she was beginning to feel serious guilt over her fixation. People in relationships didn't spend all night on the Internet reading about their clients for personal interest, especially not when they were in a relationship with someone like Bren.

While she was in Switzerland, he had been leaving her the sweetest voice mails. She had listened to one yesterday on the drive to the estate, and it still made her smile.

"This one is Yeats." He recited the poem, his voice soft and intimate. "*When you are old and grey and full of sleep, and nodding by the fire, take down this book, and slowly read and dream. . . .*"

But the car had started to pull up the drive and she'd saved the message, promising herself she would listen to the rest later. With a pang of guilt, she realized she hadn't finished it yet, or the two others he'd left her.

Even when she wasn't traveling he liked to leave her poems, from classical to contemporary to his own creations. Bren was an English professor at CUNY, a published poet, and unapologetically sentimental. They had been together for almost two years—her longest relationship to date—and she had never thought twice about another man, until now.

She began to count down the days until she left Montreux. It would be a relief to put an ocean between her and Theo. During her last week, she would wake up and sit outside on her hotel balcony, feeling the future looming across the lake, imminent and inescapable. Something was going to happen here. She could feel it. And she had no idea if she was ready.

⌒

When the last day of her assignment finally arrived, anticipation tightened inside her like a coil ready to snap. She awoke early that morning, unable to sleep, and arrived at the château two hours before her usual start time, to finish preparing all the shipments and review the letters of export.

A deep sense of melancholy hit her as she sealed the crates. Marcel had devoted his whole life to preserving these antiquities, and now they would never reside under his roof again. Disbanding a collection sometimes felt like lowering the curtain on closing night; it had to be the hardest part of her job. She only hoped that Marcel would approve of her decisions if he were still alive.

For a moment she gave in to the sadness and sat down, staring at all the crates. The longer she sat there, the more uneasy she began to feel that she'd missed something.

She got up and double-checked the official collection registry against her shipping schedules. Then she looked in all the display cases to make sure nothing had been left behind. Every item was accounted for and ready for transport. Still, anxiety consumed her.

Somehow she knew she had made a mistake.

She told herself the feeling was normal, nothing more than the stress of having to ship priceless manuscripts halfway around the world. But as hard as she tried to calm her nerves, she wouldn't rest easy until she had checked all the rosters again. Luckily, it was still morning; she had plenty of time. She would review the shipments after she had a quick coffee in the kitchen. Perhaps the chef had even made some of his fresh-baked *bürli* and marmalade. She hadn't eaten anything yet today.

When she went to set the security alarm in the gallery, her eyes landed on the wooden cabinet underneath the examination table.

Her hand stilled on the keypad.

She had never looked inside, assuming the cabinet held supplies, but it had been catching her eye all week.

She knelt down and opened the door to find an industrial safe bolted to the ground. The cabinet was just a decorative cover. It was steel-gauge with two electronic keypad locks. She tried using the gallery security codes, not sure if they would work.

To her surprise, they did, and her excitement skyrocketed. She opened the door to find only one object inside, a thick leather-bound book wrapped in linen. Goose bumps ran down her arms.

She brought the heavy book to the examining table and unwrapped the fabric to unveil a glorious codex.

"Oh my God," she whispered. The hairs on her arms rose and the silence in the room magnified. Even the air turned electric. The years this artifact had weathered seemed to radiate from it, hovering like a band of energy.

In her years of appraising she had come to understand that, sometimes, collectors kept secrets. She had just found Marcel's.

She hurried to the bathroom to wash her hands so she could touch the parchment without damaging the pages. She returned, now completely in the zone, and opened the cover with hands like a surgeon's.

When she saw the writing, her body had a visceral reaction. The penmanship was exquisite, a treasure in and of itself. The carbon-black ink remained rich and unfaded, and the script stood out from the parchment with a strength untarnished by the years.

Engraved on the first parchment leaf were four words in flowing ancient Greek script. She began to translate:

My Chronicles Through Time

The symbols resembled works of art. What was this exquisite work, and why wasn't it in the collection's registry?

Semele turned over the first leaf and gasped.

A piece of stationery was wedged between the leaves. Slowly, she removed the paper, wondering who on earth could have been so careless.

Her heart stopped when she read the note:

Semele,
Tell no one what you find written in these pages.
Translate the words and you will understand.
You can trust no one now.
Marcel

Semele felt as if she'd been touched by a ghost. She reread the note over and over in disbelief. Marcel Bossard had written to her—which was impossible. The man had died before his estate ever contacted her firm.

How had he known her name?

To my reader: I can see what time you live in, and I feel your eyes upon me. We are from different eras, you and I, and by the time you are reading these words, my ancient world will have long been buried. I am one you call a seer—someone who can divine the future and divine it well.

The power of intuition will have ebbed in your time, so you may not believe this story, or worse, think it a fable. But I assure you, my tale is true. I will begin by telling you about my life before, when I was a girl in Alexandria, Egypt.

In my youth, I did not know I had the sight. Only at certain times did the faintest glimpses of what was to come strike me like glimmers of light. Suddenly, I could see when the rains would fall, whether my brother would marry, if my father would buy me the *wesekh* collar from the market. This kind of simple knowledge would present itself, but for the most part, I thought nothing of these inklings.

Only once did a dark premonition creep into my mind. My mother was eight months with child when one night she asked me to comb her hair after her bath. I was smoothing her long tresses when the feeling gripped me. I knew I would never touch her hair again.

The next morning I heard her moans, and my brothers ran to get the old women we called the birth goddesses to help bring our new sibling into the world. For hours we huddled outside the room, listening to our mother fight for both their lives. The long silence that came afterward told me she and the baby had not won.

Perhaps if my mother had survived, she could have taught me about my gift and eased me into understanding, for I often wondered if she too had possessed the sight. Instead, she left me orphaned with searching thoughts and a precocious nature that my father encouraged. For I was a librarian's daughter—his daughter—and not from just any library, but the Library of Alexandria, the largest in the known world.

The great library and connecting Musaeum were Alexandria's pride, and had been since the city's birth hundreds of years ago. Just as our lighthouse, the tallest lighthouse ever built, could signal any ship at sea, so too was the library a beacon of light, offering its wisdom to every seeking mind.

My family's position at the library extended back to Alexandria's first days. Alexander the Great founded the city but died shortly afterward, and his trusted general, Ptolemy Lagides, had claimed Egypt as his own. It was his advisor, Demetrius Phalereus, who hatched the plan to build the library and make Alexandria the Navel of the World.

When word reached Athens that a magnificent temple to the Muses—the Musaeum—was being constructed and would serve as a prominent university, Aristotle's students began the pilgrimage from the Lyceum. One of those scholars was my ancestor. Since then, every male in my family has taken his place at the library with high honor. Even I, a young girl, enjoyed the privilege of my father's station. Librarians were close to royalty in stature, so no one dared to question me when I roamed the grounds.

Imagine that the most majestic palace from Mount Olympus had been handed down to earth. This is how splendid the Musaeum was. Marble walls gleamed like hammered pearls in the sun, and a domed ceiling arched its graceful back against the sky.

Inside, meeting halls, theaters, and an observatory composed the complex, along with a dining hall for scholars to break bread. A grand colonnade led from the Musaeum to the library's main doors, and linked pathways to the zoo and botanical gardens—each another vainglory of Egypt's new ruling family, the Ptolemies.

In the library's interior, murals depicted the creation of the world and man's quest for knowledge. Ten halls, each devoted to a specific subject, connected alcoves and circular reading rooms. These halls were massive, the size of any other city's library.

I used to pretend to go on official errands and then hide in the empty alcoves to read what the great minds had to say. I would find a cushioned seat in a quiet corner, lay out my chosen scroll, and watch dust scatter and catch the sunlight as I unrolled the parchment.

The library's works spanned thousands of years, exploring medicine, religion, astronomy, geography, mathematics, philosophy, physics, and the arts. Most scrolls and codices were either written in Greek or translated to Greek by the library's army of translators.

My brothers were appointed as both translators and transcribers—a great honor—though their excitement quickly turned to horror once they saw the never-ending pile of work. The Ptolemies confiscated the books from every ship entering our ports so they could be copied. Usually the library kept the originals, only giving back the copies. Entire warehouses at the harbor stored countless texts that had yet to be sorted and translated.

The transcribers worked at a mad pace, sequestered in small, candlelit chambers in the back of the library. The translations and annotated editions they created were exquisite, but still there was never enough time.

I tried to offer my services to my brothers, to deliver messages or food to them—anything to give me a reason to be inside those walls. How could I be anywhere else? I was a librarian's daughter, spoiled, imaginative, and a voracious reader.

But my simple life changed the day I found the key.

On my eighteenth birthday, my father surprised me with the *wesekh* collar I had seen at the market. I went to put the necklace in my mother's jewelry box, where I kept all my jewels and ornaments. A Trove of Isis, the lacquered inlay chest had been in our family for centuries. The wooden jewelry box had hidden panels and dainty drawers to hold pendants and gems.

I lifted one tray to place the collar in the bottommost compartment and discovered a panel I hadn't known existed. When I found the secret latch and opened it, my breath caught. An ornate gold key was nestled inside the nook. I would have recognized that key anywhere. Why my mother had a key to one of the library's chambers was a mystery.

When I read the inscription, a chill traveled over me. This was a key to the subterranean galleries, where the oldest works were kept away from the light. I had never visited the lower galleries—no one could except for the pharaoh and his most trusted associates.

I should have told my father I had discovered the key, but I did not. My curiosity burned. I obsessed about the key for days, wanting desperately to use it. When I could no longer withstand the temptation, I selected a day when an important lecture would be under way at the Musaeum and I knew the library would be empty.

To the average eye, the dull wooden door to the lower gallery appeared to conceal nothing more than a storage room. I only knew its location because my father had told me. He loved to share stories about the treasures in the lower gallery, and I had begged him once to show me the door. My knowledge became our secret.

I was betraying his trust by using the key. I had no right to wander down there alone, but on that particular day I could not stop myself. A sense of inevitability gripped me as I waited breathlessly in a nearby alcove for the perfect moment. When I could see no person in sight, I dashed to the door.

The key slid in easily and released the lock. My heart was beating so fast I could barely breathe. I grabbed a lantern off the wall and entered, leaving the door slightly cracked so I wouldn't be locked inside. Then I hurried down the stairwell.

I held my lantern up to the shadows and gasped in awe. Thousands of papyrus scrolls filled the gallery and extended as far as my eyes could see. The authors' names had been written on wooden plaques that hung from cords tied around ceramic canisters. Carved stones, wood, animal skins, and clay tablets lined the shelves as well. It was like tracing the history of thought back through time. Every material humans had used to cast their words had been preserved.

The number of works kept in those galleries must have been greater than the stars in our sky. As I moved through each room I could feel its hallowed ground, and when I stepped inside the last gallery, it was as though I could smell the years. Scents of faded musk and frankincense greeted me along with the reek of mold. I knew I had found the library's oldest works.

My father often recounted how Alexandria was founded by the divine lunacy of Alexander the Great, how he had a dream telling him to come to the island of Pharos. So he did, bringing with him the ancient manuscripts from Siwa, manuscripts said to have belonged to the first rulers of Egypt, the gods. The great Oracle of Ammon and the Siwan priests had protected those manuscripts for thousands of years. But when Alexander became pharaoh and declared himself son of Zeus, he took many of the works with him to the new city, to be housed like jewels in his royal library. And here they were, these priceless treasures.

I knew I should not have been disturbing such a place, but I was struck by the sight before me. I could not move. Then I saw a small stone box decorated with strange symbols sitting at eye level on one of the shelves. My hands reached out, moving of their own volition, and before I could question my actions, I opened it.

Inside lay a dainty stack of papyrus squares with pictorial-like designs. Every square had its own image with hieroglyphs inscribed at the bottom. The paintings were rich in detail, portraying a myriad of symbols: the sun, the moon, two lovers, a hermit holding a lantern, the scales of justice, a chariot racing, and an ancient mandala of the world. I counted twenty-two in all. A papyrus scroll rested beside them.

More than anything in my life, I wanted to understand what I had found. I knelt on the floor, not caring about dust or dirt, and spread the pictures out to see them together in unity. Even though I was unschooled in the art of divination, I knew I was staring at the cycle of life, from birth to death, in all its aspects.

"What are you doing?" came a hushed whisper.

I turned around with a start, frozen in terror.

A man, slightly older than me, stood in the doorway holding up a lantern. From his modest robes, I could tell he was a student. A mane of curling black hair framed his striking brown eyes. He looked like a lion ready to pounce on his prey.

"What are you doing?" he whispered again, seeming both fascinated and astounded by my behavior.

"What are *you* doing?" I retorted, keeping my voice quiet. My cheeks flamed with embarrassment and I sat up straighter. "You shouldn't be down here."

"And you should?"

"I'm investigating articles for my father."

"On the floor?" he asked, his voice rising in disbelief.

"I am Ionna Callas, daughter of Phileas," I said, as if that was answer enough.

He looked startled and satisfaction filled me. My father was one of the head librarians and his name carried weight. He held the second-highest-ranking position at the library, next to the director who was chosen by the pharaoh. He was also a scholar in his own right and widely respected for both his literary studies and scientific investigations.

I held up the key with confidence. "And you are?" I resisted the urge to sweep the papyrus back into the box.

"Ariston Betesh, from Antioch." He nodded as his gaze took in every detail about me.

I smoothed my robe, glad I had worn the sage today. The color matched my eyes, making the most of my black hair and olive skin. The faint smile hovering on his lips told me he agreed, and heat rose to my face.

"Did your father really give you that key or did you steal it?"

"This key is mine," I told him, trying to sound insulted. Technically it was not a lie. I *had* inherited my mother's jewelry box and its contents. "Why are you down here?"

"The door was open. Curiosity is the scholar's bread." He stepped forward to study the papyrus squares. "What are those?" he asked, peering over my shoulder.

"Ariston?" a hushed voice called from above the stairwell. Someone was looking for him.

Ariston turned in haste. "I'm afraid my questions will have to wait, daughter of Phileas." His words sounded like a promise, and with a wink, he left.

Not wanting to risk discovery again, I returned the papyrus and scroll to the shelf and hurried up the stairwell.

When I stepped outside to lock the door, Ariston was nowhere in sight.

⌒

That night I couldn't sleep. I could think only of the stone box, the symbols . . . and Ariston. I was certain we would meet again.

When I awoke the next morning I was gripped by the urge to re-create the first image from the box, a young man carrying a walking stick in the wilderness. My abilities would be stretched, but still I wanted to try.

I borrowed a sheet of parchment from my father's basket and used my brother's carving knife to cut a square the same size as the papyrus. Then I prepared the paint. Years ago my father had given me a special box of ground-mineral pigments: gypsum, carbon, iron oxides of red and yellow, azurite, and malachite. I mixed the pigments with water and wood resin to the right consistency and made a palette.

I closed my eyes and, with my reed brush in hand, tried to conjure the first image, but instead I saw Ariston looming over me. I dearly hoped he would not share our secret. The chastening my father would give me would be worse than any punishment from Zeus. My father might even ban me from the library forever. I shuddered at the thought.

For days I stayed away from the library and struggled to recreate the first image. I was convinced my father would barge into my room at any moment, demanding to know what I had been doing in the lower galleries. But he never came, and I knew Ariston had not said a word.

Since my misconduct had not been discovered, I decided surely this was a sign I could return again. This time I took special care in my appearance. I chose my most alluring gown, a deep crimson, and adorned the ends of my plated hair with gold beads. I lined my eyes with kohl and gave my cheeks and lips a subtle stain of red ochre. I chose one of my mother's most enticing perfumes, letting its scents of lily, myrrh, and cinnamon envelop me like a cloak.

I strolled through the entire library hoping to discover Ariston, but he was nowhere to be found. Disappointed that my efforts had earned me only the stares of several old men, I abandoned the search and headed to the secret door with my key and parchment square in hand. As I hurried with the lock, I heard a voice behind me.

"So the goddess returns."

I spun around. Ariston had been waiting for me. My heart fluttered like a bird taking flight.

"Another task for your father?" he asked, coming toward me. We both knew I had not been on official business last time, nor was I now.

Footsteps sounded on the marble behind us. Someone was coming, and there we were with the library's most secret door wide open. Ariston grabbed a lantern and pulled me inside the stairwell. We waited, huddled together until we heard the footsteps pass.

"Why have you returned?" he asked in a whisper. "Do you have a death wish?"

"I needed to see something," I whispered back. "Why are you here?"

"I needed to see something too."

We locked eyes. I could tell he meant me. Thankfully, the darkness hid my silly smile.

Then he whispered with a knowing smile, "Lead the way, daughter of Phileas."

We descended the stone staircase and I quickly headed toward the last gallery, leaving him to follow behind. I arrived at the last alcove and reached for the stone box.

His eyes grew wide when he saw the square in my hand. "You took one?"

"Of course not," I said, pleased he had mistaken my replica for the original. "See? There are no hieroglyphs."

"You painted this?" His voice rose and I shushed him.

He bent to look at my work, and the top of his head leaned so close that I could smell the juniper berries and honey in his hair. I frowned, wondering if a woman had made him such a tonic, if he already belonged to another.

"You're quite good," he said. "Yes, I see now." Then he took out the papyrus squares from the stone box, handling them nimbly. I could tell he was as taken with them as I was. He read the hieroglyph on the first image aloud.

The word sounded strange, but I refused to ask its meaning. My face, however, gave me away.

He needled me playfully. "The librarian's daughter only knows Greek?"

I could not help bristling. Most highborns only knew Greek. We were all, in essence, Greeks in Egypt. Even the Ptolemies had never bothered to learn the language of the land.

Young Cleopatra, daughter of Ptolemy XII, was the first royal ever to master Egyptian. She was my age and not only graceful but also a gifted linguist. I had heard her speak in eight different tongues fluently and quote many great works at length from memory. She was perhaps the only girl in Alexandria who loved the library more than me.

Now I wished I had attempted to learn Egyptian so I could impress Ariston, but I had to admit that I never had. "What does it mean?"

"It means 'the fool.'"

I studied him to see if he was mocking me, but he wasn't.

"I've never seen anything like them," he said. "These must have come from Siwa, from the Old Time."

I nodded, already suspecting as much. The Old Time was Egypt's most ancient history. Few works had survived from those years, but legends of secret scrolls and magical texts hidden in these caverns abounded.

"Do you see how each has a different name?" he pointed out.

"I can't read them," I reminded him, no longer trying to mask my disappointment.

"Well, I can tell you what they say," he offered. "That's simple enough."

"Can you translate the scroll?" I asked, trying not to grow too excited. His eyebrows rose at my daring. So I teased him, repeating what he had said to me. "Curiosity is the scholar's bread."

His eyes glinted with amusement and he took the scroll. "The papyrus is frayed and the writing is barely legible. Plus it's an ancient form of hieroglyph. Translating would take time."

"Still," I pressed, putting my hand on his arm, "you could do it."

"For you, I could," he surprised me by saying. "Meet me at the door every other morning, and I'll transcribe a section to translate."

"And I can study the images and try to re-create them."

"Excellent." He seemed pleased with himself. "That should take us a while."

We looked at each other and smiled. My eyes gravitated toward his lips, taking in their sensual curve. If he tried to kiss me now, I would let him. The prospect of clandestine meetings with Ariston filled me with anticipation. What we were about to do was reckless, forbidden—and also the most important task I would undertake in my young life.

Looking back, I never could have attempted to read the scroll without him. Ariston risked disgracing his family's good name to help me. Hindsight offers many treasures, clarity being one. Only later, after Ariston finished translating the scroll, would I understand that finding the key and stone box had not been an accident at all.

Ace of Pentacles

Semele squinted at the ancient Greek letters, unsure if she was getting the translation right. . . .

Was it *had not been an accident*?

Or *fated*?

Or maybe *marked by the gods*?

She took off her magnifying glasses and rubbed her forehead, feeling a headache coming on. Her translation abilities were rusty, which had made reading a slow process. She needed all three of her dictionaries to decipher every other line.

But if she had gotten the translation right so far—and she believed the story's narrator—then this memoir was written during the time of Cleopatra, who was born in 69 B.C.

Semele studied Ionna's handwriting, taking in every brush-stroke.

Paleography, dating an artifact through its writing, was her expertise. Oftentimes handwriting and the style of script were more precise measures of when a work was written than carbon dating. The shade, ornamentation, and capitalization of letters, the style of parchment, and the ink were all clues, and Semele was a master at time-stamping anything from the classical world.

Based on the handwriting alone, Marcel's mysterious manuscript looked to be from between 50 and 45 B.C. If Ionna was truly the memoirist, then Semele's estimate was not off the mark. She would be surprised if she was wrong—still, she wanted to test the manuscript when she returned to New York; she had never seen a two-thousand-year-old text so well preserved. The announcement of this discovery would send ripples through the whole industry. She had to be sure.

She turned off the examining light and leaned back in her chair, barely able to contain the thoughts running through her head.

For now she would say nothing to her client. She didn't want to create any false expectations in case she was wrong and this manuscript was simply a tale penned by a writer in the Middle Ages. It wouldn't be the first time a clergyman with an overactive imagination had written an "ancient chronicle."

Semele looked at Marcel's cryptic note again, still unnerved by his warning, and fingered the stationery in her hand. It was an engraved four-ply-cotton card, heavy stock, and clearly quite expensive.

The door opened, startling her, and a maid entered.

"I hope I'm not intruding," the young woman said with a charming French accent.

Semele tucked the paper into her pocket and forced a smile. "Of course not."

If the maid noticed Semele's suspicious gesture, she hid it and went about dusting the glass cases. To Semele the chore seemed quite pointless—every surface in the room was already gleaming. She watched the girl make a circle of the gallery, wishing the maid would go away so she could lock up and head to the kitchen for a coffee. She was going to need serious amounts of caffeine in order to make sense of this note.

Why had Marcel written to her? And how had he known her name?

"What do you think you're doing?"

Semele turned around with a start.

Theo stood in the doorway with an incensed look on his face.

She got up from her seat, at first thinking he was talking to her, but he pulled the maid aside and began reprimanding her in rapid-fire French. The maid murmured a quick apology and scurried out of the room.

Theo must have seen the horrified look on Semele's face. He shook his head, trying to calm down. "Forgive me. This room is off-limits to the house staff."

"Yes, I can see that," Semele said, although she didn't quite understand what had happened. Did he just fire the maid for dusting?

"Everything going well?" he asked, forcibly changing the subject.

Semele followed his lead and fixed a smile on her face. "Just wrapping up. I'll e-mail you the list this afternoon."

The list comprised those items she would be taking back to New York for auction. She knew Theo was waiting to find out how many pieces her firm would be selling. The heirs always were.

To her dismay, instead of leaving, Theo walked toward her. She tried not to step back as he stood next to her at the examining table.

He stared down at the manuscript. "What about this one? What do you think?"

What a loaded question—Semele was unsure how to answer. She decided to play it safe and rattled off a general analysis of the manuscript's condition, sounding more like a doctor giving a diagnosis. "The pages look fairly well preserved. Some disintegration is showing around the edges, and speckled mold is scattered throughout the text, but no more than one might expect. I also noted water damage on several leaves."

"But what do you think?" he asked again.

"Um . . . I'm actually not sure yet," she said honestly. "I only just discovered it this morning. It hadn't been recorded in the collection for some reason. Did your father ever discuss this piece with you?" she asked, trying to gauge his reaction.

"Why?" He met her gaze with the hint of a challenge.

Semele could feel heat rising to her face. "Since it wasn't

noted in the collection, I wondered if he had special instructions for it."

How she would have loved to ask Marcel why he had hidden this piece away and how he had known to address his note to her. But she couldn't—and she definitely couldn't ask Theo.

Here they were having their second real conversation, and she was horrified to discover he still made her tongue-tied. It didn't help that today he appeared energized and slightly windswept, as if he had just galloped across the estate on a horse. She wasn't sure if the strange performance jacket he was wearing was high-tech riding or ski gear. At this point she wouldn't be surprised if he was an expert in both sports and had an Olympic medal shoved in a drawer somewhere.

"I would like to take it back to New York." She cleared her throat. "I should know more within a few weeks. The piece could potentially generate a large sum at the auction." *That* was an understatement, she thought.

"Good. Please take the utmost care with it. This manuscript was special to my father."

His admission surprised her. So Marcel *had* discussed the manuscript; Theo just didn't want to discuss it with her. Which begged another question: Did Theo know about the note? There were so many things she wanted to ask him, but Theo had turned away and was now absentmindedly surveying the room.

"I can see you've been quite industrious. How much longer do we have the pleasure of your company?"

Semele frowned, not sure how to take the remark. "I fly back tomorrow, thank you," she answered, knowing she sounded stiff.

He gave her a faint smile, and his gaze trailed over her face again.

She could feel her cheeks starting to burn and fought to control it, becoming annoyed with herself.

"Do keep me informed of your progress. You have my numbers and can call me anytime."

Again, he looked as if he wanted to say something more, just as he had at their first meeting and every day since.

She waited, the knot of anticipation tightening in her stomach. But the words never came.

"I'm afraid I leave tonight on business." He went to the door. "Please take every precaution and safeguard my father's collection. I'm sure you know better than I do, but there are some very special pieces in this room."

Semele nodded, about to reassure him, but then he was gone.

What a strange man. Of course she would safeguard the collection. Why else was she here?

Text message to VS—

She found it.

Reply from VS—

Excellent. We are in play.

The High Priestess

Semele's instincts told her she needed to make a copy of the manuscript right away. Usually flagging an item for digitization meant involving a preservation manager, a collections manager, and a photographer. They would all discuss handling issues, customize the cradle to hold the manuscript, and come up with contingencies to avoid any undue stress on the parchment. That was the ideal scenario. But occasionally when working in the field, she needed to digitize a work before transporting it back to New York—like today.

She set up her tripod, which had a pan-tilting head so she could shoot the image flat on the table. Then she mounted her camera, along with a special scanning camera, and positioned her portable high-intensity discharge lamps to provide a continuous light source.

She kept waiting for Theo to barge in and question what the hell she was doing, just like he had to the maid. Her hands became unsteady and she could feel the frown locked on her face. The quality of several leaves looked tenuous. Two thousand years were weighing on this parchment like invisible stones; it was a heavy burden to carry.

When the last page had been digitized, a wave of dizziness hit her and she closed her eyes until it passed.

She had been working with unwavering focus for several hours. Now she was completely drained. But when she opened the file on her laptop to double-check her work, what she saw made her whistle. The quality of her scan was a hundred times better than any image from a commercial digital camera. Every blot of ink and speck of dust had been captured in the minutest detail: it looked like an exact replica.

She dismantled all the equipment and then carefully packed the manuscript in the last remaining crate, her mind still reeling from her eleventh-hour discovery. What if she hadn't looked in the cabinet?

The thought that she might have left Switzerland without finding this jewel horrified her. She still couldn't believe there was no mention of the manuscript in the official registry.

The grandfather clock in the hall struck four and she glanced at her watch in surprise. The day had vanished. The courier would be here soon, but there was one more thing she had to do before leaving the château. She needed to make sure Marcel was really the one who had written her the message.

She pulled Marcel's note from her pocket and studied it again. The writing had a distinctive right-slanted scrawl with wide spacing, connected letters, and restricted loops. Her mind automatically began to list the defining traits: he was larger than life, generous but cautious, and signs of tension marked his penmanship. She needed only to see a small sample to be sure.

Hurrying across the gallery, she ducked into Marcel's personal study. She usually passed through the room to access the kitchen, but today she stopped and closed the door. The chances of one of the staff coming in were slim, but she couldn't risk anyone seeing what she was about to do.

She rushed to the sixteenth-century mahogany writing desk and opened all the drawers, where she found ledgers, letters, even an old appointment book—more evidence than she needed.

Within seconds she had her answer. All the handwriting was identical to the note. Marcel *had* written to her. Now the question that remained was why.

But there was nothing more she could do here. She needed

to discuss the situation with Mikhail when she got home. He would know how to handle the dilemma.

She was about to leave when her eyes settled on the family photographs hanging above the fireplace. They ranged from daguerreotypes taken in the 1800s to pictures that looked quite recent. She didn't know who all the people were but she could feel the love, the sense of friendship that emanated from them.

In a grand house such as this, her favorite room would be this one, and she was certain it had been Marcel's too. She felt as if she had gotten to know him through the weeks she'd spent here.

She studied a picture of a much younger Marcel with his wife. Theo stood wedged between their legs, only five or six years old. An older woman, most likely his grandmother, hovered to the side. Semele looked at the other photos of Theo. There was one with his mother that appeared to be the most recent. She knew that Mrs. Bossard had passed away three years ago from breast cancer. In the picture Theo had his arms around her and was laughing. He didn't look like his current self at all.

Semele couldn't stop staring at the picture. Something about it made her wistful.

The desire struck her to go visit a few of the other rooms one last time before she left. Her only opportunity to explore the château had been on that first day. There was a small reading library upstairs, where she'd spied several jaw-dropping first editions perched on a bookshelf, including an *Orbis Sensualium Pictus,* the earliest picture book for children, first published in 1658. She had to know if it was an original.

It would just take a minute. Surely no one would mind—Theo was gone and the housekeeper had already said her good-byes. The only person left was the chef, who was probably in the kitchen drinking wine and watching his favorite Swiss cooking show. But as she ventured up the sweeping staircase, she began to second-guess her nerve—*Orbis* or no *Orbis,* she felt like an intruder. Halfway down the hall, she was ready to turn around when she saw that the bedroom door directly across from her was open. What she saw inside made her freeze.

Theo was sitting on a king-size bed in the middle of a room that looked like it had been plucked straight out of a Tudor manor. He was wearing only sweatpants and sitting cross-legged, meditating with his eyes closed and an open hand on each knee.

He looked like Leonardo da Vinci's *Vitruvian Man* come to life and reclining in repose. The air around him felt charged.

Semele stood watching him until a glimmer of awareness finally returned to her and she realized how this must look. She was a professional, one of the best in her field, and here she was hovering at her client's bedroom door like a Peeping Tom.

Tiptoeing backward, she fled through the hall and ran down the stairs, jumping the last two. She dashed back to the gallery and closed the door. "Jesus!" That had been completely ridiculous.

Mortified, she put her hands to her face, still in a panic. If she had been discovered . . . She tried to calm down but spent two solid minutes pacing the room.

Needing a distraction, she grabbed her laptop and made her way to the kitchen for a visit with the chef and a cappuccino. When he offered her a glass of Petite Arvine from the local vineyard, Semele changed her mind.

The debacle upstairs called for wine.

She perched on a stool at the kitchen island and sipped the golden white. The chef tried to offer her a late lunch, but she declined, too worked up to eat.

She opened her laptop to try to take her mind off Theo. What she really wanted to do was read more of the manuscript, but she didn't feel comfortable working on the translation in front of anyone. What if Theo came downstairs? Just the thought made her stomach do a somersault.

Instead she logged in to her company's server, where there was a running news stream of sales happening at various auction houses around the world. She forced herself to focus on the recent highlights.

Sotheby's had sold twelve items of a collection she was quite familiar with for $14.9 million. One of her associates at the firm, Fritz Wagner, had managed the auction. She made a mental note to send him a bottle of champagne when she got back.

A copy of the Torah had set a record, selling for $3.85 million, and a *Titanic* letter had sold for $200K. It seemed like all the usual suspects were up for grabs this week. Writings from Abraham Lincoln's journals—the man wrote more than a million words in his lifetime—and works by Thomas Jefferson and the Beatles too. And it looked like Bonhams had just sold the second of two known copies of the first edition of *The Wonderful Wizard of Oz* for $100K.

The next listing grabbed her attention.

Sotheby's had auctioned off an entire private manuscript collection for $2.5 million. The collection was billed as "a representation of the history of the written word in Europe" and contained pieces from Early Antiquity to the Renaissance, including several rare works from the Dark and Medieval Ages in a myriad of languages: Latin, Hebrew, Greek, Syriac, Armenian, and Old English. The catalog would be an excellent reference. Semele studied the list of all sixty items and started to take notes.

Half an hour later she reached for her wine and realized she had finished it. When the chef asked if she would like another, she slid the glass forward.

As she watched him pour, she noticed he wore a Geiger watch like her father's. She had been meaning to ask her mother if she could have the watch as a keepsake, only they weren't speaking to each other now.

With a sigh she sipped the wine and moved on to checking e-mail. There was one from Bren letting her know he had made a reservation at La Grenouille for tomorrow night.

Her eyebrows rose as she read—the place was a landmark, where Elizabeth Taylor, Frank Sinatra, and Salvador Dalí had all dined by candlelight and roses. Semele and Bren had been to La Grenouille once before on a business dinner with a collector her firm was courting. Over Grand Marnier soufflés Bren had whispered that he'd bring her back for a special occasion. Semele was beginning to wonder just what he had in mind.

Was he planning to turn dinner into something more than an anniversary celebration? An image of him placing a ring-sized box on the table took shape in her mind. Surely he wasn't going to propose. They weren't at that stage yet. She brushed the thought aside.

In his e-mail he had attached a funny picture of himself holding a handwritten sign that said LOST AND LONELY. It made her smile.

They had barely spoken the past three weeks. Whenever she tried to call, she got his voice mail because he was tied up in class. Switzerland was five hours ahead, so most of their conversations ended up happening over e-mail and texts. But Bren understood how consumed she was by her assignments. Out of the twenty days she had been in Switzerland, she'd allowed herself only one day off to play tourist.

Last week she had strolled the gorgeous lakeside walk to Château de Chillon, the famous island castle on the edge of Lake Geneva. The castle looked like it was literally rising from the water; its construction was a marvel of architecture and steeped in a thousand years of history. It had been everything from a Roman stronghold to a royal summerhouse to a prison.

Semele spent the morning touring the grounds, looking out Gothic windows and wandering along the sentry walks. She visited the Clos de Chillon wine cellar, where monk François Bonivard, the hero of Lord Byron's famous poem, had been imprisoned. She did a small tasting of their Grand Cru and bought a bottle to take home to Bren. At the gift shop she also found a leather-bound copy of *The Prisoner of Chillon*. Wine and Lord Byron would be perfect anniversary gifts. She planned to give him both tomorrow night.

Semele's fingers flew across the keyboard as she sent Bren a reply—perhaps a sappier one than usual to atone for her unexpected feelings upstairs. Then she finished off her drink and thanked the chef for a wonderful stay. As soon as the courier came, she would be officially done at the château, and she was ready to head home.

She waited for her computer to shut down and zipped it into its case.

Feeling mellow from the wine now, she wandered back into the gallery. A sharp pang of guilt hit her as she realized she'd been half hoping Theo would come downstairs. Although they had said their good-byes this morning, he was still here . . . and so was she. . . .

In a bit of a haze, she shut the door and leaned back against the heavy wood and closed her eyes.

"Daydreaming?"

Startled, she turned to find Theo standing in the doorway of his father's study. He was waiting for her. He had changed into slacks and another sweater. Her eyes reflexively swept over him, but then she caught herself.

"Did you have a chance to take a last tour around the house before you're off?" A knowing look danced in his eyes.

Semele's heart hammered in her chest. *He had seen her upstairs.* "I-I . . . I wanted to look at your *Orbis*. . . ." She hesitated, thinking that didn't sound right.

"Did you? Look?" He walked toward her.

She watched him close the distance between them. "Is it really an original?" She hated how nervous she sounded. Her conscience screamed for her to back up, to look away, to figure out how to leave the room, but she couldn't resist the spell that was weaving itself around them.

"I'm afraid this house is full of surprises," he said softly. "God knows I shouldn't be down here." His hand came up and trailed along her cheek. "Tell me to go."

The desire in his eyes made her forget every thought running through her mind. She wanted him—had wanted him from the first moment they met. Their lips locked, seeking each other, and the tension that had been building between them all these weeks turned into an insatiable dance. It was as though a hand reached inside and turned her like a spinning top.

"Semele," he whispered and lifted her up.

She felt the table beneath her and his hands as they slid along the silk of her stockings. She leaned back, taking him with her as the kiss deepened. They were almost unable to stop.

It was Theo who pulled away. His breath sounded ragged as he ushered an apology. "I'm sorry."

Those two words jolted her back to reality. She was lying across the examining table in her client's arms.

Semele opened her eyes and saw a myriad of emotions play across Theo's face before his gaze shuttered and the connection between them was severed.

He backed away and gave her room to stand. Her legs wobbled, her whole world off-kilter. She had no idea how to handle the situation—she couldn't find her voice.

"Forgive me," he said, sounding like a repentant gentleman from the 1800s. His stilted manner made everything worse. She could barely focus on what he was saying. "I'm afraid I let myself get carried away." He seemed to be waiting for her response.

"Me too," she stammered like an idiot.

Before she could recover, he said, "Forgive me," once more and strode off toward his father's study. "Safe travels, Miss Cavnow."

The door closed behind him with a definitive click.

Knight of Swords

After Theo's exit, Semele crashed back to reality. Her first thought was of Bren.

How could she have done this to him? A flush spread over her as she pictured herself with Theo.

She berated herself while she waited for the courier to come pick up the crates. An endless hour of waiting. Nothing like this had ever happened to her before. She was half tempted to call Bren right then and confess.

Tomorrow marked their two-year anniversary. Now she had this—this nightmare, this shame—blackening everything.

A million times she questioned why he had kissed her.

Theo Bossard was a client. They had barely spoken the whole time she was here, and now he dared to leave her with *that* send-off? It wasn't as if she could have a fling with a man who lived four thousand miles away, even if she weren't with Bren—and she was.

The more she thought about it, the more she was convinced that Theo had seduced her for sport. If she hadn't had that damn wine, none of this would have happened.

For the rest of the evening she tried to forget. She ate dinner back at the hotel without tasting a thing. She packed her suitcase on autopilot and then stood under the shower, eyes closed, hoping Theo's memory would wash away with the water.

She didn't know how she could tell Bren or how he'd react.

The past year had been difficult for them. They had been about to move in together when her father died and they'd agreed to put their plans on hold. Bren had helped her through her father's death and the rift that had occurred between her and her mother when, after the funeral, Semele had discovered the secrets her parents had been keeping from her.

She kept thinking at some point she and Bren would return to how they were their first year together, before her family had fallen apart. They had been "that couple" in the park on Sundays, lying on a blanket and taking turns resting their heads on each other's stomachs, while reading books in the sunlight. They cooked dinner together, went grocery shopping together, and for Valentine's Day they even took a couples' massage class to learn each other's pressure points.

All that had changed after the funeral.

Semele mourned by losing herself in her work. It was perhaps the biggest source of tension in their relationship. Bren tried to be patient. They still had their own apartments even though they usually spent the night together.

She knew talk of the future would come up again tomorrow night over dinner. And here she was, sabotaging everything.

Lost in thought, at first she didn't register the strange noise outside the bathroom.

She heard the shuffle again and turned off the water. *Someone was in her hotel room.*

She stood paralyzed in the shower until instinct kicked in and she reached out to secure the bathroom lock.

She waited breathlessly, dripping wet, with her ear to the door.

Outside there was a sudden swoosh of movement and the quiet click of a door closing.

Frantic, she wrapped a towel around her body and looked for a weapon. She grabbed the only hard thing she could find—the hair dryer.

The adrenaline coursing through her was a rush unlike anything she'd ever felt before. She undid the lock and charged out with a scream.

The room was empty.

Still charging, still screaming—she whipped open the door and ran down the hall, clutching the towel around her while holding her hair dryer out like pepper spray.

The hall was empty too.

She stopped running and turned a full circle, then lowered the arm holding the dryer. She looked deranged.

An elderly couple stepped off the elevator, and the three stared at each other for an awkward moment. Then the old man gave her a wink.

With an embarrassed smile, Semele hurried back to her room, but not before hearing the woman whisper, "American."

Semele locked the door and moved the dresser to block the entrance. If an intruder tried to come in again, they'd find a wall of fake oak. Still frantic, she checked her things and found her purse, wallet, computer, and iPad all where she'd left them.

She sat down on the bed and let out a shaky breath, trying to calm down.

Had she imagined it? Had someone been in her room at all?

At this point, she was willing to believe she had been mistaken.

It was almost eleven now and she had to be up early to make her flight, but she knew she wouldn't be able to sleep. Between the image of Theo looping through her brain, her anxiety about Bren, and now fending off a phantom intruder with a bathroom appliance, she just wanted to get the hell out of Switzerland and go home.

She was about to turn off the light when she looked at her laptop and froze. Her computer was on, which was impossible. She had turned it off before she'd left the château. She remembered doing it in the kitchen. But now the screen was lit and staring back at her.

The manuscript file was open.

Someone had been looking at her scan. They knew she had a copy.

Semele stared at the ancient Greek script glowing on her computer screen like puzzle pieces waiting to be fit together.

This entire trip she had sensed an invisible shadow following her, and now it had showed itself. She didn't understand what was happening. The only thing she was certain of was that this manuscript was more than it seemed.

Marcel had tried to warn her.

I must share with you my last days in Alexandria before I can tell you a different tale. For there is more to this story. My journey as a seer truly began when I read the Oracle's scroll. The day Ariston gave me his translation was also the last day I would see him in Alexandria.

I found him waiting for me in the library, in a reading room that held works on anatomy. He was usually in that chamber.

Ariston had come to Alexandria to study the great works of Herophilus, the physician who founded Alexandria's school of medicine hundreds of years ago. The library housed all his research. Herophilus had devoted his life to dissecting the human body to gain knowledge of its inner mysteries, and he had written countless texts on the subject. Ariston had been studying Herophilus' collection so he could take the knowledge back home. Ariston's father was a renowned physician in Antioch, and Ariston was expected to follow the same path.

Each year thousands like him made the pilgrimage to Alexandria to research and leave their work alongside masters. They were honored to have their names printed in the library's illustrious registry. The prestige carried weight, even back in their homelands. Soon Ariston's time in Alexandria would be over. I could not bear to think of life without him.

When I met him in the reading room that day, he gave me such a perplexed look, as if I had suddenly become a mystery to unravel. Then the question in his eyes vanished and he smiled.

We went outside and headed toward the harbor, which had earned Alexandria its reputation for being the grandest port in the world. The market of vendors with wares from faraway regions stretched along the seawall like bands of colored thread. Spices wafted and danced in the air, obscuring the smell of livestock. We passed by stalls where artisans performed their trades and musicians played for coin.

Ariston bought two roasted dates and we strolled south toward the Gate of the Sun. Lake Mareotis glistened in the distance.

I didn't think the moment could be more perfect, but when I looked over at him, he was staring at me strangely again.

"I finished the translation," he said after a long pause. "The scroll was written by the Oracle of Wadjet."

He let this news hover in the air. For a moment I couldn't speak.

The Oracle of Wadjet existed thousands of years ago. Wadjet was a goddess, one of the earliest deities ever recorded. She had been the daughter of Atum-Ra, the creator Sun God, and as legends went, she had been transformed into a cobra to protect the pharaohs, the land of Egypt, and the all-seeing Eye of Horus. Regarded as the world's first seer, Wadjet influenced every oracle to come, including the Greek Oracles of Delphi and Dodona over a thousand years later.

Oracles supposedly had a direct connection to the divine, and the Oracle of Wadjet had been a powerful beacon in the ancient world, but her writings and her prophecies had become lost three thousand years ago when Egypt moved its epicenter to Memphis. Ariston's discovery was beyond incredible. We had found a set of symbols she had used and a scroll written by her hand.

"She wrote the scroll knowing . . ." He trailed off.

"Knowing what?" I asked. I was filled with trepidation. He had read something in the scroll that changed the way he looked at me.

"It's not for me to say. Read my translation when you get home."

Part of me wanted to go home and read it right away. But that would cut short our afternoon together and I didn't know how much longer Ariston would remain in Alexandria. I had a sinking feeling his time at the library had come to an end.

"You promised to show me your uncle's newest invention," I reminded him, trying to dispel the gloom that had settled over us.

"Are you sure you still want to see?"

"Of course I do!"

We tacitly agreed not to discuss the scroll any further. Instead we took off, hand in hand, toward the Royal Quarters and Emporium, where countless temples encompassed the heart of the city. On any one street people could pray to a variety of deities, Zeus and Jupiter, Isis and Osiris, the Jewish god Yahweh, the Persian god Mithra, or Serapis, a god the Ptolemies introduced to bind themselves to the Egyptians and their mysticism.

Too many temples existed, I thought, for any one prayer to possibly reach its destination. In Alexandria every temple relied on a certain number of worshippers, so the competition to gain the attention of a passerby was fierce. Spectacles rivaling the best theatrical shows would erupt outside temple doors throughout the day. Ariston's uncle, the one he was staying with, was a purveyor of such wonders, and his work was in high demand. Alexandrians loved anything to do with magic, so each temple's keeper would try to outdo the others with marvels that often revolved around fortune telling.

Ariston's uncle had just finished building his latest contraption, a magical fish that spewed gold-painted coins from its mouth. Each coin had a fortune carved upon its face.

We arrived just as the mechanical fish was being hoisted into the air, with an aquamarine banner flying behind its fins like an ocean wave.

The device drew a crowd as coins rained from the fish's mouth, and a sea of hands reached to catch them. Some came flying toward me, glinting in the light. I caught one and squealed with laughter.

Before I could read the fortune, Ariston cupped my face with his hands and kissed me full on the mouth, a stolen kiss, bold and lustful. His arm wrapped around my waist and he pulled me against him. I came alive and claimed him with equal passion.

"Marry me," he whispered. "Come with me to Antioch. I leave tomorrow."

I could not speak. How I wanted to shout yes to the crowd, but I could not. I was a girl of eighteen, several years past the usual age of marriage, and now my father and two brothers depended on me to run their household. The thought of abandoning my family was unthinkable. They would never forgive me.

Ariston took my silence for his answer. He dropped his hands and stepped back.

"My father—" I started.

"Don't." He stopped me gently. Words would have tarnished the moment even more.

I nodded, too distraught to speak. He had already known my answer, yet he had asked me anyway.

From his robes he pulled out the codex that contained his translation. "Read the Oracle's scroll and look for me in your magic symbols." Without another word he turned away and walked toward the library.

I couldn't fathom that this moment was good-bye. My hands gripped the codex as I watched him go. He turned back to look at me, his face full of longing, and then disappeared into the crowd.

I ran home and wept for hours. When my father and brothers returned I found it difficult to look at them. They had no idea the sacrifice I had made, that I had changed the course of my life for them by not changing it at all. I tried to join in the playful banter at dinner and listen to them recall the day's events. But my laughter rang false and the wine tasted bitter. My mother had left her sons and husband in my care, and sitting in her chair that night was the first time I resented her for forcing me to take her place.

Later, in my room, I lit my reading lantern and opened Ariston's translation to find out what a seer from thousands of years ago might have to say. As I read I began to understand why Ariston had looked at me so quizzically.

The Oracle of Wadjet had known my name.

The Empress

The plane's descent into JFK forced Semele to stop reading. She had been immersed in the manuscript since takeoff eight and a half hours ago. As hard as it was to pull herself out of Ionna's story, she powered down her computer and packed everything away in the bag under her feet.

When she glanced up, she saw a man from the next row looking at her, and she gave him a polite smile. She stared out the window, watching the plane touch down. Being back in New York felt surreal.

She checked her cell phone on the cab ride to her office, irrationally thinking that Theo might have called her. When she saw her voice mails she grimaced.

She had three, and two were from her mother:

"It's me. Are you back in town yet? I really do need to talk to you. Please call me back."

The second was more of the same: "Darling, we can't go on like this. If you could just call me so I can explain everything. I know you're still upset—"

Semele deleted both. She didn't want to think about her mother right now. Their issues were insurmountable, although Semele knew at some point she'd have to call her back and discuss what happened. There was also a voice mail from Bren. She didn't want to think about that either.

—

The cab pulled up to her office building on the Upper East Side. The sleek, modern exterior contrasted with the classical European structures around it. Kairos Collections Management took up the top three floors of the twelve-story building.

Semele hurried inside to get out of the windy drizzle. November in New York was always unpredictable, but it seemed colder and wetter than usual. She couldn't have planned a grayer, more dreary homecoming.

She headed to the executive offices on the twelfth floor to drop off her things, thinking she would grab an espresso in the break room. The jet lag was already kicking in.

When she rounded the hallway corner, she stopped—her office door was wide open when it should have been locked. She could hear the sharp clicking of high heels on the floor inside and then caught a cloying whiff of perfume.

A second later Raina stepped out.

"Oh, you're back," Raina drawled in her lilting Russian accent, looking neither guilty nor apologetic for being caught in Semele's office. Instead, she gave Semele a scathing once-over.

Raina was wearing her usual power dress, which showed off her collarbone and a lot of leg in a way that seemed calculated. From the moment Raina had arrived from Moscow, with her cascade of auburn hair and privileged air, Semele had called her Russian Barbie.

She returned Raina's stare with a cocked eyebrow. "Was there something you needed?"

"From you? Not at all." Raina brushed off the question in a condescending tone. "I was dropping off recent catalogs."

Semele frowned, knowing Mikhail's assistant usually did that.

"How was the trip?" Raina folded her arms with her hands out to show off perfectly manicured nails.

"Excellent." Semele had nothing else to say. She would discuss the collection and how to proceed at auction with Mikhail.

"Have your expense report on my desk by Friday." Raina turned to leave. "And tell Mikhail you're back."

Semele kept her face expressionless. Raina was easily the most annoying person she knew. "Is Cabe here?" she asked innocently, enjoying the flash of jealousy in Raina's eyes. Cabe headed Restoration at Kairos and was one of Semele's closest friends. Raina couldn't stand that their friendship predated her.

"Of course. He's busy working." Translation: *Don't bother him.* Raina walked off.

Semele tried to brush off the exchange, but whenever she talked to Raina it put her in a foul mood. She dumped her bags in her office and looked around to see if anything seemed out of place. A stack of glossy catalogs sat dead center on her desk, along with a mountain of mail. Still Raina's excuse for being there was flimsy.

One handwritten envelope stood out from the pile—she would recognize that handwriting anywhere.

Tomorrow. She would deal with her mother's card tomorrow.

Semele took the stairs down to the restoration labs on the eleventh floor. Cabe's ten-speed was propped against the wall.

Cabe stood hunched over the humidification chamber. His gloved hands were unfolding several brittle-looking letters. He was dressed in shorts despite the weather and had exchanged his biking shoes for flip-flops.

"Looks serious." Semele nodded toward the chamber, taking a peek.

He looked up and grinned. "Oh, cheerio, you," he said with a fake English accent. "Welcome back. Got me here so'more spy letters to Georgie-Porgie."

Georgie-Porgie was their nickname for George Washington. They had countless others for historical figures and artifacts: Linny was Lincoln, Mo was Mozart, and Elvis was the Declaration of Independence.

"I had to completely revamp the sodium carbonate elixir to treat the invisible ink. Epic fail. This batch is taking me forever." He continued working the papers apart like a neurosurgeon.

"Don't worry. You'll get it done."

When it came to salvaging the unsalvageable, Cabe was a rock star. He had a graduate degree in both chemistry and forensic biology and oversaw every Kairos lab. He was also the only person Semele trusted when she had a palimpsest—parchment on which the original text was written over. Cabe always unearthed the writing without fail.

"How was Switzer-vonderland?" he asked, attempting a vague German accent.

"I saw our client half-naked and an intruder broke into my hotel room," she deadpanned.

"Is that why you didn't call me back?"

"I already gave you my advice on Raina. Run away."

He gave her a sheepish look. "Kind of can't do that."

Semele could only stare at him, at a complete loss. "You're kidding me. While I was gone?"

He laughed at the look on her face. "Believe me, it's blowing my mind."

Semele could only gape in horror. Russian Barbie was dating one of her closest friends? Semele didn't know what to say. Even worse, Cabe looked happy. But right now she was too tired to find out how bad the damage actually was. "We'll do dinner soon," she promised. "I just stopped by to let you know I've got a special piece coming in with the Bossard Collection I need you to look at."

"Sure. Bring it." He saw the look on her face. "What?"

Semele hesitated. His news about Raina had completely derailed her. "Just see what you can find out."

"You got it. Oh, hey, I need to test your DNA. "

The abrupt request made her laugh. Only Cabe. "God, no."

"Come on. I'm doing everyone at the company." He moved to his workstation.

"Do I want to know why?" She watched him load a program.

"Mark needed a favor."

"Mark? Our Mark?"

"He's now head programmer for one of the largest ancestral DNA companies in the country."

"And he needs our DNA why?"

Semele and Cabe had become friends with Mark almost a decade ago when they were all on fellowship at the Smithsonian in the Conservation of Museum Collections program. Semele had worked on conservation research and Cabe and Mark in scientific analytical studies and technical support.

Cabe typed in several commands. "I'm helping him troubleshoot a program glitch by running profiles using three different patches. You all get to be the lucky guinea pigs."

She rolled her eyes. "Of course we do."

"Come on. It's a cheek swab." He opened the kit on the table. "You get your own ethnicity chart."

"Lucky me."

Cabe grew solemn. "Sorry, Sem. I'm an idiot."

"No, it's fine, really," she said, trying to reassure him. "Swab away."

Her family background had become a touchy subject lately, and Cabe was one of the only people who knew why. After her father passed away, she had spent days helping her mother locate important papers. In her search, she had unearthed adoption papers in an old file—her adoption papers.

She joined him at the table. While he swabbed her cheek, she noticed his bike in the corner. "You know you shouldn't bike when it's slick outside."

"Already back and giving orders," Cabe teased. He put the swab in a plastic capsule and labeled the sticker. "Wanna grab dinner tonight?"

"Can't. It's our anniversary."

"How are you and Bren the Pen?"

"Good," she said quickly. At least they were until yesterday. She would have loved to tell Cabe what happened in Switzerland, but she owed that confession to Bren, and only to Bren.

The Emperor

Bren had gotten new glasses while she was gone, square tortoise-shells that had a distinctive professorial air. Semele kept staring at him during dinner, wondering how a pair of glasses could be throwing her off so much. The frames made his face, the angles, look completely different. She much preferred his oval wire-rimmed glasses; they had more character, looked antique.

His chestnut hair was officially longer than hers now after the month they'd been apart. He had tucked the unruly waves behind his ears. Tonight he was wearing a suit instead of faded jeans and one of his quirky T-shirts. She had never seen him wear the suit and wondered if he had bought it for tonight.

She had donned a silk 1960s cocktail dress, paired with ruby lipstick and a clutch from the 1940s that reminded her of Dorothy's slippers in *The Wizard of Oz*. They sat nestled in a back corner, hidden behind an enormous spray of orchids. So far she hadn't found a way to confess what had happened. Her conscience and good intentions had left her when the salmon tartare and Veuve Clicquot arrived, but still she knew she had to tell him.

"You look far away." He gave her hand a lingering kiss.

"Sorry, just thinking about work."

"How was the trip? Did you have a chance to make it to any of the places I recommended?"

"You love to imagine that my trips are more glamorous than they are," she teased. "I spend all my time in libraries and attics."

"Please. You were holed up in a château in Switzerland. Nothing happened the whole month?"

Her conscience screamed at her to tell him, but a muddled sound emerged from her mouth instead.

"Did you listen to my poems? Or were you saving them?" he asked, seeming sure she'd done the latter. "The truth."

"Saving them, mostly."

"And that's why you've been acting guilty all through dinner." He looked slightly upset.

She hesitated. This was the perfect time to tell him—or the worst. There wouldn't be a better opening.

The moment sailed by without her.

"I did make a point to listen to them on the flight home, all of them. They were beautiful." God, she hated her lack of courage. Why couldn't she tell him? "How's the new book coming? Did you get a lot of work done while I was away?"

Bren searched her eyes. "You know . . . I don't want to talk about work either. Let's talk about us." He squeezed her hand.

She swallowed. She already knew what was coming.

"I don't want to wait anymore. Let's be done with it, combine furniture, closets, the whole thing. Just move in. Don't you think we've waited long enough?"

His request hovered in the air between them.

Semele knew that at their age, moving in together meant a proposal most likely would come next; it could be six months or six years from now, it didn't really matter. Once they were on board, things were pretty mapped out. Her father's death had been an excuse not to hop on, and then afterward, her assignments were, which sent her all over the world, sometimes for over a month at a time.

Before Switzerland she had been in Italy, sequestered in the damp, moldy library of a wealthy grandmother who possessed a trove of manuscripts, a few even penned by Catherine de Médici, the queen of France. Semele identified several astrological charts that had been written by the queen, along with personal letters to her friend Nostradamus. She had no idea how they had ended up in Florence, the city of Catherine's birth, but the letters had been a thrilling find. In New York the collection sold for a huge sum at Sotheby's. The family was elated that "Nonna's treasure" had been rescued from the attic and returned to the world.

This was just one electrifying moment in a career that had many of them. She knew without a doubt her calling was to rediscover and help preserve history. The problem was she didn't know what a future with Bren looked like alongside that. A small part of her wondered if she was subconsciously sabotaging her chance at happiness, if she was afraid of commitment.

"Okay," she said, regretting her answer as soon as it was out of her mouth.

Bren leaned over and gave her a kiss she could barely feel; her thoughts were too scattered. She'd have to give up her beloved apartment in Brooklyn Heights for Bren's condo in Williamsburg, which had twice the space. But she could live with carpet instead of parquet floors. Why was the thought even in her mind?

"We can start tonight and move some stuff over the weekend," he said.

Tonight? Her heart sank. Already he was moving too fast. She tried to backpedal without seeming too obvious. She needed more time.

"I'd love to," she said, "but there's a manuscript I need to finish translating, and I'm so tired from the trip." In other words, they were not spending the night together.

His face fell in disappointment "Right. Of course."

He'd agreed, but she could see the hurt in his eyes. She had chosen work over him, again.

"I'll make it up to you," she promised as the waiter arrived with their entrées. "Let me just deal with this account." And Theo . . . he would be in New York next month for the auction.

At some point she was going to have to face the thoughts about Theo running rampant in her mind. Deep in her bones, she knew they had started something that day in the gallery that was far from finished.

Message to VS—

Back in Brooklyn

Reply from VS—

Maintain surveillance. Wait for instruction.

I read Ariston's translation of the Oracle's scroll, and a shiver ran up my body. Wadjet had foreseen that her treasured box would be forgotten in a cavern of our library. She had asked me—by name—to make sure her symbols survived time. She tasked me with many things I had no idea how to accomplish.

At the time I didn't know what to think, being singled out by a voice from a world that had long ago faded away. Not only had Wadjet foreseen that I would find her treasured box, she said I was born with the ability to divine the future. Her symbols, she said, were mine to master. The scroll explained, in detail, the meaning of each divinity symbol—how they worked together to form the geometry of life, and how within that ever-changing geometry, I could discern the answer to any question.

To appease my doubt, I spent untold hours in the library, researching divination in earnest. I read the stories written by famous oracles and seers who had attempted to bridge the barrier between humanity and the heavens. I found the seers of the past to be the most powerful.

In the long-ago world, seers believed divination to be the mother of all knowledge, the soul of philosophy, and the heart of religion. Their mysteries had been preserved in the library's caverns, wisdom from the ancients who knew how to access the primordial knowledge that surrounds us.

I read countless scrolls that detailed how to interpret dreams, how to read birds' signs in the sky. I read about powerful seers who had gone to war with their generals and foretold the future of battles before a single sword was ever wielded. I read lists of omens and portents. I learned about the differences between soothsayers—those who made predictions—and oracles, those who spoke from altered states of mind, such as the Pythia at Delphi. I studied accounts from seers who could interpret nature, who could read the messages hidden in a crash of thunder or a bolt of lightning, and the ones who were gifted with prophetic knowledge—the most rare seers of all.

As I read I became even more unsure of where I belonged. Wadjet believed I had the sight. She had written to me directly, as a teacher would a student. But how could I be a seer? Seers were from the families of wealthy politicians and were apprenticed at a young age to those who were already masters. I did not have the charisma or ambition to travel from city to city, gaining followers and prominence. I was just a girl who had found an ancient set of symbols.

If I were truly to become the seer that Wadjet had portended, then I needed to know more. So I began to spend all my time in the lower galleries, learning everything I could from seers whose accounts stretched far back into the shadows of time.

As I put myself through the rigors of my private studies, I failed to notice Egypt was in the midst of even greater turmoil. Perhaps if I had, I could have foreseen the tragedy that was to come.

❧

When Cleopatra's father, Ptolemy XII, died, Cleopatra took control of the throne and married her ten-year-old brother, Ptolemy XIII. They were husband and wife in name only, so they could rule together.

Overnight she transformed into the goddess Isis herself. No longer did she wear simple gowns and roam the library freely with an open scroll in hand, as she had in childhood. Instead she dressed as if she were part of a pageant that never ended.

She adorned her body with ornate jewels, armbands, and necklaces. Even her wigs were works of art.

At my family's dinner table I learned about the gossip—the struggle for power between sister and brother, the manipulations of the royal ministers, who were determined that Cleopatra remain only a figurehead. But Cleopatra was too strong-willed, too smart, to let that happen. She could debate a man four times her age and win.

Cleopatra fled Egypt for Syria to escape the plotting of her ministers. Her plight and the people's outrage over her exile caught Rome's eye.

The Ptolemy who had ruled before Cleopatra's father officially bequeathed Egypt to Rome in his will. But instead of assuming control, Rome had allowed the Ptolemies to continue their reign under its watchful eye: the empire was too busy with problems of its own. When Caesar arrived in Alexandria to assess the situation, Cleopatra seized the opportunity and snuck back into the city to plead her case. Caesar had the power to decide the fate of her country.

No one had ever denied Cleopatra, and it seemed Caesar couldn't either. She was twenty-one now, a woman in her full glory and revered by the people as their queen and a living goddess.

News quickly spread that Caesar had become Cleopatra's lover and protector. He returned Cleopatra to the throne and reestablished the joint rule she once shared with her brother. But Caesar had miscalculated the royal ministers, who were secretly fortifying the Egyptian army to sever their ties and end their subservience to Rome.

Caesar had not come to Alexandria with enough men to fight, and his reinforcements from Syria would not arrive in time to save them from defeat. So when the ministers' treachery became apparent, Caesar picked the most strategic place in the city, a cluster of mansions by the water, and barricaded himself there with his troops. He took control of the adjacent isle of Pharos, where the great lighthouse stood. After securing the entrance to the port, he ordered that both harbors be burned.

Alexandria was the finest port city in the world, with deep waters. Its two harbors could hold a thousand ships, which lit like kindling and stoked the fires for days. We tried to continue on while flames engulfed the ships on the water.

In the throes of worry, I didn't think to consult the Oracle's symbols. It's true but I didn't think of myself as a seer back then. Seers grasp the future and pull it back into the present, while the rest of us wait for it to find us. I waited. No one knew what tomorrow held. No one knew who would win this war.

The night the flames took the city I joined my father outside our home to watch the harbor. We lived in the Brucheion near the royal complex and had a clear view of the port.

Before us an endless sea of red fire stretched across the water like a titan's arms, traveling in all directions. The flames leaped, full of rage and a strange kind of beauty that both repelled and mesmerized me at the same time. I would never see anything so magnificent again.

Then the sea breeze shifted and the black smoke began to roll toward us like viscous waves, causing me to choke.

"The winds are turning," my father said, his voice filled with dread.

For days, ever since Caesar had given the order to burn the harbor, everyone worried that the fire would make its way to the library. The wind was now full of malice.

My father called to my brothers. "Ring the bells!" Then he ran after them to the library. He was too seized with panic to notice that I had followed.

Within minutes, the bells were ringing. My brothers had been quick. Soon crowds of people came running to help.

Imagine the flames of Hades. I have no other words to describe the devastation.

We all rushed inside together like a Greek chorus, suddenly players in an unbelievable tragedy, grabbing every scroll and codex we could carry in our arms. Outside we threw the bundles high into the air and far into the distance, hoping to get as many of the works as we could to safety.

I raced back inside to the lower gallery, intent on saving the Oracle's box. As I rounded the corner, I saw my father unlocking the secret door to the lower gallery. I called out to him. When he turned, I saw the truth in his eyes. He knew I had a key, and he knew I had been down there before. He had let me go with his blessing.

"Stay back, Ionna!" he yelled.

Then I saw him disappear down the stairwell. I screamed and tried to run after him, but a shelf fell in front of me, blocking the entrance.

A man called out behind me. His robes had caught fire while he was trying to save a collection of scrolls. He ran toward me, but a wall of flames enveloped him.

I stood crying, waiting for my father to return, but the smoke forced me to go back outside. I collapsed on the ground and gasped for air. People dashed past me carrying buckets of water. At least a third of the library had already been destroyed, if not more. People were still trying to salvage what they could.

The Oracle's stone box, her writings and symbols, were now surely gone. My father must have known what priceless treasures the lower galleries held. That was why he'd risked his life to save them.

I don't remember when I was told to leave or by whom. My clothes were singed and covered in ash. When I arrived home, I fell asleep on a pallet by the door so I could hear when my brothers returned and, with the gods' will, my father.

⌣

The next morning stillness greeted me.

I rose to wash my hands and feet and wiped my face. I changed robes and drank two cups of water. Dizzy, I sat down. I wanted to cry but knew if I started to weep I would never stop. What the day would hold, I could not fathom. I had foreseen my mother's death, but not this.

When I returned to the library the blackened walls told the story. An eerie calm rested in the air, as if a great storm had blown through, and then left us.

In one night, nearly all the knowledge, all the dreams of dreamers had been extinguished like stars in the sky no longer shining. I saw bedraggled men staggering from exhaustion as they tried to organize the salvaged scrolls and codices blanketing the lawns. The wreckage was a giant puzzle that could never be put right again.

The director of the library saw me, and his face fell. "Ionna, go home," he said gently. "I will have my daughter come."

His daughter was of my mother's generation. I did not understand why he would send her to me.

"Thank you, but there is no need," I said. "We will be fine."

He did not speak, but the anguish on his face told me my brothers would not be coming home either. I backed away, unable to believe that, in one night, I had lost them all.

I don't remember where I went. I just remember the deep well of grief. For days I moved in a stupor. Eventually the director's daughter did come with food and wine. She cooked and cleaned and offered me a place to stay with her family. But I didn't want to abandon my house, the last remaining piece of my life.

The director felt a responsibility to me. My father was a life-long friend and close assistant. Most likely, he would have taken over the library when the director passed away. Now all that had changed.

While I mourned, Alexandria worked hard to restore order. Caesar had been victorious against the Egyptian army, so we were forced to forget our losses and celebrate Caesar and Rome's ingenuity. The war ended by January, but the city had paid a price. The library was hardly the only casualty.

Our people accepted this fate. Hundreds of libraries had existed throughout our history, many achieving great prestige and then perishing. I grew up listening to their stories by candlelight—all true, my father insisted. My favorite was about the library in Persepolis, the great city in Persia. Their library contained the Avesta, a sacred book that, supposedly, could grant man immortality.

"Is the book in our library now, Father?" I would ask him, wide-eyed.

"Oh no, no, no." He would shake his head gravely. "When Alexander defeated Darius III, he burned down the library out of vengeance and the Avesta was destroyed."

My father would stare into the fire with a sad, faraway look as if he had witnessed the act himself. Alexandria's library would be no different from those that had fallen before it. I imagined a girl, like me, being told our story far in the future.

How would the record remember us?

My father's favorite saying had always been "Sweet is the truth." With so much of it now gone, I could taste only bitterness. He believed that knowledge could never be lost, that other libraries would rise to fill the void. But could the same words be written? Hundreds of thousands of scrolls were lost—our recorded history wiped away in one night.

Aristarchus had tried to prove that the earth revolved around the sun, and that the universe was many times bigger than we had thought. His research was supported by the ancient Babylonian texts our library had housed, all of which had been destroyed in the fire. Every year volatile debates broke out about whether or not the earth did in truth revolve around the sun; Aristarchus' scrolls and the Babylonian texts were the proving points. Now students would never read those theories.

How Seshat, the goddess of knowledge and the written word, must be weeping. Our library had been a House of Life, and now that life was gone.

The Hierophant

The blaring alarm jarred Semele awake. She was sprawled on her stomach, using her laptop like a pillow. She sat up with a groan and opened her eyes. Her whole body screamed in protest. A combination of jet lag and lack of sleep was taking its toll.

After dinner with Bren last night, she unpacked and faced her overflowing basket of laundry. Between cycles, she worked on translating more of the manuscript and continued well after the laundry was finished. She'd clearly fallen asleep at her computer.

She shuffled to the bathroom and would have laughed when she saw herself in the mirror if she hadn't been so tired. A huge, angry sleep mark from her keyboard ran down the right side of her cheek to her chin. Her laptop was literally imprinted on her face. *Lovely.*

A shower helped revive her and gave her time to think about Ionna's account of the fire. Semele knew of Alexandria's history and the legends surrounding the library's destruction. She had taken a course on ancient libraries of antiquity at Yale; it was also one of her father's favorite topics.

The Library of Alexandria's demise had always been plagued by controversy—debates raged over when it had happened and who caused the destruction. Many historians believed that when Caesar set fire to the ships, he caused the first fatal blow. Others insisted that only books in the warehouses near the waterfront were destroyed. Each camp cited countless historical references to back up their claims. In all the years, there was still no single narrative that historians could agree upon.

Semele ran down the list of culprits. If Caesar wasn't responsible, then it was likely Queen Zenobia of Palmyra, who notoriously persecuted Alexandria's librarians and burned books while at war with Roman emperor Aurelian. Less than thirty years later, Diocletian had purged the Library of Alexandria of every single magic and alchemy book and burned all the scriptures. Then, in A.D. 391, Pope Theophilus' decree destroyed the Serapeum, where the remaining works from the library had been moved.

And between all those wars, nature had played her hand as well. Earthquakes caused major destruction over centuries, and every day the elements brought on a slower degradation. The most moderate theorists claimed that a combination of these factors caused the library's demise.

Semele knew there wasn't one simple answer, and yet here was an account from a person who lived through it. Just the thought rejuvenated her. She was wide awake now and couldn't wait to get to the office.

She needed to talk to Mikhail.

She arrived almost late for her meeting and with no time for coffee. She hurried down the hall to Mikhail's office. His assistant, Brittany, was sorting auction catalogs at her desk outside the imposing double doors.

"You can go right in," she chirped, but then squinted her eyes. "What happened to your face?"

Semele gave her a tired smile and entered Mikhail's office right as he was finishing up a call. He motioned her in, so she took a seat and waited, listening to him speak softly in Russian.

Mikhail had been head director of the Hermitage Museum in St. Petersburg before coming to Kairos. He was somewhere in his late fifties and had the dramatic look one expected to see in a portrait of a Russian cossack soldier hanging on a museum wall.

He said something quietly and hung up the phone. Semele had no idea if the call had been business or personal. With Mikhail she never knew.

"Welcome back." His voice had only the slightest hint of an accent. "You look tired." He assessed her with sharp eyes; then his face relaxed into a smile.

"A bit jet-lagged," she said, downplaying her fatigue.

He pressed his intercom. "Brittany, please bring Semele an Americano, one sugar."

Semele flashed him a grateful smile.

"And ask Raina to join us."

Semele's smile fell. Why was Raina coming to their meeting?

"So!" he said, clapping his hands. "I hear Switzerland was a success."

She nodded, now slightly off-kilter. "The collection's here. We can go down. I just need to double-check the roster and get a few more items to the lab. . . ." She trailed off when Raina strutted in.

"That won't be necessary," Mikhail said, shooting Raina an appreciative glance as she sat down and crossed her legs.

Semele all but rolled her eyes at Raina's daring hemline and stilettos. No wonder Cabe was a tangle of hormones.

"What's not necessary?" she asked, returning her focus to him.

"There's been a change of plans. Fritz is going to handle the Bossard account."

It took Semele a moment to process what Mikhail had just said. He might as well have been speaking Russian again. She looked at Raina, who seemed just as surprised.

"You want to give my account to Fritz? To Fritz?" Semele asked twice in disbelief. Fritz was the company's blond-haired wonder boy from Vienna and technically the most senior consultant on staff. He was also the one who had just handled the $14 million auction.

"I think it's a wise decision," Raina interjected, obviously taking pleasure in Semele's discomfort. "Especially with such a high-profile collection."

"The Bossard account is mine," Semele said to Mikhail, stressing the word "mine." He had never given one of her accounts to someone else. She was too stunned to say anything else.

The door opened again and Brittany entered. She reached to place the coffee on the side table next to Semele.

"I'll take it," Semele said gruffly, not even letting her set the cup down. She took several fortifying sips while she waited for Brittany to leave. She kept her eyes on Mikhail and ignored Raina entirely. "Why would you want to take me off?"

"Fritz handled the Galli account beautifully last year," he said. "The board would like to see the same results here."

"The Galli Collection?" Her mind drew a blank.

"The dowager in Bern," Raina reminded her with a patronizing tone.

"The sheet music?" Semele asked, growing more astounded.

A wealthy widow in Bern had amassed a rare collection of sheet music and ledgers from the Renaissance and Baroque eras. Both collections were in Switzerland, but their similarities stopped there.

Why Mikhail would want Fritz to take over the Bossard account was not only beyond her but also an insult. A fleeting thought crossed her mind. "Does Theo Bossard have an issue with my work?"

"Not at all." Mikhail shook his head. "On the contrary, he's been full of praise."

The thought of Theo speaking to Mikhail about her was just as unsettling. What had he said?

"We have a new account you need to jump on right away." Mikhail handed Raina the open file on his desk. "Set it up."

"A new account? Are you kidding me?" Semele finally let her anger fully surface. "I'm in the middle of one I happen to care about!"

She and Mikhail were supposed to spend the next several hours going over the collection and hammering out potential strategies for the auction next month. She had also been anxious to discuss the manuscript and Marcel's note. And now her account was being handed over to Fritz?

"What if I say no?" she asked. Raina laughed and Semele wanted to throttle her. She shouldn't even be here.

"I'm sorry, Semele." Mikhail met her eyes.

During the five years they had been working together, she and Mikhail had developed a strong mutual respect as well as a shorthand for communicating with one another. He was telling her the decision was final.

"Where is the client?" she asked.

"Beijing," Raina informed her with barely disguised glee as she reviewed the file.

Semele closed her eyes. She couldn't believe this was happening. Part of her wondered if this was some sort of plan to get her out of the picture. Why Beijing? Why now? She should be swamped with preparations for the auction. Now she was being shipped off to China.

Raina stood up to leave. "I'll get with the new clients and set up your travel," she said and sauntered out.

Semele waited until the door closed and then turned back to Mikhail. "Is this a roundabout way of firing me?"

Mikhail let out a surprised laugh. "No, I give you my word. I know this seems out of the ordinary. But sometimes I have to make decisions for the good of the company. The Beijing account is more important. You're needed there."

Semele refrained from questioning him further. She sipped her coffee instead and tried to make sense of what was happening. She didn't see how an account in Beijing could be more important than Bossard. And Mikhail didn't even know about the manuscript yet. She needed to broach the subject.

"There's one piece in the collection that I think is going to be significant."

He cut her off. "Turn your notes over to Fritz by this afternoon and he'll sort out everything. Why don't you take the rest of the week off?"

Mikhail was already walking toward the door. Semele stood in a daze and followed him.

"Recharge, get rested," he said. "We'll discuss Beijing first thing Monday morning."

Semele looked from him to the open door, not ready to walk through it yet. "Seriously? You're giving me the rest of the week off."

His eyes softened at her bewildered look. "You've earned it."

Her mind was in a tailspin. Yes, she had earned it. But she didn't want to go anywhere next week.

This was all so unlike Mikhail. Normal Mikhail would want to go over each piece of the Bossard collection with her immediately. He would follow her down to the tenth floor and get so caught up that he would cancel his afternoon appointments so they could keep talking. Normal Mikhail would never want her to take time off, and he would never reassign a collection.

"Give Fritz your files and I'll see you Monday," he said, holding the door open for her to go.

Semele left, knowing her face betrayed her hurt and confusion. She couldn't help thinking this turn of events was because of the manuscript. Ever since she had found it, she'd been on edge. Her gut told her someone knew she was reading the memoir, and clearly Mikhail didn't want her to discuss it.

"Semele," he called her back.

She turned around and saw the concern on his face.

"There will be other collections," he said gently. "Let this one go."

She nodded, not sure if she could.

Could I have saved my family if I had only foreseen the fire?

The question haunted me until I read Wadjet's scroll. She explained how the future had a course, yet our lives remained fluid like water, leaving us with a choice in all things. Life's greatest mystery was how these conflicting truths existed in harmony. It was the reason why intuition existed at all.

Perhaps pain was a teacher. After the fire, I began to cast the Oracle's symbols to divine the future. I no longer questioned what they were telling me, and my intuition grew stronger.

I began to prepare for the journey they foretold. I had to believe that from the ashes of this tragedy, a new life was waiting for me.

The director of the library handled my father's and brothers' funerals and negotiated with the embalmers. I waited for seventy days for their bodies to be returned. All who knew them judged their lives as virtuous, and I was assured their place in the afterlife was secure.

My father's wealth paid for each sarcophagus, and I buried them in our family tomb. I sewed what remained of his fortune inside my cloak. With luck I would have ample funds for my travels to Antioch, as well as means for several years if I lived frugally.

When I heard *The Grebes,* the largest Roman merchant ship ever to enter our harbors, had docked, I wasted no time.

My father had known the ship's captain. He once saved the man's personal books from being confiscated by the library and instead kept the transcribed copies for the library's collection— something my father was prone to do when he could. He did not agree with the Ptolemies' edict and believed one of life's greatest tragedies was for a man to have to part with his books. I hoped the captain would remember my father's kindness and grant me voyage.

"Of course I remember, girl!" the thick, barrel-chested man bellowed. "Now why are you bothering me?"

Amid the shouts and orders as the ship readied to sail, I spun my tale—that my husband waited for me in Antioch—and added that I was with child, for good measure. The captain looked at my slim frame and frowned but did not question my story.

"Pay your way and stay out of my way, and we'll have you in Antioch by the week's end. Now get on. We'll be leaving shortly."

"But I need to get my things."

"Hurry up then. I won't wait."

I could tell he would leave me if I wasn't back in time. I ran home calling on the speed of Hermes.

With no time to consider, I stuffed my bag with every valuable I could seize. First I emptied my mother's jewelry box. Then I packed her comb, hand mirror, and perfumes, along with my father's favorite reed pen, a huge stack of parchment, and my brothers' *sistrums*—percussive instruments used in the festivals. They had no value or use, but I had to take something from each of them. Then I bundled the pottery jar holding the Oracle's symbols in a swath of silk, along with Ariston's translation. I laced the gold key on a cord around my neck and tucked it inside my gown. The metal felt cold against my skin.

The library key was now my talisman. Wadjet had chosen me to safeguard her symbols and help them survive. Now all that remained was my set of painted replicas and a translation of her words from a fledgling physician. In my eyes I had already failed.

I ran all the way back to port and boarded *The Grebes* only moments before she pushed off.

The captain saw me dash down the plank and laughed. "I've never seen a woman with child run so fast."

I blushed and hastened to place a hand upon my stomach. The old man chuckled and turned back to his business.

Once on deck, I stood in awe. The ship was massive, bigger than it appeared from the docks. The hull stretched 130 feet long, and the vessel had three masts instead of one to accommodate the tonnage of its cargo. There was a complex system of ropes and knots rigging the square sails; it looked like one of the magical contraptions Ariston's uncle had crafted.

I walked down the middle of the deck, trying to keep out of the way. One of the ship hands nodded gruffly and motioned "Passengers over there."

A handful of men clustered in a corner: three scribes, a merchant, two priests, and a Nubian warrior with a goat. I nodded to the motley group with confidence, as if young women traveled alone all the time. Then I took a seat on the bench. The Nubian's goat came over and nuzzled me.

The warrior surprised me by addressing me. "She smells the spice in your perfume." He spoke softly.

I looked up at him and nodded, hesitant. Nubians had earned the hard-won reputation of being the fiercest fighters in the world. They were not to be crossed. I decided to let his goat lick my hand as much as the animal wanted.

Among all the merchant ships, *The Grebes* had one of the finest reputations—it carried Egypt's wheat to Rome, wood from Lebanon, oil and wine from Greece, and delivered papyrus throughout the Mediterranean—but still, a week aboard any vessel was a long time. We would travel along the coastline to Antioch, stopping along the way in Damietta, Ascalon, Tyre, and Tripoli to unload cargo, and then finally dock in Seleucia at the mouth of the Orontes River. From there I would take a barge up the river to the city.

The idea of traveling alone both thrilled and terrified me. As the ship pulled away from port, the key hung heavy around my heart. The library shrank smaller with a distance impossible to bridge, for I knew I would never return to Alexandria again.

We passed the lighthouse and I forced myself to face the sea.

My old life was behind me, and my one chance at happiness existed in an unknown future. Antioch was a growing metropolis, often called the Rome of the East. I tried to imagine what Ariston's home was like and began to worry that, in a city of over half a million people, I would never be able to find him at all.

As if the Fates could sense my fear, the voyage seemed doomed by the end of the first day. High winds threatened to batter us into the coastline, and a relentless storm followed overhead, meting out punishing rain and claps of thunder.

Fear took root inside me. What if I died at sea? No one would be there to bury me, and I would never find my way to the afterlife. Shipwrecks were a frequent occurrence, and by the second day all the passengers, everyone except the Nubian, were convinced we would die.

I watched him look out to the water, his stance straight and regal against the rain. Was the warrior unafraid of death, or did he simply know he would not perish on this voyage? I had no such certainty.

It was the knife at my neck that woke me.

"Make a sound and you're dead," a crewman hissed in my ear as his hand reached under my cloak.

The knife cut into my skin and the blade burned as blood ran down my neck. When I whimpered he pressed the blade deeper. I could feel his body against me, and bile rose up in my throat.

The man stopped groping when he felt the coins hidden inside my cloak. "What's this? The nymph comes with gold?"

He moved the knife away from my neck to cut a coin from my cloak. The moment the blade lifted, a slicing sound blew past me and an arrow landed in his chest. The man made no noise as he slumped to the side.

I was free of him and looked up with terrified eyes. In the darkness I saw the Nubian, bow in hand, kneeling on his pallet twenty feet away.

He came over with the stealth of a cat, picked up the dead man, and lowered him over the side of the boat. It all happened so quickly. When the Nubian was rid of him, he took a piece of cloth from his bag and wrapped it around my neck.

"The wound is not deep," he whispered.

Shock took hold of me and my body began to shake. In a panic, I looked around to see if anyone was watching. The Nubian did not seem concerned.

"Why are you traveling alone?" he asked.

My teeth chattered as I shivered uncontrollably. "My family is gone. . . ."

"And the husband you are joining?"

So he had heard my story. His eyes held surprising gentleness. I shook my head, unable to fathom the outcome if he hadn't intervened. My eyes dropped to the intricate necklace banded around his neck.

"Thank you," I whispered.

He helped me stand and moved my pallet to be closer to his. "I have a daughter. May the gods watch over her as they do you."

I lay down near him, and his goat licked my arm in a show of welcome. Filled with gratitude, I stared at the vast balcony of stars glittering above me, while beneath me the ocean rocked, lulling me to sleep as a mother would a child, and my fear vanished.

Five of Swords

The knock startled Semele; she'd been immersed in translating. She opened her office door to find Fritz gloating like a blue-eyed Bavarian boy. She fought the urge to slam it in his face. He had wanted the Bossard account and now it was his. She couldn't believe she had considered buying him champagne.

"Don't screw it up," she snapped.

Fritz chuckled and wagged his finger at her. "Temper, temper. Someone's milk got spilt today," he said with a heavy German accent. She gave him a withering look he seemed to enjoy. "Anything I should look at first?" he asked in a more serious tone.

"All of it?" she answered sweetly.

She didn't include the scan of Ionna's manuscript in the USB drive she gave him, nor did she mention the manuscript's existence. Let Wonder Boy find that gem on his own.

He took her files. "Don't worry. I'll make sure the auction is the highlight of the year while you're eating egg rolls."

"You know I'm ready to kill you."

He laughed. "Sorry, Semele. You're just too irresistible. What in the world did you do to piss off Theo Bossard?"

She looked at him blankly. "Nothing," she said, knowing she sounded defensive. Maybe Mikhail wasn't being honest and Theo really was behind her reassignment.

By the time Fritz left her office, she was in a black mood. She ignored all the mail that was still piled up and picked up her mother's letter. She may as well open it. Nothing could possibly make her feel worse at this point. It was probably a belated birthday card with a check to go shopping. Usually her mother took a train to the city to give Semele the check in person. They would hit her favorite antique markets and vintage clothing stores in Chelsea and Williamsburg for the weekend. But not this year.

Semele hadn't talked to her mother in six months. She knew she needed to call—the holidays were coming soon. But her mother would only start crying and apologizing again. Semele didn't know if she could take the drama. Something in her had broken the day she found the adoption papers, and she wasn't sure it could ever be fixed.

With a sigh she ripped open the envelope to find a fancy Papyrus card decorated with kaleidoscope patterns and flowers.

Her heart sank when she saw her mother's penmanship. She could tell by the extended word length and spacing, the height of the letters and strokes, that her mother had been drinking when she wrote this. Even her signature looked shaky and weak, and the angle slanted downward. Her writing carried all the signs of someone struggling with depression and their sense of self-worth.

Semele returned the card to the pile, wishing she had never opened it. It actually made her feel worse.

She grabbed her purse and laptop and turned off the light. Her mother, office politics, and China could wait. She was officially done with this day.

—

She was headed toward the subway when her cell phone rang. She glanced at the number and stopped walking.

"Semele Cavnow," she answered in a clipped voice.

"Semele, it's Theo. I was calling to check on the delivery."

"The delivery was fine." Her tone hardened. "You'll be pleased to hear I've been taken off the account."

There was a pregnant pause. "What are you talking about?"

"Our senior consultant, Fritz Wagner, will now be overseeing your father's collection, per your request—"

"I didn't request anything." Theo cut her off. "I don't want anyone else handling my father's collection but you. Only you."

Semele didn't know what to say. So much for Fritz's theory. Now she had made things worse by upsetting her client—ex-client.

"This is unacceptable," he stressed.

"Mr.— Theo, I'm sorry but it wasn't my decision. I thought it was yours. . . ." She trailed off.

"No, Semele. It wasn't mine."

The warmth in his voice reached out to her. Thousands of miles apart and it was as though they were back in the gallery.

He let out a pained sigh. "I'm afraid I didn't handle our goodbye as I should have. There are things I need to say."

She waited for him to continue.

"Semele . . . I'm struggling."

His admission twisted her inside. She wanted to tell him she was struggling too, and had been ever since they'd kissed. But saying so felt like cheating on Bren all over again. Instead she said nothing.

A long silence passed between them.

"Let me handle Kairos," he said, sounding frustrated again. "I'll call you back," and he hung up.

Semele stood rooted on the street as people rushed past. Was Theo actually going to demand she be put back on the collection? Here she was trying to forget what had happened in Switzerland, and just hearing him say her name like that wasn't helping.

She was sure Mikhail would figure out a way to get Theo to accept Fritz: her boss was a master at handling difficult clients. Maybe it was better if Fritz took over. Fritz would be the one to review the collection piece by piece with Theo after all the appraisals were finished; he'd be the one taking him to client dinners and holding his hand through the auction process. The more she thought about it, the more it seemed like Fritz was the better choice. Theo Bossard made her make very bad decisions.

She still couldn't figure out how to tell Bren what had happened.

The truth was, her life had been unraveling ever since she had found Marcel's note and the manuscript.

Message to VS—

Potential problem.
No longer overseeing the collection.

Reply from VS—

Unexpected.

Message to VS—

Assigned to Beijing.

Reply from VS—

Continue surveillance.
I'll handle Beijing.

I could see why Poseidon was the patron of Antioch. Elaborate mechanical fountains performed dances everywhere I turned. The city stole my breath with its magnificence. Mosaics decorated the buildings and the marble glinted like rainbows in the sunlight. Known as a mecca for the legal minds of the East and a doorway to Asia, the city was steeped in wealth and luxury.

I walked the main street, a two-mile stretch bustling with traders and artists. A covered colonnade extended on both sides, offering shade, and a broad carriage road created a thoroughfare in the center.

Cheers from the Hippodrome reverberated in the distance. Much like the infamous Circus Maximus in Rome, the chariot races at the Hippodrome drew over eighty thousand spectators a day. I could also hear the sounds of flutes and tambourines signaling some kind of wild merriment nearby, and I began to understand why they said Roman soldiers stationed in Antioch refused to leave.

For hours I wandered through the maze of the market, stopping to buy provisions as I made my way to the center of the city. There was only one place I could think to go, and I wanted to make it before I lost the day's light. My father had known many a scholar from Antioch who had traveled to our library. I hoped to find someone at theirs who knew him.

Because I had grown up a librarian's daughter, I knew that all libraries had a book depository. These rooms were prized but frequently forgotten—vaults where countless codices and manuscripts were stored before being cataloged or translated. Antioch's would be the perfect place to hide.

The depository was always located in the back of a library and unlocked during the day. With the ease born from a lifetime of sneaking through alcoves, I skirted past questioning eyes until I found the door. I ducked inside and let my eyes adjust to the dark. Then I moved several stacks of crates, creating a hidden corner that would be my bed for the night.

I dug through my satchel and pulled out the food from the market. I feasted on flatbread with peppered *çökelek* cheese and a kebab dusted with pistachio and lemon sumac. Nothing had ever tasted so delicious.

I drank it down with *salgam*. The woman selling the purple refreshment told me it was made from pickled-carrot water flavored with half-fermented turnips. My lips felt the sting of the turnips, but the drink tasted delightful and my body was restored.

Thoroughly satiated, I leaned back against the wall and closed my eyes. I must have dozed off, because when I awoke, the door was closed.

I tried to ease my growing panic. Surely someone would return tomorrow morning to unlock it. They always did at our library. After they came, I would wait for the right moment and sneak out. Then I would find a scholar who knew my father and ask for his assistance. I would need help if I was going to rent a room. So long as I lived modestly, the coins in my cloak would last while I searched for Ariston.

My eyes grew heavy as I looked at the shadows of the scrolls and manuscripts, towering above me like mountains. I felt like a scroll that had been lost and deposited among the rest.

That night I had strange, vivid dreams of lying on the floor of a cave. When I awoke the next morning the dream felt important, but I didn't know why. The sound of the lock turning jarred me awake.

Suddenly the door opened and one of the *hyperetae,* the assistants responsible for registering the books, came in to make a morning deposit. I huddled deeper in the corner, not daring to move.

The sands of time in the hourglass seemed to stop as I listened to him stack manuscripts. Had a *hyperetae* ever moved slower?

Finally, the man finished and left. I waited a while longer to be sure, then sat up and gathered my things. I drew my cloak tightly around me to hide my travel-worn gown. I could not risk changing into the fresh clothes I had in my bag. Instead, I combed my hair into a Greek knot, making a thick bun at the bottom of my neck, and strategically decorated it with golden adornments. I removed my favorite *wesekh* collar from my jewelry pouch. The gold and lapis shimmered where my cloak opened at my neck. Then I doused myself with my mother's most expensive perfume made from spikenard, a prized root from the Himalayas. The aroma conjured a certain sense of status, and there would be no mistaking its spicy musk. Now I looked more like a librarian's daughter than a homeless waif.

After carefully sneaking from my hiding place, I toured the reading rooms. The spikenard successfully masked my odor from a week at sea. I set my face in a regal look and acted so entitled that no one questioned me.

Behind my facade, I studied each scholar, searching for a familiar face. After strolling for hours, I finally gave up. I bought more food at the market and returned to the book depository.

I did this for three days.

Like a scampering mouse, I grew more and more desperate. I had no home, no family. I had simply left one library for another—and what existed beyond these walls terrified me.

When I awoke on the fourth day, I clearly remembered my dream from the night before. I did not question its meaning. Instead, I packed my belongings and left the depository for good.

And there, in the last alcove, I found Illias sitting just as he had been in my dream.

～

Illias was one of the head librarians in Antioch. He looked frailer than when I had seen him last. His back was now curved and stooped with age, and his hands shook as his fingers guided his eyes to the next line of text. He had stayed at our home for several months on his last trip to Alexandria eight years ago. I could only hope he remembered me.

I approached him discreetly and hovered next to his stool. "Excuse me, sir?" He looked up and squinted at me. "I don't know if you remember me, I'm—"

"Come closer, girl. Speak up!"

I leaned in until I was practically on top of him. "I'm Ionna Callas, Phileas' daughter from Alexandria—"

"Ionna? Dear girl!" His face lit up. "I didn't recognize you." He stood in excitement. "What North Wind blew you to Antioch? Where's Phileas?"

He looked behind me, expecting to find my father. For a moment I had trouble speaking. He saw my distress and his smile vanished. "Oh dear. Oh dear." He led me to his stool and helped me sit.

Sequestered in the private alcove, I told him the whole story. He had heard about Caesar's fire, but he did not know my father had died. He listened without a word, though his eyes grew bright.

When I finished, he patted my hand. "You will come live with us. My wife, Aella, will be overjoyed to have a girl in the house again." His generous offer surprised me, but I did not demur. I was too overcome with relief.

Illias gathered his scrolls and led me outside, where his servant waited with a donkey-led carriage. A wreath of dangling ribbons decorated the donkey's hair like a strange rainbow on display.

I stared at the spectacle, unable to hide my astonishment.

"My wife's doing," Illias explained with a defeated wave of his hand as we climbed onto the seats.

The carriage traveled south along the colonnade and then on to Daphne five miles south of the city. We passed exquisite fountains, public parks, and sculptures all along the road.

"I'm getting too old to walk to town, but I refuse to give up the trips and stay at home. To do so would be a fate worse than Hades," he said with an amused smile. "Aella wanted a grand carriage—a huge expense. I said no so she punishes me by decorating the donkey's hair." He looked over at me. "Wait until she gets ahold of you."

My eyebrows rose. "Your daughters are no longer there?" I remembered that he had three girls not much older than me.

"Lucky birds flew the nest, all married and with their husbands. Aella needs someone to shower with attention. You'll do fine." He sounded so pleased; my apprehension grew.

The carriage left the main road and entered an enchanted-looking forest with leaves as green as emeralds. Never had I seen such a grove. Illias explained how every tree in Daphne was considered sacred and it was unlawful to cut them down. Apollo had pursued the nymph Daphne through this countryside, and now the forest bore her name. In the legend, Daphne had turned into a beautiful laurel tree, and those evergreens stretched as far as my eyes could see.

I caught my first glimpse of the Temple of Apollo towering in the distance above the tree line and I gasped.

"The Jewel of Antioch," Illias said proudly. "Many a ruler has traveled here to consult the Oracle, though not as much anymore. Now people come to the bazaar at the temple to buy charms and blessings from the vendors . . . and other entertainments." He glanced at me. "It's not safe for a woman to go alone."

"What are those tents?" I pointed to the outskirts of the market where rows of tents had been erected.

"Those are the dream chambers," he said.

"Like Saqqâra!" I exclaimed, growing excited.

In Egypt we had Saqqâra, the City of Dreams, at the necropolis in Memphis, a place where seekers could sleep in chambers and dream the answers to their questions. Dream interpreters could be hired to sit with the patrons and explain the signs.

"Perhaps I could go to the chambers too?" I asked hopefully. The power of dreams had begun to preoccupy me. I wondered if I needed to practice the art of dreaming to understand Wadjet's message.

Illias raised his bushy eyebrows and looked at me. I could tell he was wondering why I wanted to undergo such an experience.

"I read Hippocrates' treatise on dreaming," I said, trying to explain my interest.

He laughed, clearly tickled. "Ah, you are Phileas' daughter!"

It was true. I had read Hippocrates along with many other teachings on the ancient practices of Asklepian dream questing. Dreams were considered messages from the heavens, divine wisdom imparted to guide our lives. To try to understand the world of dreams was a serious endeavor. After I was settled, I decided, perhaps I should undertake my own journey.

The road soon turned along a sloping hill and descended into a lush valley. I could hear a trickling stream nearby.

"Here we are." Illias pointed past two statues of Apollo and Daphne sitting on either side of a tiled pathway. The elaborate statues were colorfully painted and seemed better suited for a festival parade. "A bit audacious, these two," Illias said as we passed them, "but Aella could not be dissuaded."

We traveled down a path studded with flowers that ended at an enchanting villa in the center of an orchard. The house had a sculptured fountain of Aphrodite in repose with two swans spouting water over her head.

I heard high-pitched, girlish singing coming from inside the house.

Illias smiled with a tolerance born either from years of weariness or love. "Come out, o' goddess," he announced. "We have a visitor."

The door opened and out flitted one of the loveliest creatures I had ever seen.

Her hair was a dazzling golden-white and the long tresses had been teased into a cascade of curls and braids and laced with flowers and jewels. I had never seen such an intricate hairstyle. She circled around me like a dancing muse.

"A girl! You brought a girl!" Aella squealed and hugged us both. I wasn't sure how to respond, suddenly feeling like a new pet.

I assumed Aella must have married Illias very young, for she looked at least twenty years his junior. But soon I found out that was not the case. Aella had an obsession with beauty regimens and retained her glowing youthfulness by applying unusual concoctions and elixirs, which had their origins in distant places: some came from Egypt, others from Rome and China. She had a special *cosmetae,* a servant whose only job was to attend to her hair, makeup, and perfumes, and she devoted her entire morning to bathing and dressing. She loved to soak in milk with rose petals because she had heard Cleopatra did the same. When I told her I knew the queen, she adopted me as a fourth daughter then and there.

"You poor little dove. To survive the perils of the fire and the journey at sea alone." She forced me to recline on a chaise and hastened a servant to bring me a hot cup of kaynar, a sweet cinnamon drink sprinkled with crushed walnuts. I sipped the delicious brew and felt its warmth spread throughout my body. Sitting there, I couldn't help thinking that my mother had guided my dream last night to help me find them.

⌒

By the week's end, Aella had pulled girlish secrets from my heart as only a woman could. I confessed that Ariston had proposed, but I had rejected him because of my family. She hung on to every word as she clutched a facial cloth in her hand.

"We will find this Ariston Betesh. Do not worry, my dove."

In the days that followed, Aella and her *cosmetae* subjected me to countless ministrations, while assuring me that a servant was searching for Ariston.

Lemon and vinegar treatments soon brightened my hair to copper gold. For my facial treatments, the *cosmetae* frequently referred to an enormous scroll, a manual written by an influential woman in Antioch detailing the most powerful mixtures to halt wrinkles, sunspots, and other unfortunate blemishes. The facial masks she applied smelled like rotting onions and often consisted of things like ground horns, marrow, eggs, and animal urine. Poor Illias would walk around the house muttering, "The smell, the smell!" I vowed that when I left Aella's care I would never put another foul-smelling paste on my body again.

After finishing my beauty treatments, I usually pleaded exhaustion and escaped to my room. I would take out Ariston's translation of the scroll and cast the Oracle's symbols. What I kept seeing in their patterns made my heart grow lighter. I would find Ariston before the next moon.

The house servant returned two days later with news that Ariston had been found. Aella jumped from her chaise with a singsong squeal, and the *cosmetae* went scurrying off to prepare one of her robes. They chose a Grecian-style gown for me with ornamental clasps made from mother-of-pearl, and the gold border along the fabric's edges glittered when I moved. Aella informed Illias that he would have to forfeit his trip to the library that day because I needed his carriage. He mumbled under his breath but did not refuse us. Aella and her *cosmetae* stood by the gate to see me off.

"Do not worry, my dove. He'll say yes!" Aella exclaimed as she waved her facial cloth in the air.

She was not speaking of a marriage proposal but of the dinner invitation I was to extend. To dine at the house of an Antioch librarian was a great honor, and Aella instructed me to have Ariston and his family come at the week's end.

The carriage traveled north through the market, past the palace where Seleucid kings once ruled, before Antioch was annexed by Rome. I marveled at its seven high doors of iron-plated gold and the enormous columns of mottled red-and-white marble. The basilicas and Hall of Records towered with equal grandeur nearby. I thought Antioch might just be the most beautiful city in the world.

Ariston lived near the oldest quarter of Antioch, and his family's home also served as a clinic and medical school. A stone wall sequestered the enormous grounds and decorative gates opened to the courtyard. The property must have been in the family for generations.

When I entered the courtyard, a young student hurried to greet me. He acted as if I were a dignitary. He assumed I was there to see Ariston's father, no doubt because of Aella's dress and the eccentric carriage. I blushed and tried to keep hold of my courage.

"No, his son, Ariston. Could you please tell him he has a visitor?"

The young man assessed me with keen eyes. I turned away to admire the fountain, beginning to feel like I looked as foolish as the donkey.

The boy left but soon returned with disappointing news. "I'm afraid Ariston isn't here. Do you wish to leave a message?"

My face fell. What could I say? I was there to accept a marriage proposal he was sure to have forgotten? Tears filled my eyes and I shook my head.

I berated myself as I rode away. Why hadn't I left my name along with Aella's invitation to dine? Now Ariston would never know I was in Antioch unless I borrowed Illias' carriage and called again.

I was debating whether to turn around and go back when I saw a band of young men walking toward us. They were laughing and in the midst of a debate.

My breath caught when I spotted Ariston. How much he had changed in the year we had been apart. He still had that same mane of hair, but he seemed stronger, more virile, as if he had fully become a man.

His friends noticed me, the overly decorated maiden, as I was about to pass.

One called out, "Aphrodite is upon us! Oh, hail!"

In a moment of panic, I leaned forward and opened the sun parasol on the side of the carriage. Just before the umbrella opened, Ariston's eyes met mine. Confusion flickered across his face. My heart hammered in my chest as the carriage continued on.

Had he recognized me? What was I doing? I had come so far to find him and now I was hiding behind a parasol, all because I could not bear the possibility of his rejection—that a year might have been too long.

I closed the parasol as we made our way south. I could hear the Fates laughing at my faint heart—to see a future and not have the courage to embrace it. The jostling of the carriage seemed to echo their mirth as the road became rougher under the wheels. Then I realized why. I was going the wrong way.

"Driver, stop!" I leaned forward. "We must turn around."

Aella's servant looked back at me. "But we're almost to Daphne's Gate."

"I need to go back, please," I begged before what little courage I had deserted me. The driver did not seem willing.

"Ionna Callas!" a voice behind us called out. "Daughter of Phileas!"

I looked behind to see Ariston running toward us.

I stood up. "Stop the carriage or I will jump!"

The servant stopped and Ariston was beside us within moments. "You're in Antioch," he said, drawing in deep breaths from running. His face was full of wonderment.

"Yes . . . I am." My voice was barely a whisper.

"You just left my house?" he asked, confused.

I nodded, now completely mute.

He shook his head, not understanding. "Then why were you running away?"

I stared at my hands, unable to look at him. "I was afraid. . . . So much time."

"Ionna." He took my hand. "How I have longed for this day."

In his eyes, I could see the same love shining that had been there before, on the day he asked me to marry him. This was Ariston, my Ariston. Time had not separated us. I still had his heart.

~

On that day in Antioch my new life began. Just as I can see you searching for your way, unsure if you should trust the future pulling at you inside, know you will walk the road ahead of you whether you are ready or not.

You have been translating these words, trying to deny that they have been written for you—but they have, Semele. Your life and mine are entangled.

The Chariot

Semele stopped reading. There was no way she had gotten that right. Her eyes returned to the Greek symbols and she translated the line again.

Her name. Ionna had written her name.

She tried to ignore the goose bumps rising on her arms and reminded herself that the name Semele had ancient origins. Her father had picked it.

In Greek mythology, Semele was Zeus' lover and the mother of Dionysus. She was also the only mortal ever to be the mother of a god. But Semele was killed by Zeus shortly before giving birth, her death brought about by her own foolishness. Zeus had granted her one wish, her heart's desire, and given his oath he would grant it no matter the consequence. Her wish was to see Zeus in all his glory; however, no mortal could look upon him without bursting into flames. Zeus was forced to keep his promise and show himself, and Semele died by fire. In the end, Zeus rescued the unborn Dionysus and sewed him into his thigh until the baby was ready to be born.

Semele still had no idea how on earth her father had sold her mother on the name. The fact that it also appeared in Ionna's manuscript had to be a coincidence. She sighed and continued translating.

Your father did not choose your name. Your grandmother did—the one who severed your family tree at the time of your birth to protect you. But you must understand, Semele, that those roots remain.

Semele jumped off the couch as if her laptop were on fire. "Holy shit!" she yelled to the empty room.

A rush of adrenaline coursed through her as she stared at the glowing computer screen, now completely petrified.

Did that just happen? Did a two-thousand-year-old manuscript actually talk back to her?

She ran to the bathroom and splashed water on her face. She had slept only a few hours. Maybe her exhaustion and jet lag were making her delusional. The possibility that Ionna was communicating directly with her violated every law of the universe.

She turned off her computer without even closing the file. She had to get out of her apartment. Now. She grabbed her cell phone and called Bren. He answered on the second ring, and she could hear the happiness in his voice.

"Hey, you." Then he hesitated. "You're not calling to cancel tomorrow, are you?"

Semele laughed. Even to her ears it sounded shrill. "No, silly." She never said "silly." "I was calling to see if you're busy tonight."

"Just waiting for my girlfriend to move in with me," he reminded her. "Was it my message this morning?"

Semele thought fast. Had he left Emily Dickinson on her voice mail today? She really needed to start listening to those poems.

He began reciting it: "*Wild nights—wild nights! Were I with thee—*"

She cut him off. "Definitely in the mood for one of those."

"Seriously?"

He had no idea. She was teetering on the edge and would rather jump off than stay there.

They met at a small hole-in-the-wall in Williamsburg. The place hosted spoken-word nights, poetry slams, house parties, DJ battles, and even stand-up comedy. Bren had done a poetry reading there for his first book of poems, *Duende.* It had technically been their second date. He had gotten up onstage and spun words with a vulnerability that had made her dizzy. Afterward they cuddled on busted leather couches drinking tequila and beer and danced until three in the morning. The whole night had been her best date in years and cemented the start of their relationship.

Semele never confessed to Bren that she'd had to look up "duende." The word had many meanings: magic, spirit, and the passion that roused creativity. The next day she bought the book and spent the rest of the weekend reading each poem several times. Bren was publishing a new collection this year called *Soaked in Bourbon and Lit on Fire*—in honor of her, he teased. She had to admit that sounded more up her alley.

Tonight, the club seemed like the perfect place to go.

Bren was tongue-tied when she walked through the door. She was wearing her sexiest dress, a little black number with burnished red piping that made her feel like the star of her own burlesque show. The dress molded to her body, exaggerated every curve, and showed more leg than anything else she owned. Her hair gleamed like obsidian and curved into a wink right at her jawline. The total effect of the red lipstick, thick mascara, and eyeliner made her look exactly like she felt—dangerous.

She surprised Bren with a long kiss and led him to the bar, where she ordered them both martinis. She planned to have several.

Bren leaned closer to her. "Hi, I'm supposed to be meeting my girlfriend here tonight. You look a lot like her," he said, raising his voice over the music.

"I get that a lot." She clinked his glass.

"Hard day at work?"

"You have no idea." She pulled him onto the dance floor.

The music pulsed, compelling her body to move. She lost herself in the rhythm, dancing to song after song. She kept flitting to the bar for drinks, hoping to catch a buzz, to turn off her thoughts—anything not to think—but she couldn't get drunk tonight no matter how hard she tried.

Her mind was sharp, on edge, and her thoughts amplified. Seeing her name in the manuscript had completely derailed her. And for a split second, she'd really felt Ionna reaching out to her.

Did that make her crazy?

She went to order another martini and couldn't help thinking that she resembled her mother tonight. Helen could outdrink anyone at a party.

"Sure you want another?" Bren asked.

Semele laughed and shook her head. She grabbed his hand and they abandoned the bar. They took a cab back to her place, kissing in the backseat like teenagers, their arms like pretzels around each other.

Bren whispered, "Sem, you're driving me crazy."

"Good." When they arrived at her apartment, she led him inside and up the stairs. They were already pulling at each other's clothes before they had even closed the door.

They made love for the first time since she'd been back. Semele moved like liquid as she straddled him, kissing him deeper, possessively. Her body took over, forcing her mind to shut off.

The desire inside her spiraled, bringing forth thoughts—an inner knowledge—she had secretly suppressed. She stared into Bren's eyes, unable to look away.

Like a window opening, she saw glimpses of his future, a string of moments, his life in montage. Never had she experienced anything like this before.

She saw two boys that looked like miniature versions of him running across the park and squealing as he chased them.

Other images flashed by her in a flurry of time.

She saw Bren's future was filled with love—those beautiful boys—and a wife who wasn't her.

∞

My abilities blossomed after Ariston and I married. No one but he knew I was a seer.

I did not need to claim fame or glory. I continued to cast the Oracle's symbols in the privacy of my rooms, where life settled in around me. I began to see how a day's events would play out. I could tell Ariston what patients he would see that day and what ailed them. But still I could not see how to protect Wadjet's symbols through time. I feared I would fail her.

After a year of daily training I could stretch my mind's eye as far as a week, and after two years I could see one month into the future.

That is when I saw what I needed to do.

I will admit I was nervous, but it was finally time to delve into the world of dreaming. I wasn't sure how to tell Ariston of my intent, so I waited until after we had made love the next night. I shared my plan while we lay in each other's arms.

"You want to go on a dream quest at Mount Starius?" He looked at me as if I had transformed into Medusa with snakes for my hair. "Now?"

I nodded and waited for his full displeasure. The idea was mad, I knew. Last month I had discovered I was with child; after nearly two years of marriage we had finally conceived. Going on a journey was the last thing I should be doing.

"It's not far." I tried to assure him. "You can come with me."

"Of course I'll come with you!" he all but shouted. "I'm not

about to let my pregnant wife go traipsing around the moun-
tainside alone like some Gilgamesh!"

I laughed. "I wouldn't be traipsing."

"That's not the point!"

"Mount Starius lies right outside the city. It's not far!" My
voice rose to meet his and I tried to calm down. We were both
sitting up, glaring at each other.

"Why Mount Starius? Why not go to the temple of Apollo,
where we can pay for a tent?"

"I don't want a tent. I want a cave."

"What in heaven's name is wrong with a tent?"

"Because I need to be alone and not have all of Daphne outside."

I had read about Mount Starius in my research. In antiquity
it was considered a sacred place, its hidden caves used for dream
questing for over a thousand years. And I had already seen us
there. Twice I had dreamed about the cave, first in the book
depository and again just the night before. Finally the dream
made sense.

"Ariston, I must go. I've foreseen it."

"So everything you foresee you must blindly trust and follow?" he asked, exasperated.

I took his hands and tried to help him understand. "I have
not yet solved the Oracle's riddle. She said that when I am with
child, I will understand what I need to do to accomplish what
she has asked of me. My fear of failing her casts a gloom over
my happiness. Even with you. But I have seen a clear path to
that cave. I know I will find answers there. Now is the time."

Ariston grew still and stared at me. I could see I was reaching him.

"I must go this month. You, of all people, know I did not ask
for this gift. It is my burden and I need you to help me. At Mount
Starius I will understand what to do."

"But why now?" he beseeched. "You have your whole life to
discover the answer."

"I cannot control what I see any more than I can control time. Please help me." I kissed his hand. A shadow passed over his face and he looked as if he was going to object again, but I reminded him, "You were tasked to help me." Wadjet had not called him out by name but she had called upon my husband to aid me.

His expression softened and he kissed the tip of my nose. "I'm the one who translated it, remember?" he teased. But I could tell I had won.

We departed a week later, explaining to his family that we were going on a pilgrimage to pray for the baby's birth.

When I told Aella and Illias of our trip, of course they wanted to come with us. Aella said she would bring the servants and her *cosmetae*. I dissuaded her and promised we would be back soon. But my heart was touched by the gesture. Even after my marriage to Ariston, Aella and Illias continued to watch over me and dote on me like a daughter.

At Mount Starius I found the isolated cave I had dreamed of, and we made camp outside its opening. It felt strange arriving at the present from a future I had already foreseen.

Ariston wrapped a blanket around me, enveloping me in its warmth. "May the answers find you," he said. "Dream well."

Then he kissed me with such tenderness, as if I were leaving for a faraway journey. I knew it wasn't possible to love him more.

"Thank you," I said. He saw the lines of concern etched upon my face.

"Do not worry," he said softly. "Whatever you see, we will face together."

I looked up into his eyes in surprise. He too understood the gravity of my mission and had the same fear I did—that I would be forever altered by what I saw. I kissed him again, and steeled my courage.

When I entered the cave, the darkness greeted me with heavy silence.

I took off my sandals and walked forward, feeling answers waiting for me beneath the sleeping stones. I spread out my pallet, lit a candle, and settled in to dream.

As I lay there, never had I been more aware of time and all its trappings. Every small working of my body—thirst, hunger, physical discomfort—railed against me. Dreaming with purpose meant leaving the briars of daily life and entering the fallow lands of the mind. Dream questing is a Herculean task.

My time in the cave was the most difficult of my life.

For the first day I thought only of water, swallowing the dry air until my throat ached. By the second day my stomach clenched and clawed for food, and by the third my skin itched everywhere as my limbs twitched from their desire to move. I was hot and cold all at once; my body had become a stranger. I wanted nothing more than to end my suffering as I drifted in and out of consciousness. But I could not.

To divine is to imagine the world rightly, to see past the illusion that we are separate from the entire fabric of reality. Here I was attempting to have a waking dream of the future—all because an ancient oracle had seen me do so. The only problem was I had no idea how to accomplish such a feat. In all my research, I had read how to quiet the mind, to still the body, and to banish all doubt so the dream would come. But beyond that was a mystery. Waking dreams are not the usual dreams of sleep, but something far more potent.

I floated in a temporal realm for days, until the silence, the waiting, no longer existed. Then, without warning, the string of my thoughts snapped like a severed thread and my mind opened.

With incredible clarity, I saw the Oracle's symbols pass from hand to hand as they traveled through the future, and I saw those hands as one unbroken chain: those hands became my own, those stories became my story, and it is this tale that I will share with you now.

As you read my account of the future, you will ask how I came to know it. The best explanation I can offer is that time and memory go hand in hand. Without our memories, time would not exist. What we perceive as the world is really memory in motion. The visions I had in the cave were memories yet to happen. And any memory that has yet to happen is a prophecy.

But prophecies can be dangerous. The greatest prophecies have been hunted by kings and coveted for their power to bestow knowledge that does not yet exist. I won't deny I feared what would happen if I were to commit my vision to paper, and I did not do so after we returned home. Instead, I waited.

When I emerged from the cave after seven days, Ariston rose to his feet, visibly relieved. He could tell I was altered, but he did not ask what I had seen. There was so much I wanted to tell him, but I couldn't yet. The knowledge I now possessed was too great. In that moment I didn't know if I could ever share what I had seen. So we simply embraced and he took me home.

For several days I lived in a daze; everyone thought I was fatigued from our travels. Aella came to our home to care for me and ordered me to rest, barely letting me out of bed.

One day, after I'd begun to recover, I took out my father's parchment and reed pen from Alexandria. I now understood why I had brought them with me. The time had come to use them.

I began to write with the greatest speed, committing my words to paper as though my pen were flying on the wings of Nike, for I have foreseen that I will not survive my child's birth.

King of Cups

Semele clicked back to the previous page and double-checked the time line. On one page Ionna made a shocking revelation, that she would die in childbirth, and on the next she wrote of a couple journeying through the Zagros Mountains to Gundeshapur, a city founded several hundred years after Ionna's lifetime.

Semele frowned. She must have made a mistake when she was photographing the manuscript—or worse, several pages were missing.

"Hey, you're up early," Bren said from the doorway.

Ignoring the crisis on her computer screen, she turned to him and tried not to look as frustrated as she felt. She didn't want to deal with reality right now.

He leaned over and gave her a lingering kiss. "Working?"

"Yeah, sorry." She gently pulled away. "I've got to have this finished before . . ." She trailed off.

Before what? As of yesterday she wasn't even handling the Bossard Collection. So why did this matter? Technically it shouldn't, but she wanted to know the rest of Ionna's story—she needed to know why her name was in the manuscript. Deep down she knew this wasn't a coincidence. And that was what bothered her the most.

Bren sat next to her on the couch wearing only his jeans. "Sem, last night was wicked." He took her hand.

Semele avoided his eyes. Last night had been wicked. She had been the one at the cauldron and she had conjured up an image she wished she hadn't seen.

She woke early that morning to find Bren asleep beside her, his leg and arm across her body like a barricade—as if even in sleep he knew the realization she had come to. The clarity of her vision last night had stunned her by showing her what was already in her heart. It felt like turning around and looking into a mirror, already knowing what she would see.

She had lain there in bed, trying to figure out what the hell to do, until she couldn't stand it anymore.

Without waking Bren, she'd grabbed her robe, tiptoed from the room, and quietly shut the door behind her. After a double espresso, she returned to translating. Even after everything that had happened last night, Ionna still had her undivided attention.

She tugged her hand away. "I need to go to the office."

Bren gave her a searching look. "You're acting weird. You know that, right?"

She gave a weak nod.

"Why?" The hurt in his voice made her wince. "It's me."

"I know. I just . . ."

"Just what? Talk to me."

How could she tell him there was a ticking clock on their relationship, that they weren't going to last?

"Sorry, I'm really stressed over work."

"Of course." Bren threw his hands up in surrender. It wasn't the first time he'd heard this excuse. He tried switching to a brighter tone. "Just don't forget about the dinner tonight with my folks. I was thinking I'd come by at seven. The reservation is at seven thirty."

Her heart sank. She'd forgotten that his parents were in town from Florida for the week. It was their first time visiting Bren since he and Semele had started dating, and she knew he was excited to introduce her. She couldn't fathom the idea of spending an evening with them now.

"Bren, I'm too tied up with this deadline to make the dinner."

A range of expressions played across his face. "You're kidding. My parents have been looking forward to meeting you for months."

"I know. I'm sorry. I really am, but it's a bad time."

Bren stormed into the bedroom and came back with his shirt. He dressed rapidly and grabbed his wallet and keys off the table.

"Don't be mad," she pleaded.

"Don't be mad? What the hell, Sem?"

Her eyes welled with tears. God, she hated this. The truth was that even if she hadn't seen his future without her in it, she and Bren would still be standing at opposite ends of the room, a gulf between them.

"Did you meet someone in Switzerland?" he demanded. "Is that what's going on here?"

Semele hesitated. Theo wasn't the reason.

"Because ever since you came back it's like you're a different person."

"Like I said"—Semele crossed her arms—"I'm stressed over work. I don't want to fight."

Bren shook his head, completely bewildered. "You seriously can't go tonight?"

She nodded, avoiding his eyes, and made a big deal out of packing up her computer. She needed to go to the lab and check the manuscript. "I'm sorry. I know it's lame."

Bren let out a pained sigh of resignation. "I guess we'll have to do it next time. I'll tell them things are really crazy on your end."

She wondered what he would say if she confessed that a two-thousand-year-old manuscript was talking to her. Crazy didn't come close.

Queen of Swords

Semele got off the elevator on the eleventh floor, purposefully avoiding the twelfth, where she might run into Mikhail or Raina.

She found Cabe at the humidifier chamber again. "Still busy with Georgie?"

He muttered, "Our first president is high maintenance." He glanced over to her and smiled. "You're looking rad-trashed."

She grimaced. "Thanks. I need to ask a favor. Has Fritz inventoried the Bossard Collection?"

"Yesterday. I got the short list this morning."

The short list wasn't really a list. It was more like a mini-collection, comprised of items that needed authentication, closer examination, or possibly restoration. Semele knew the manuscript would be one of the works singled out. She had logged the piece with several question marks about its origin and date.

"Back table." Cabe motioned. "But I thought you weren't on the Bossard Collection anymore."

"I'm not. I just need to take a quick look at something."

She headed toward the sink and was washing her hands when her cell rang—her mother, again. There was also a voice mail from Bren, no doubt fishing for the reason behind her emotional withdrawal this morning. She saw Theo had left her a message too and quickly played it.

"Semele, Mikhail's insistent that Fritz handle the auction. It's not ideal, but he feels it's the best course. I'd still like to meet when I come to New York next month." He hesitated. "I'll be in touch soon."

Semele's pulse quickened and she listened to the message again. Theo wanted to see her. She had no idea what to make of that, and she would never find out—she would already be in Beijing when he came.

She put her phone back with a little sigh and washed her hands once more for good measure.

There were twelve pieces on the back table, including Ionna's manuscript. She carefully opened the leather binding to examine the first leaf.

"I agree," Cabe said when he saw what she was handling. "That one's quite the stunner. I'm doing a DNA rundown."

"Good. I was hoping you would."

DNA testing had become one of the most precise methods of dating a work, though there were several handicapping factors. Usually the parchment was made of an amalgamation of animals' skins from different time periods, which made pinpointing its exact origin and date difficult. Handwriting analysis would always remain a vital tool in the process; unlike DNA testing, it didn't require samples.

"Call me when you have the results."

"Sure. But why?"

"I've been reading it," she confessed. He gave her a quizzical look.

"I made a digital so I could hone my translation skills." She wanted to downplay her interest, and this wasn't a lie. She hadn't done a translation in years. "I think some of the leaves are missing."

Cabe shrugged. "The translator will find out soon enough."

Semele frowned. The idea that another translator would be reading Ionna's story bothered her. But in less than a month a buyer would acquire the manuscript, and Semele would move on to another collection in another country. For the first time the thought made her weary.

She leaned down to study the binding where she had stopped reading this morning and saw the evidence.

Pages *were* missing.

They had been carefully cut out right at the spine, where the leaves were stitched. She leaned even closer and discovered that quite a few had been removed.

"What are you doing?"

Raina's voice made Semele jerk upright. Raina was standing in the doorway, her hands on her hips.

"Hey, Renie," Cabe interjected.

Semele looked at him. Did he just call her "Renie" and smooth out his stained T-shirt? Semele looked back to Raina and noticed the slight flush on her face. She would have laughed if she wasn't so irritated.

Semele stepped away from the table. "Leaves are missing from one of the Bossard manuscripts. It's an important piece." She tried not to sound like a thief caught in the act. Why should she feel guilty for looking at a manuscript she had authorized to be transported here in the first place?

"Mikhail gave you the rest of the week off," Raina said, crossing her arms in that disapproving way of hers.

Semele stared at her without blinking and forced herself not to mimic her gesture, though she desperately wanted to. She didn't say a word, her spine stiff with anger.

"Fritz has already noted that some pages are missing and informed Mikhail and his client. He's very thorough," Raina said in a clipped voice.

Semele caught the subtext—*and you're not.* She decided to make an exit before she said something she would regret, and headed for the elevator. "Excellent. Ciao, you two." On her way out she shot Cabe a stern look, which he purposefully ignored.

As the elevator doors closed, she caught a glimpse of Raina

and Cabe sharing an intimate kiss. The sight of them felt like a punch in the gut, and it only reinforced the distressing thought that was running through her mind: she was about to lose her friend.

Message to VS—

Manuscript has missing pages.

Reply from VS—

Was it him?

Message to VS—

Unclear. Will dig deeper.

Reply from VS—

Dig quickly. Assemble a team.

All her life Elisa had received premonitions and she believed those visions were gifts from God.

She attended mass every day at the Golden House, a magnificent church that surpassed every building in Antioch. Built in the shape of an octagon, it had a gilded dome roof decorated in gold, brass, and precious stones that towered in the sky like God's crown.

Elisa's father was a great physician in Antioch, and last year Elisa had married one of his pupils, an earnest young doctor named Mathai. Mathai had loved Elisa from afar for years before gathering the courage to seek her hand. His mother ordered him more than once to choose a different girl. "She cannot bear a child. Look at her. She will snap in two!" she proclaimed with a grim shake of her head. A woman who had mothered four sons felt entitled to say such things.

Fortunately, as the middle child, Mathai was often overlooked. So when he decided to marry Elisa, his mother finally relented. It was Elisa's father who took issue: he thought Mathai weak and doomed to mediocrity and had hoped for a better match. There had always been tension between the two men. Only Elisa knew she could convince her father to let them marry.

One day, when she was helping her father clean his medicine box, she confessed she had foreseen her future as Mathai's bride. Not knowing how her father would react, she rushed to assure him she had also foreseen how, over the years, Mathai would stay dedicated to his studies and rise in prominence. More importantly, she promised that Mathai would treat her like the most priceless treasure in the world.

Her father listened while polishing his medicine vials, never once looking at his daughter. Even if he hadn't believed in his daughter's gift—which he did—he had never been able to say no to Elisa, his gentle daughter, whom he adored above all else.

He expelled a soft breath and nodded. "So it will be."

At the end of their first year of marriage, Elisa confided in Mathai about her gift.

"Husband?" she called to him softly as he was leaving to go to her father's school.

Mathai turned around and smiled at the sight of her sitting at the kitchen stool, her stomach just beginning to show with child.

"On the way to my father's you might run into your old friend. Do ask him about his leg. It needs mending."

Mathai was in too much of a hurry to question her strange request. But on the way to his father-in-law's school he did run into his old childhood friend. Even more astounding, his friend was limping. Mathai never would have asked why if Elisa had not warned him.

His friend showed him a cut across his knee that had festered. Mathai brought him to the clinic, and his morning was spent cleaning the wound, stitching it, and applying salve. When Mathai returned home he found Elisa waiting for him on the same stool.

He stared into her eyes and realized she had just told him her secret.

From then on, every morning before he left, she would tell him something about his day. And it would always come to pass. After a month of being privy to her foresights, Mathai believed that, indeed, she was blessed. So when Elisa came home from the Golden House that day in tears, barely able to speak, Mathai listened with grave attention.

While kneeling in prayer, she had seen the walls of the church crumble around her and the stones turn to sand. Then she saw a great earthquake level Antioch to rubble. A firestorm raged through the city for days and the Golden House was destroyed. Hundreds of thousands of people perished and the city was demolished.

Her words sent chills through his body. He was horrified that she had foreseen these catastrophic events with such clarity.

That night the family gathered at Mathai's insistence and Elisa recounted her vision. When she finished, no one spoke for a long time. Mathai held Elisa's hand while her mother wept.

Finally her father said, "You must leave Antioch. Right away."

Mathai frowned. "But the baby."

Elisa's hand moved protectively to her stomach. She would give birth soon, but she knew it would not be in Antioch. "Mathai, we must leave. We all must leave." She pleaded to her parents.

Her mother shook her head. "We are too old, Elisa. Our place is here."

Elisa's eyes welled with tears. She would spend the next several days begging and pleading for her parents to come with them. She also knew that, in the end, they would not. Only her desperation to save the child in her womb would make her consider leaving them behind.

Mathai sat brooding. "But where would we go?" he asked helplessly. "Our lives are here. Our family, my work . . ."

"We must leave. For the baby," Elisa said with conviction.

"But where will we go?" Mathai repeated.

"To Gundeshapur," his father-in-law said in his commanding voice. "I will write to the academy with your introduction."

Mathai looked at him in astonishment, and long-buried ambitions began to stir inside him. He had heard of opportunities arising in Gundeshapur, the glittering jewel of the Sassanid

Empire. But never in his life had he thought he would make the journey. Now Elisa's father was willing to write to the academy there on his behalf. The Academy of Athens had lost its funding from the emperor, triggering a great exodus—not only from Antioch, but also from Edessa and Athens—to Gundeshapur.

Only the brightest scholars and doctors were granted tenure. Gundeshapur boasted a medical training center, a hospital, an observatory, a library, and its own translation house. Built by the hands of Roman prisoners of the Persian dynasty— many of whom were skilled architects, masons, and artists— Gundeshapur's buildings supposedly rivaled those in Rome and Antioch in their magnificence. To work there would be any-one's dream.

Mathai watched Elisa's father pen the letter. "Thank you," Mathai said, his voice choked with gratitude. Elisa's father looked up at Mathai with sharp eyes and pointed to his daughter. "I do this for her."

Mathai nodded earnestly. "I'll work hard. I'll give our child the best life."

Elisa swallowed the lump in her throat and took her husband's hand. She already knew he would.

⌣

They left before the week's end. Elisa looked back at her city for the last time. She prayed to God once more for her vision to be wrong.

She and Mathai journeyed east, then south. They stopped at Aleppo and Rusafa before continuing the long stretch down the Euphrates to Dura-Europos. Elisa rode on their horse while Mathai led the donkey with all their possessions.

The Zagros Mountains loomed in the distance and Mathai calculated they would reach Gundeshapur in three days' time. Elisa was growing weaker and weaker; today she had not said a word at all. Mathai feared she could not keep riding.

Their horse carried her gently, as if he understood her fragile state. The baby would come soon. Mathai tried to convince her they should stay in one of the passing towns until the child was born, but she insisted they keep going. His position at the academy was not guaranteed, and the longer they delayed, the more tenuous it became. He was not the only physician to come from the west seeking work.

Elisa let out a small moan and Mathai stopped the horse. He hurried to give her water. "Drink, Elisa. Drink." He held up the leather bag but she did not take it.

Her eyes glazed over as she stared into the distance. Then her body went limp and she listed toward him, tumbling off the horse.

As Mathai rushed to break her fall, the horse startled, poised to run. "Easy, Zaman," Mathai said gently. "Help me now."

Zaman remained still but neighed with agitation. Mathai held Elisa in his arms and tried to think of what he should do.

He laid her on the ground and led the horse and donkey to a nearby tree. Then he went looking for branches to construct a makeshift litter, which he covered with one of their blankets. He laid Elisa on top and tied the litter to the horse. Only a few hours of daylight remained, so they had no choice but to continue on.

They traveled for two more days, barely stopping to rest. Only when he knew Elisa was asleep did Mathai show his fear. Her vision had forced them to flee Antioch, and he struggled to suppress the thought that his wife and child would not survive the journey.

⁓

When they finally arrived in Gundeshapur, Mathai closed his eyes and whispered a prayer.

They wandered through a residential district and Mathai tried to get his bearings. He assumed the medical school would be south, near the city center, but he wasn't sure they could travel any farther at this point. Elisa had begun to whimper in pain hours before, and now she could barely stifle her screams. They would not have time to seek lodging from the academy before the birth.

Mathai placed a cloth in Elisa's mouth for her to bite on, in the hope it might distract her from the pain. She opened her eyes and looked up at him, pleading. Mathai swallowed and squeezed her hand. "We have made it to the city. I will find help," he assured her; though he wasn't sure how.

He led Zaman and the donkey down the street. From the looks of the houses, they were clearly in a wealthy district. The architecture of the city felt foreign, from the colonnaded porticoes and square towers, to the pointed archways and trapezoid doorways.

He passed an old woman on the side of the road selling fresh yogurt and asked if any physicians lived in the nearby houses.

The woman only spoke Pahlavi, but she saw Elisa's distress and pointed to the villa farthest down the street, the one that looked like a palace. Mathai thought he understood.

"Thank you," he said. But since he was not buying anything, the woman just shooed him away.

Mathai led the animals through the villa's archway into a courtyard. Countless sculptures littered the yard, and towering columns circled the fountain like a temple. Mathai had never seen a more extravagant, or cluttered, garden.

A house servant came out to greet them. Mathai tried to communicate with the man, but had no luck. The servant signaled for them to wait and disappeared inside.

Not a good start. Mathai rubbed his hands together, trying to figure out how to gain entry to the home. The family who lived here surely had a house physician. Mathai only dealt with injuries to the skin. Bringing a baby into the world required select skills he did not possess. The physicians of wealthy families delivered all their patrons' children. This house would be Elisa's best chance.

Soon a large man who looked to be in his fifties emerged. He was yelling in Pahlavi with the booming countenance of a much younger man. Mathai couldn't understand his words but thought he must be asking, "Why are you at my house?"

"Sir," Mathai interrupted as politely as possible. "Do you speak Syriac?"

"Of course I speak Syriac!" The man switched to Syriac immediately. "I speak Greek too. Do not come to my doorstep to insult me!"

"Forgive me . . . ," he said. Elisa let out a shrill moan from the litter. Mathai hurried on. "I've been told you have a physician."

"If I let every stray and straggler into my home, then the whole city would be at my door. Be gone!" The old man turned to head inside.

"Please," Mathai called to him. "I have many treasures I will give you in return. My family's medical journals." The journals were among his most prized possessions and he needed them for his work, but now was not the time to worry over such things.

The old man turned around. "Show me."

Mathai rushed to the donkey and opened the bundle. "They are the finest copies—Galen, Hippocrates, Dioscorides' *De Materia Medica*, which is a collection—"

"I know what *De Materia Medica* is, boy! Every doctor is toting the same."

In desperation, Mathai riffled through another bundle and pulled out a thick codex. "No one has this." He held out the manuscript. "From my wife's family. Very old."

The man opened the binding to examine the first parchment leaf and squinted. "Greek?"

Mathai nodded. He could not read Greek and knew very little about the manuscript. Elisa's grandmother would often read parts to her and translate the words into Syriac. "It was taken from the Great Library of Alexandria before the fire." Mathai wasn't sure if that was exactly true, but whoever had written the work had seen the fire. That much he knew.

He almost offered the unusual divinity symbols that went with the manuscript, but the old man would not be interested in such a collection. Plus his wife seemed quite attached to them.

Mathai looked toward Elisa with relief. Her eyes were closed and she seemed oblivious to the exchange. He didn't think she would be angry if giving away the codex would save her life and the child's. The manuscript looked to be in perfect condition and would be a prize in any man's library.

"Done," the old man agreed, and suddenly a cluster of servants appeared in the courtyard to assist the newcomers. Mathai and Elisa were now guests.

The servants showed Mathai to their quarters and carried Elisa to the bed. The house physician appeared within moments and quickly began his examination. Mathai was relieved the man spoke Syriac. He had been told many physicians in Gundeshapur did.

"The baby will come soon. The birth will be difficult," the man said.

Mathai met his gaze and saw the worry, the hesitation in his eyes. The words he had left unspoken struck fear in Mathai's heart. The doctor wasn't certain if Elisa or the child would survive.

"Until the time comes, she must rest," he ordered, and then assigned two female servants to attend to her.

Mathai found their things had already been unloaded from the donkey and brought to their rooms. He unfolded a fresh robe for Elisa, which he gave to the servants. Then he located a clean tunic and pants for himself.

The house had the luxury of a private bath, and Mathai took great pleasure in washing away their journey. While soaking in the water he closed his eyes and prayed again for Elisa's safety. He could not find a place to put the fear inside of him.

After his bath, he passed the dining room where the old man

sat alone at a long table covered with platters of food. The savory scent of lamb made Mathai light-headed and he realized how long he had gone without a meal.

"Come!" his host ordered with his mouth full. "You must be hungry after such a journey."

Mathai hesitated. "My wife . . ."

". . . needs her rest. I insist. Share my wine."

The feast looked more suited for a wedding banquet than an everyday meal, with so many dishes to choose from: eggplant with onion and mint, sun-dried yogurt, stuffed grape leaves, barberry rice, and a savory stew topped with grated walnuts. Mathai couldn't believe such a meal had been prepared for one person, but he had yet to see another member of the household.

"Will your family be joining us?" Mathai asked.

The old man kept eating, ignoring the question. Instead he wanted to know about Antioch; he said he had visited years ago. Mathai learned the old man's name was Admentos and that he had been one of the first Greek scholars to make his way to Gundeshapur.

Mathai listened and did his best to answer Admentos' questions. During the lulls in their conversation he could hear Elisa screaming. The labor had begun, but Admentos would not let him leave.

After dinner he insisted on showing off his personal library. Mathai found the library as crowded as the courtyard. So many manuscripts and scrolls burdened the shelves that some hung precariously off ledges and others had fallen to the floor. Piles of codices were stacked in the corners of the room, too many to count. The man was a hoarder. Mathai wondered if he had even read half his works.

When Mathai saw Elisa's manuscript shoved between five others on one of the reading tables, he was astonished. What had been a prized possession for them was merely another token in Admentos' library.

For Mathai, standing there in that room, his life suddenly felt like it belonged to a stranger. Just as the manuscript had ended up in a place it did not belong, so had he.

He should be at the academy right now, meeting with the director and discussing his future. Someone should be unloading their things and placing them in one of the small quarters reserved for the staff. Elisa should be resting in their new bed and preparing for the birth. Instead Mathai had to suffer the company of a greedy old man who cared little that his wife was fighting for her life.

Elisa's screams grew louder. When she called out his name, Mathai backed toward the door. "Excuse me," he interrupted. He no longer cared if he offended the man. Elisa needed him.

～

The next hours were the bleakest of his life. He had heard gruesome tales of childbirth, that it demanded every bit of a woman's spirit. He watched Elisa fight and knew his mother had been wrong about her. Elisa's body might be frail, but she would not give up until the baby was born.

He knelt beside her and held her hand.

Elisa tried to speak to him. "Promise me, Mathai . . ." she said, but she could not continue. She screamed and her body contorted with pain.

His eyes grew wet and he choked back a sob. "Elisa?" She couldn't hear him.

When her pain subsided again, he tried to bring her back.

For a moment, clarity returned to her eyes. "Give our child my mother's symbols." She gripped his hand hard.

Mathai thought back to the trade he had made with Admentos and thanked the heavens he had not also offered the divinity symbols. "I will. I promise."

"And the story. Tell her the story."

Mathai did not know the story, but he couldn't break his wife's heart by confessing what he had done. Before he could answer, Elisa screamed again and did not stop until the baby's cries joined hers. Then she fell back on the pillows and closed her eyes.

It was evening now and soft moonlight fell on Elisa, calling to her from the window. She looked over to the light. She saw that in time, Mathai would settle in Gundeshapur and rise in prominence to a degree that would have made even her father proud, just as she had promised him. Mathai would remarry and have several more children; though his first daughter would always remain his favorite. His new wife wanted to resent her but couldn't, and she ended up loving the child as her own.

Mathai kept his promise to Elisa. He gave their daughter the divinity symbols when she was old enough to understand. He explained that they were a family heirloom from her birth mother and had come from the Great Library of Alexandria. Mathai only asked that she not look at them in front of him; he did not want to be reminded of his beloved first wife.

On occasion the girl would take them out in private before she went to sleep. She would study the mysterious images and imagine what her mother had been like. The girl would stare at the moon, not knowing that its light connected them beyond the years.

～

Elisa was my last descendent to know my story, now lost in a stranger's library in Gundeshapur. That you are seeing my words is testament to the seams of time.

You must look up now, Semele, and stop reading. Someone is watching you.

Strength

Semele almost fell out of her chair.

Several people nearby shot her annoyed looks. She was sitting in the Rose Room in the New York Public Library and had been completely absorbed by Ionna's story when she stumbled upon her name again.

Her gaze shot up and landed on a man three rows ahead. Their eyes met and he quickly glanced back at his book. Semele scanned the other seats around her, searching for anyone who seemed conspicuous.

This was the second time Ionna had called her out by name. It just wasn't possible that she was communicating with her. Ionna had to have known some other person named Semele. Maybe Semele was even the name of her daughter.

The name is Greek, Semele grimly reminded herself, trying to calm down.

But then how was it possible that Ionna knew about Gundeshapur, a city founded several hundred years after her time? Unless this manuscript was a fake and had been written years later. She needed to talk to Cabe and find out what the DNA test revealed about the manuscript's date of origin.

If, in fact, this manuscript was written during the time Ionna lived, or said she lived, Semele had a real problem: a woman living in the time of Cleopatra had foreseen the rise of the Sassanid Empire, and this alone would make the manuscript priceless.

Semele glanced around the room again and saw the man who had just caught her eye. Why did he look so familiar?

Her computer beeped—her battery was running low. She took it as a sign. She had been sitting there all day translating Ionna's manuscript, and seeing her name again had completely unnerved her. She needed to get out of there.

She bent down to put her things away in the bag by her feet, when it came to her.

The man had been on her plane. He was the man who'd been staring at her from the next row on her flight from Switzerland.

A surge of adrenaline hit her, but she tried to remain calm as she gathered her things.

She looked at the man again discreetly, trying to remember every detail about him: forties, knit sweater and thin metal glasses, short hair, clean-shaven. Possibly German or Swiss, if she had to guess. There was nothing sinister about him. He had a preoccupied look, the kind that made people forgettable. If she hadn't caught him staring at her, she never would have noticed him.

Without turning around again, she grabbed her things and hurried to the exit. But right as she was leaving, she couldn't resist the urge to look one more time.

The man's seat was empty.

Eight of Swords

Semele hit the street running, besieged by questions.

Had he been following her since Switzerland? Did he know where she lived? And how the hell had Ionna known?

Semele felt more than a little crazy, but Ionna had warned her. There was no way she could deny it.

Glancing over her shoulder, she scanned the street. She saw no evidence of the man. But still, she was afraid to go home. She fished her phone out and hit the second name at the top of her favorites. Calling Bren was out of the question.

Cabe answered on the last ring before the call went to voice mail. "Hey, stranger."

"Hey. Can I come over now?"

"Sure. Everything okay?" he asked.

Semele took a breath and tried to keep the tremor from her voice. "Stressful day." That was putting it mildly. "I'll explain later."

"I've got my award-winning pasta going. Come on over."

"Great, see you in a bit." She hung up.

Cabe lived about a fifteen-minute walk from her place in Brooklyn. She would go to his apartment and then figure out what to do. They'd been planning to catch up since she'd gotten back, and they would have already set a dinner date if she hadn't been so preoccupied with Ionna's manuscript.

Semele rang the bell to Cabe's building, out of breath from her demented-looking power walk down the street. She glanced up and down the block again, clutching the bottle of cabernet she had bought at the liquor store around the corner like a weapon. Cabe buzzed her in and she ducked inside, relieved to be behind a locked door. She made her way to his apartment at the end of the hall, where the smell of garlic greeted her.

Cabe swung his door open and she held out the bottle of wine. "For the chef."

"*Graci! Buongiorno, buongiorno . . . ,*" he said in a flurry and disappeared into the kitchen. "Step into my house," he called out with a bad Italian accent.

Semele took off her shoes in the tiny entryway and squeezed past Cabe's ten-speed. The chain on the bike scratched her leg as she brushed past. She looked at the run in her stockings and grimaced.

"I hate your bike." She padded the five steps into the closet-sized kitchen. "Smells amazing."

Cabe poured her a glass from the bottle he had already opened. "Cheers." They clinked glasses and he continued stirring the bubbling Bolognese.

"Ooh, this one's nice," she said, tasting it again. "Oliver?" His brother, Oliver, was a sommelier in the Hamptons and always sent Cabe a case of his current favorite for his birthday. Semele took another sip and nibbled on a piece of aged Gouda he had put out on a board.

Slowly, the trauma of the past hour began to loosen its grip. For now she was safe. She could worry about the man later—right now, she wanted to pretend her life was normal. She was hungry and the wine and cheese tasted delicious. She took another sip, moving the velvety red across her tongue. Cabe had made one of her favorite salads, an arugula, candied-walnut confection with feta and aged balsamic.

"Were you already cooking all this before I called?" She asked. He had quite the gourmet spread going.

Cabe shot her a pointed look. "Raina may stop by."

Semele's jaw dropped in horror. Raina was coming here? "Tonight? Why didn't you tell me?"

"What, you can't eat together?"

"I'd prefer not to!"

Cabe stopped cooking. "You know, I've been trying to be cool about this little aversion you've got toward her, but really, what has she done to deserve your judgment? You barely know her. It's so unlike you."

Semele hesitated. In all honesty, she couldn't answer that. She knew her reaction to Raina wasn't rational. She struggled to come up with an answer. "Have you seen her handwriting?"

The first time she got an expense report with Raina's comments, Semele had been absolutely perplexed. Raina's handwriting was flat-out ugly and bore all the marks of an introvert with serious emotional baggage. Her letters were unbalanced and sprouting all over the place, like a yard with too many weeds.

"So what, Miss Quantico, it's a little messy. Ever analyze your own handwriting?"

He had said it half-jokingly, but it still stung. Of course she had analyzed her own handwriting. Every day she saw what her pen revealed naked on the page. The large inner loops on the right-hand side of her circle letters all but announced the secrets she was hiding; the figure eights lacing her writing showed an abnormally strong fluidity of thought; and her backward crossed T-bars highlighted the critical nature she had toward herself. Only an expert graphologist would be able to tell.

She tried to dial her emotions down. Cabe did too and softened his tone. "Just give her a chance. Please, for me. She really is different when you get to know her."

Semele doubted that but held her tongue. She'd had Raina pegged by the end of her first week at Kairos—fake. Over a year later, her opinion hadn't changed. Raina would tear Cabe to shreds. That he couldn't see it was mind-boggling.

"What about you and Bren the Pen?" Cabe asked, changing tack. "He called me, you know."

"I don't want to talk about it."

Cabe's eyebrows shot up. He was close with Bren too, so Semele didn't feel she could be totally honest, but she tried. "Let's just say, I'm starting to have doubts. It's complicated," she said.

Bren had left her several messages and she had yet to return them. She was being absolutely horrible, the kind of horrible that could not be forgiven. Deep down she knew that was the point. Cabe was right. She was sabotaging herself.

She tried to change the subject. "How's Oliver?" she asked, pouring herself more wine and studying the label. It was a 2011 Barbaresco from a boutique winery, incredibly smooth. She really should e-mail him a hello. She'd become friendly with Oliver after she had tagged along with Cabe to the Hamptons once.

"He's fine. And don't change the subject." Cabe pointed his finger at her. "Bren is the best damn thing that's ever happened to you." The pasta bowls clanked together as he set them down on the table.

She let out a sigh. How could she explain that ending her relationship with Bren was the right decision? The idea of women's intuition had been distilled into a vat of ridiculousness for centuries and was usually scoffed at—and she knew she'd sound crazy if she told Cabe the full story. While her time with Bren would always have a place in her heart, that time was over; her premonition had helped her see it.

"Let me just say one more thing and then I'll shut up," he advised. "Don't be stupid."

"You know I'm not like Allison," she said softly. "Even if Bren and I don't last, I'm not like her." Allison was Cabe's ex-fiancée. She had dumped him at the altar right before Semele moved to New York. Cabe had moped on Semele's new couch, curled up in a fetal position, for weeks.

"But something did happen in Switzerland, didn't it?" Cabe asked. It didn't sound like a question.

Semele could feel the weight of his judgment. First Bren and now Cabe. Did she have "something happened in Switzerland" tattooed on her forehead?

Yes, something had happened in Switzerland. The problem was it was more than kissing Theo. She couldn't begin to tell him that a prophet was speaking to her through an ancient manuscript, or that she had started to see the future. Thinking about any of it made her head hurt.

"Can we move on?" she asked, picking up her fork. Cabe's doorbell sounded as if on cue. The thought of Raina made her lose her appetite.

Cabe jumped up to buzz her in. "Oh, hey, I got the DNA test back on that manuscript," he said on his way to the door.

"And?" Semele asked, her heart stopping and starting again. She wasn't sure she was ready to know.

"It's from right around 46 B.C. at the latest, no question," he said and promptly disappeared into the entry hall.

Semele sat back and let out a long breath, glad she had a moment alone to process. Those results were staggering. Ionna really had known about Gundeshapur, a city founded over two hundred years after she had written the manuscript. What else had she known? Semele was barely halfway through Ionna's story.

She could hear Cabe and Raina talking quietly in the hallway. Then Cabe came back alone, looking irritated.

Semele glanced toward the door. "What happened?"

"She had an emergency pop up and could only stop by for a minute."

That sounded unlikely. "Who shows up for two minutes and leaves?" Semele could tell by the look on Cabe's face that she was the reason Raina had bailed on dinner. "Was it because of me?"

"No, not at all."

She could tell he was lying. "Cabe, seriously. Who gets jealous like that?" she asked, feeling disturbed.

"She wasn't jealous." Cabe sounded peeved. "It's just dinner."

Semele nodded and tried to eat. But she couldn't help feeling that Raina was driving a wedge between them. She might as well have still been in the room.

Cabe was completely distracted and most likely wishing Raina was there enjoying his culinary efforts, not her. For the first time, Semele felt like an intruder and the feeling didn't sit well. But she had come here for help. She needed to confide in him.

"Cabe, I'm in the middle of something serious. I think the manuscript I'm reading . . . is special."

That got his attention. "What do you mean?"

"The person who wrote it talks about history that hasn't happened, like a prophecy."

"Like Nostradamus or something?"

"Kind of." Except unlike Nostradamus' predictions, Ionna had recorded facts and names without codes, quatrains, or rhymes that needed to be deciphered. Semele didn't want to get into the details right now. "Someone knows I'm reading it. I think I'm being followed."

"What?" Now Cabe was completely with her. "Hold on. Back up. From the beginning."

"I found a manuscript that Marcel Bossard had kept secret, and I made a copy in Switzerland. The night before I flew out someone broke into my hotel room, but they didn't take anything. They opened the file on my computer." She hurried to explain, feeling her anxiety returning. "Then today I went to the library and caught a guy watching me—and he was on my flight from Geneva. I know the Rose Room is a serious tourist destination, but what are the odds? He was on my flight." *And he had shown up in the Rose Room right when Ionna had said Semele was being watched.*

Semele didn't feel comfortable sharing that part of the story. But if she couldn't tell Cabe, who could she tell? If her father were still alive she would have taken the first train to New Haven and shown him the manuscript. He would have known what to do.

"That's why I called," she confessed. "I was scared to go home. I didn't want him to know where I lived."

"Jesus, Sem, you should have told me."

"I'm telling you now." They stared at each other. "What do I do?" she asked. Her fear was threatening to overwhelm her again.

Cabe rubbed his chin, looking equally worried. "Well, for starters, if some guy is following you, you're staying here tonight. We'll walk over to your place in the morning and check things out."

Semele felt her body droop with relief. Tomorrow was Saturday. Soon it would be Monday and she'd be back at work prepping for Beijing. Suddenly putting six thousand miles between her and a stalker didn't seem like such a bad call.

They went back to eating in silence. "You know, maybe you shouldn't read any more of it," Cabe said.

Semele didn't answer right away. If Ionna was predicting the future, did she really want to know the rest?

A strange sense of inevitability took hold of her. Yes. Yes, she did.

Message from VS—

The missing pages?

Message to VS—

Still searching.

From VS—

Find them.
Anything else u r not handling?

Message to VS—

Manuscript being translated this week.

From VS—

Do not let that happen.

The Hermit

The next morning Cabe and Semele strolled to her place with coffees and pastries from a nearby café in hand. As they walked, Semele watched all the pedestrians around her, on alert for the man at the library.

She looked over at Cabe. "Do you think a person can predict the future?"

Cabe considered the question. "Well, it seems impossible when you grant that reality is just a complex web of particles colliding with each other all the time."

Semele snorted. "It was a yes-or-no question."

"Then no. Life is based on the uncertainty principle. If we can't even measure a particle's velocity and position at the same time, how can we know where anything will be in the future?"

"Let's pretend I haven't seen every *Star Trek* episode like you. What about people who have premonitions that come true? How do you explain that?"

Cabe hesitated. "Okay. There are at least ten dimensions that we know of so far. Maybe psychics—I'm talking real ones—if they exist, have the ability to see an interdimensional spectrum of space-time that we can't access."

"Interdimensional space-time?" That didn't help.

"The thing that's always bothered me about the idea of seeing the future is that it negates free will. If the future is already set, what's all this?" He motioned to the street. "Was it set in stone that I was going to eat this blueberry scone for breakfast, or could I have gotten a chocolate croissant?" He took a bite of the scone from the bag he was carrying. "Can we change the future, or does it unfold by cosmic design?"

"Quit spitting crumbs on me," she said. "Those are all good questions. I don't disagree, but then how do you explain the manuscript?"

For a second he looked stumped. "Is it really a prophecy?"

"Cabe, she knew about a city that hadn't been created yet."

The more Semele thought about it, the more mystified she became. Semele knew the history of Gundeshapur. The city had been a pivotal force in the ancient world and flourished for hundreds of years. When Justinian all but closed Plato's academy in Athens, the Greek philosophers moved to Gundeshapur. So did the Nestorian Assyrians, when they were seeking refuge from religious persecution in the Byzantine Empire.

After the fall of the Roman Empire, so many of antiquity's greatest works were lost. It was only because of cities like Gundeshapur that they survived at all. The Persians and their Arab inheritors studied Euclid, Pythagoras, Aristotle, Plato, and countless others before those writings found their way back to the West centuries later, heralding the dawn of the Renaissance. Semele had studied this path of knowledge; one only had to track the great libraries of the ancient world to do so. When one library perished, another was born, and the river of knowledge rushed to the new source. Her father had taught her that.

"I'll give you a copy of the translation when I'm done." She hooked her arm in Cabe's and gave it a squeeze, suddenly not feeling so alone. "I'm going to need your help on this."

"Abso-freaking-lutely." He squeezed back.

⁓

When they arrived at Semele's apartment, Cabe made a big show of looking around. First he threatened the closet before whipping the door open, shouting, "I've got Mace!" Then he addressed the shower curtain and the space under the bed too, trying to lighten the mood.

"All clear."

"Thank you. That was amazing," Semele said, teasing him.

"Seriously, you get scared, call me and I'll come right over. And if you see that guy again—police." He gave her a pointed look. "You really should tell Bren."

"No." She shook her head adamantly. Bren would demand she stay at his place, and that was the last thing she needed.

After Cabe left she double-checked the lock on the door and pulled down the shades. There was enough coffee on hand and food in the freezer to last her until Monday. She didn't plan to leave her apartment for the rest of the weekend.

She took a long shower and changed into her favorite old leggings and house sweater. She had just powered up her computer when the phone rang.

She let the answering machine pick up.

"Honey, it's me." Her mother's voice filled the room. "We have to talk. Really. This has gone on long enough."

Semele bit her lip, debating whether to pick up.

"Your father wouldn't like this. . . ."

Semele let out a deep breath. This was the first time her mother had played the "your father" card.

"I really do need to talk to you . . . and tell you I'm sorry . . . so sorry. Can you come home for Thanksgiving?" Her mother's voice trailed off. She was crying.

"Shit." Semele swore under her breath and grabbed the phone. "Mom?"

But she had already hung up.

Semele almost rang back, her fingers lingering over the keys. She would call her before she left for Beijing. She would be out of the country for Thanksgiving, but maybe she would go home for Christmas. They could talk then. Her mother was right. Her father wouldn't be happy. But he also wasn't here anymore.

∞

I tell you Rabka's story because every tree has a branch that rots.

The stars were in great disharmony at the moment of her birth. The houses of the zodiac declared war, and the astrological signs faced one another in opposition. When you are born at such a discordant moment, you can either overcome your misfortune or become chained to it. Rabka chose to embrace the dissonance and, over the course of her life, to allow her spirit's light to dim.

Her father, Ahmar, was a prodigy at the Academy of Gunde-shapur and came to Baghdad at Caliph Harun's invitation. Ahmar, a linguist, philosopher, and scientist, could read and write fluently in over six languages. Caliph Harun needed such men to help run his new empire.

Harun's grandfather, al-Mansur, founded the new capital of the Abbasid Empire: Baghdad, the City of Peace. It was built in a perfect circle to reflect the harmony of Euclidian geometry. Euclid was an ancient scholar from Alexandria whose theorems had created a whole new system of mathematical thought. He had mastered plane geometry and the geometry of the three-dimensional world using intuitive axioms to show the properties of physical reality.

The caliph's most astute astrologer had studied Euclid. He chose the city's precise location, and the palace and mosque were constructed at the center of the circle to symbolize this new nexus of power. When the time came for al-Mansur's grandson, Harun, to rule, Baghdad had become the jewel of the world.

Harun believed educated men ranked after God and angels. So he beckoned them to Baghdad, and Ahmar embraced this opportunity. The Academy of Gundeshapur, like a candle battered by the wind, was waning. Ahmar carried its light to Baghdad, along with his wife and young daughter, Rabka. He brought other graduates with him and three hundred camels to carry their books.

In Baghdad, the ink of a scholar was considered holy. Chinese papermaking had made its way to the capital, creating a flourishing new market for the written word. Scholars made up the new aristocracy, and within this elite Ahmar flourished.

Rabka was raised in luxury within the walls of Caliph Harun's palace and surrounded by opulent gardens and pavilions that surpassed most people's dreams of paradise. Crafted by the finest artists of the day, the palace's vast rooms were filled with entire landscapes built to enchant the senses. Rabka had a gift with words and wrote poems describing the palace's splendor, its fantastical forests, bridges, and waterfalls. Her poems centered on court life as well, announcing births, weddings, or other social events.

"Very few women have this talent, Rabka. I will not dissuade you from your writing," her father said.

Very few women were allowed the opportunity to discover their talents, Rabka thought, but she kept that opinion to herself. "One day I will become as exalted as Ulayya," she boasted. Ulayya, Caliph Harun's sister, was a celebrated poet and musician, a rare feat for a woman. "One day I will be the same."

Rabka's father would only nod and smile, obviously disagreeing, but he did allow her to recite poems to the *rawi* who worked for him. *Rawis* memorized poems and performed them for large audiences, since many people could not read or write. A good *rawi* had over two thousand poems memorized at any given time and could recite them all at once.

When Caliph Harun died, Rabka composed her first *madih,* a poetic tribute to their new patron, al-Ma'mun, gaining her the attention of the court. Baghdad had undergone a civil war after

Harun's death as his two sons struggled for the caliphate, and al-Ma'mun emerged victorious. The position of Rabka's family was secure once more, for al-Ma'mun loved learning above all else.

Rabka grew into an alluring young woman and adorned herself with as many jewels as Harun's most beloved wife, Zubaidah. Zubaidah wore so much jewelry that two servants had to help her stand. She had thirty servants just to care for her pet monkey, and one hundred slave girls to recite the Koran at all hours to prove her piety. She would only eat off plates of precious metal and drink from golden goblets. Witnessing such excess only fueled Rabka's passion and twisted her desires as the time neared for her to marry.

Soon she would no longer have the protection of her father. Rabka prayed every day and night for a good match, for someone who would allow her to stay in her beloved palace and write poems for the court. Her family had obtained immense wealth through her father's accomplishments, and Rabka expected even greater glory with her future husband.

On the day of al-Ma'mun's wedding to the vizier's daughter, Rabka had her first premonition and saw the answer.

"Who is he?" she asked her servant, Aadila. Rabka motioned to the man across the hall in deep conversation with al-Ma'mun.

"Khalid al-Amin. A rising star, that one."

"Is he a scholar?" Rabka asked, anxious.

Aadila nodded. "He has already been appointed the caliph's most trusted *nadim*."

Rabka felt her heart bloom. Her father had been Caliph Harun's *nadim*. As a *nadim,* Khalid would visit the caliph several times a week to debate science, philosophy, and religion, to tell stories, to play chess or backgammon. In return the caliph would grant Khalid an enormous salary, the highest status, and private apartments within the palace.

Rabka continued to scrutinize her husband-to-be, for she had foreseen their marriage as clearly as if Allah had handed her a mirror of the future. Khalid would be remembered as one of the greatest minds in Baghdad—a gifted scholar, orator, translator, and jurist—and become even more exalted than her father. With Khalid, Rabka would be royalty in all but blood.

Aadila watched Rabka and flashed her a wicked smile. "So you've set your sights on that one?" The old woman had served many in the course of her life and understood Rabka's heart well. Rabka didn't answer, but her eyes shone with greed. Like all women, she didn't have a say in whom she would marry, but Rabka was certain she could steer her father toward Khalid.

Aadila clucked her tongue. "'Tis a shame he is to marry in three months. He'll have a First Wife."

Rabka's eyes turned to slits of anger. She looked at her servant, twisted one of the sapphire and diamond rings off her finger, and placed it in Aadila's hand. "No, he won't," she said. The two women understood each other perfectly.

Al-Ma'mun's wedding celebration lasted seventeen days and was the most extravagant anyone could remember. Over a thousand tables were set to accommodate the guests, and a hundred dishes were served each day. Rabka made sure Khalid noticed her during the festivities. She dressed in brocade tunics gilded in precious stones and silk trousers that moved like liquid gold. She looked like a glittering al-'Uzza, the ancient Goddess of the Morning Star.

"Khalid al-Amin is the man I should marry," she instructed her father in private. "He is the only man who can carry on your legacy." She knew exactly how to sway an arrogant man like her father, who wanted nothing more than to be revered forever. For good measure, she persuaded her father's *rawi* to recite a *ghazal* she had written for the wedding couple. It was a romantic poem, nostalgic and complex with perfect meter and rhythm. The *ghazal* surpassed anything she had ever composed, and its delivery was her greatest triumph. By the end of the applause, Khalid had eyes for no other.

On the last day of the celebration, Aadila snuck into the bedroom of Khalid's future wife and cut off the girl's nose. She put poison on the end of the *janbiya* to make certain the blade would be deadly. The bride-to-be died a week later and no one ever knew Rabka had been the one to strike. Now free of obligation, Khalid married Rabka, and the future unfolded as she foresaw it.

Rabka should have been happy that she had obtained her desires, but she had not divined that she would have to move out of the palace. When Khalid told her, she broke every mirror and bottle of perfume in her bedroom. The smell of frankincense lingered with her grief for weeks. She raged to Rusa, the goddess of fate, and recited incantations of ancient sorcery in an attempt to change her future's course, but the talismans and spells were useless.

Khalid tried to assuage her. "The caliph has gifted this house to us. It is the finest in the city."

"I despise the city!" She sobbed, her eyes swollen from days of crying. "Am I to live with the stink?"

Outside the palace the city was a melting pot. Over a million people—Arabs, Persians, Jews, Christians, Indians, rich and poor alike—lived together in the capital.

"But the mansion has the finest architecture, equal to the palace!"

The design included wind ventilation and there was also running water on the walls to keep the house cool. Its front doors were made of ebony and precious metal. But when Rabka walked through them she hated every room. Only simple flowers—lilac, jasmine, and violets—lined the inner courtyards, and the trees weren't plated in gold. Even the roof, which transformed into a grand bedroom under the stars on the hottest of nights, did not appease her. Rabka was a queen without a palace, a poet without a court.

When she gave birth to her first child, a daughter, she wrote a poem, one she never shared, about a wife who was secretly the mythical dragon, Azhi Dahāka, ready to breathe fire until her bones turned to ash. By the poem's end, the wife stood beside the ruins of her former self, unable to return to the girl she was once was. It was the last poem Rabka ever wrote.

As they settled into married life away from the palace, Khalid tried to ignore Rabka's misery. They had three daughters, not the son Khalid desired. But still Khalid never took another wife, for he was unable to fathom the thought of more Rabkas. Instead he devoted himself to his work.

Caliph al-Ma'mun had dreamed that Aristotle visited his bedside. When he awoke he realized what it meant: that it was his duty to build the largest treasury of books yet so he could safeguard the knowledge of the world. This new center of learning, Bayt al-Hikmah, the House of Wisdom, would be both a library and an academy. He appointed Khalid to be one of the directors.

On the caliph's orders, Khalid sent scholars to the four corners of the earth to bring back all the ancient texts they could find—the first expedition ever of its kind. For years Khalid oversaw the translations of lost and forgotten manuscripts from Greek, Persian, and Sanskrit into Arabic in an attempt to unify what distance had divided. As Rabka foresaw so many years before, Khalid became the most honored scholar in all of Baghdad. But his star ascended without her.

Even so, his spirit grew restless. Of Khalid's three daughters, only the youngest, Maisara, noticed. One night after the servants had cleared the table, Khalid sat thinking, his mind so far away his body may as well have not been in the room. For twenty years he had been faithful to Caliph al-Ma'mun, helping him build his legacy with the House of Wisdom, but he no longer found solace in his work.

He saw his daughter watching him. "I am covered in dust, Maisara," he said in a tired voice. He motioned toward his chest and his head. "This heart and mind are covered. Perhaps the time has come for me to go walk in the desert and brush off the sand."

"What do you mean, Father?" Maisara asked, trying to understand.

Her father smiled and beckoned her to his study.

She followed with growing excitement for she had never been invited there before. She waited while he unlocked the cabinet where he kept his most treasured possessions. He pulled out a long scroll and unrolled the parchment.

"What is it?" Maisara whispered in awe. She had never seen anything like it.

"A map of the entire world," Khalid said with satisfaction. Caliph al-Ma'mun had tasked geographers with traveling the globe and taking measurements to create the most accurate map of all time. Khalid possessed one of the few copies. They were priceless.

"Here is the circle of the city, the breadth of the empire, and all that lies beyond our borders." He showed her how the oceans created one body of water. He showed her the seas, the great rivers, and the deserts.

She listened, almost afraid to breathe lest her father stop talking. He had never spoken to her of such things; in fact, he rarely spoke to her at all. But that night he showed her the vastness of the world.

"This is the journey I will make." He traced the path to the desert with his finger.

Maisara made a silent promise that one day she would do the same.

～

Caliph al-Ma'mun died unexpectedly a month later. Khalid risked the dragon's fire and told Rabka he was leaving for the Arabian Desert to follow the way of the Sufi. He needed to see beyond the constraints of earthly life.

Rabka erupted with the rage of a thousand storm demons. She screamed and called him the vilest names ever to cross a woman's lips. But still Khalid left with only the robes he was wearing and a case the size of a scroll on his back. Maisara knew it surely held the map.

After Khalid had gone, Rabka grew silent, now a whirlwind without force. Her daughters were terrified. In an instant, their world had broken. Rabka sat down in Khalid's chair at the head of the table and laughed so hard tears watered her eyes. She had seen everything but the ending.

They had no income and no male to protect them and, with the caliph's passing, no relationship with the new ruler. Soon they would be destitute.

At first they survived by selling Khalid's prized belongings. Rabka sold off his library. He had thousands of books and rare works, including copies of the Vedas Scripts from ancient India, alchemy books written by Babylonian priests, and original texts from the Chaldean and Median Empires.

Rabka wanted none of it. Her most important task was securing her daughters' futures. With Asma, the eldest, Rabka worried there might be difficulty. The girl had ugly teeth, a wandering eye that could be disconcerting, and her father's bulbous nose. After months trying to find her a husband, Rabka gave up in despair. Then a new opportunity presented itself.

One of the only female trades was the textile industry. Rabka found Asma employment as a fabric dyer and spinner in nearby Baqdara, working alongside other women and children.

"The wages will be poor," she informed Asma, "but at least there are wages."

"Please, please let me stay," Asma begged.

Rabka turned deaf ears to her pleading and ordered her remaining daughters to sort through Asma's belongings to see what could be sold at market. She didn't think a fabric dyer needed much.

Rabka sold her own beloved gowns and jewels to pay their exorbitant taxes and buy food. No longer could they afford pears from Nahavand, figs from Hulwan, or limes from Egypt. They couldn't serve grilled lamb with Rabka's favorite pomegranate sauce, or grilled anything for that matter. Meat was too expensive. Olive oil from Syria and honey from Mosul soon became distant memories.

Baghdad had the most opulent cuisine in the world, and Rabka had been raised in the caliph's court watching Harun taste thirty dishes a day with two servants standing beside him. One servant would hold thirty clean spoons so Harun could taste each dish, while the other servant waited to collect the dirty ones.

What heights she had fallen from! She let their chefs go, along with all their servants. Now when food was set on the table, her daughters would snatch it like falcons.

Maisara was the one who cooked and cleaned. She learned how to use each cooking vessel in the kitchen. She would spend hours washing pots and beating them with brick dust, then potash. Her hands became rough from all the labor, but she didn't complain. She spent hours alone in the kitchen dreaming of how she would leave Baghdad one day. The room became her map as she plotted her escape.

Rabka prohibited her second daughter, Alya, from performing any labor, for in Alya, Rabka saw her best chance. The girl was quite lovely, a gazelle, thin as a willow with high breasts, a long neck, and a curtain of hair that fell to her feet like silk. The son of an esteemed family Rabka knew from her days in court was traveling to China soon as an ambassador for the caliph, and he needed a bride.

"Do not send me so far away to such a strange land! I will die there! I know it!" Alya screeched and threw herself at her mother's feet.

"Better to die *there* than in the slums of Baghdad with the beggars and the cripples," Rabka said with fierce conviction.

Now Maisara was the only daughter who remained. Out of all the sisters, she suffered the most, for poverty led Rabka slowly into madness. Rabka's worst nightmare had come true. She was destitute.

At night Rabka would recite her poetry in weeping bursts, with only the deaf ears of the city to hear her cries.

Secretly, she began to prepare for her death. Even her funeral would cost money, and she had only one thing of worth left to sell: a deck of beautiful hand-painted picture cards that had been in her family for generations.

"But your mother made you promise to take care of them," Maisara tried to reason with her. "They belong to us." Maisara had always hoped the cards would one day be passed to her. She was the only daughter who stayed behind.

"They belong to me!" Rabka hissed. She knew they would fetch a high price, especially with the tale she could spin about their origins. Playing cards had become quite popular in the empire, particularly after the Mamluks brought their card games down from the high steppes of Mongolia. Many scholars had begun to collect cards from Mongolia, India, and the farthest reaches of China. And the collectors paid handsomely.

⌣

Rabka found the perfect merchant. Men like Jamal Azar had helped build the Muslim empire into what it was. He had traveled to Cordoba, Cairo, and explored the sea route to China. He knew every trade route—but he had never seen cards like Rabka's.

"These cards came from Egypt in the time of Caesar." Rabka held them out to him. "They survived the Great Fire in Alexandria and have been passed down through my family for centuries. Look at them!" She fanned the cards out on the table. "The artist was the same man who painted the pharaoh's personal holy books."

Jamal bent over to study the cards with his optical glass while Maisara looked on wide-eyed at her mother's story.

"The paint is real gold," Rabka added, "and worth twice as much."

Jamal didn't know if what Rabka said was true, but after careful examination he decided these cards would be a prize in his personal collection, the one he showed others to make his wares seem more expensive. He paid Rabka several gold coins but knew it was a good investment.

When Rabka and Maisara returned home, Rabka lay down on her pallet and Maisara covered her mother with a blanket.

"Was the story true?" Maisara asked.

"How would I know?" Rabka dismissed. "I wasn't there."

Rabka stared up at the ceiling for a long while. Then she let out a strange cackle and said, "This is my punishment for taking another woman's husband."

That night while Maisara slept Rabka took out a different bundle, one she had kept all these years. She unwrapped the Chinese silk and touched Aadila's *janbiya,* the dagger her servant had used to kill Khalid's betrothed. Rabka fingered the blade with only one regret: no one would witness her final act. Her death would have made a glorious poem.

When Maisara awoke the next morning, she found her mother dead with a Delphic smile on her face. She cradled her in her arms and cried tears so acrid they burned her skin. Now she had no one.

She paid for the burial with the gold coins her mother had fetched for the cards, and keeping the promise she had made to herself, set off for the desert like her father had done so many years before. She would walk the way of the Sufi and brush the sand from her heart.

⌣

With Rabka, my progeny severed our connection to the Oracle's symbols. Rabka's daughters went in three different directions, like a disbanded constellation that no astrolabe could measure. I often searched my mind's eye for those lovely stars, but I never found them.

The cards, however, I could still see.

They left my descendents' hands and were caught in the current of time like a piece of driftwood. I had to have faith that they would one day find their way to shore.

Wheel of Fortune

When Semele got on the train to work Monday morning, she felt like she'd entered a time machine back to the present. She had been translating all weekend. The past two days had literally flown by. She had turned off her cell phone and ignored the Internet—she'd ignored Bren too. She still owed him a call but couldn't quite face him yet.

Right now she didn't want to deal with the office either. She couldn't care less about her meeting with Mikhail. They were supposed to discuss Beijing, but her focus on work was gone; at this point she barely had a grip on reality. She was immersed in Ionna's story, still unable to fathom that Ionna had envisioned the birth of Baghdad and the House of Wisdom.

Had Ionna also seen the library's annihilation in 1258 when Genghis Khan's grandson razed the city? And what had happened to the Oracle's cards? Where did they go after Rabka sold them to Jamal Azar?

Semele's mind raced with possibilities. She was reading a bona fide prophecy, and the more she read, the more Ionna's words were affecting her. Semele could no longer deny the sense of purpose that had begun to fill her. She was meant to find this manuscript. Two thousand years ago Ionna had foreseen that Semele would read her words, and Marcel had left them to her, knowing she was a part of the story.

How much did Theo know? This was the question burning in her mind now—and her gut told her he knew more than she did.

He is coming to see me on Friday.

Where did that thought come from? Goose bumps traveled down her arms. Was he really? And, if this was true, then why? The whole idea was unsettling. Even worse, she couldn't stop the feeling that, before Friday, something terrible was going to happen.

⌒

A policeman stood at the entrance of Kairos' building. "Ma'am, I need to see some identification before you can go in."

"What's going on?" Semele asked, digging out the work badge buried in the bottom of her purse. The officer scrutinized her picture and didn't answer.

"Sign here," he said. He held out a logbook and finally allowed her to enter.

Semele joined the huddle of people in the lobby, then spotted Cabe coming off the elevator. They made a beeline for each other.

"Hey. What's going on?" she asked him.

"Didn't you get my message?" He looked astounded. "I called you like five times."

"Sorry, no . . . I had my phone off," she mumbled, starting to feel light-headed.

"There was a break-in last night. On ten," he stressed, lowering his voice. "That manuscript you told me about was taken."

Semele covered her mouth in horror. The manuscript was gone? She could feel tears threatening to form and furiously held them back.

"I think you should tell the police you were being followed," Cabe said.

"What? Why?"

"What if it's the same guy?"

"That's crazy."

"No, this is crazy." He motioned to the chaos in the lobby. "We were robbed. By professionals. Do you know how much security this place has?"

Semele did know and her head was spinning. She looked around as if the thief were still there. Of course the man following her was connected to the theft. He had to be. And now she had the only copy of what they had taken.

"Listen," she said, lowering her voice. "Don't tell anyone I made a digital."

Cabe scowled.

"Promise me," she insisted. "It's safer if no one knows."

"I don't know." He let out a deep breath. "This doesn't feel right."

"You're telling me," she agreed. Mikhail got off the elevator and headed toward her. In all her time working for him, she had never seen him this stressed.

He sounded rushed. "Semele, I uploaded the Beijing file to the server. We're going to have to meet tomorrow." His eyes scanned the lobby. "I'm dealing with the FBI and insurance agents today. They've closed off all the floors."

"You mean, I can't go upstairs?" She needed to see Marcel's collection, to see for herself that the manuscript was really gone.

Mikhail shook his head. "Keep your phone on. There's a chance the investigators will want to question you."

Semele nodded, though the possibility of being questioned made her stomach lurch. She had brought the manuscript to Kairos. *And she'd made a secret copy.* She glanced over at Cabe.

"Fritz is handling things—for now." Mikhail noticed their silent exchange. "But the investigators may want to speak with you too. Cabe, you're with me." He hurried to go shake hands with a suited man who had just entered the building, most likely the insurance agent.

Semele shot Cabe a look. They'd talk later.

⌒

Semele hurried to the subway station, looking up and down the street with a growing sense of panic. If she had the only known copy, would whoever stole it come after that as well?

Her cell phone rang and the number flashed across her screen. Holy hell, why was Theo calling?

She picked up. "Mr. Bossard, I'm so sorry. Have you been informed about the incident?" she asked, floundering. She had no clue how to handle this call.

"Mikhail called me," he said. "Are you all right?"

The question caught her off guard. "I've only just heard the news. I'm so sorry." She apologized again. "I hope the investigators recover the piece."

She waited for him to respond, but there was only silence from his end. She hedged. "Mikhail and Fritz will be following up with the investigators and keeping you apprised." She heard him sigh, but still he said nothing. Just what did he want her to say? Why was he calling?

He finally spoke. "Semele, I'm afraid I haven't been entirely frank with you about my father. This isn't happening like I expected."

A chill burrowed deep inside her. *So he knew.* He had known all along about Ionna's manuscript.

It was as if the veil between them was falling away.

"There are certain things I need to share with you, but it's best to do so in person. I'm in Rome right now but can be there by the end of the week."

"Friday," she whispered. The thought she'd had this morning was coming true.

"Yes. Until then, be careful."

"Theo," she said, her voice sounding shaky, "if you're trying to scare me, it's working."

"You're in the middle of something you don't understand. I'm not even sure I understand it." He sounded frustrated. "I'll call you when I'm en route. Please be careful." Then he hung up.

Semele stood on the corner and a cold wind whipped around her. She was afraid to go back to her apartment, and reading the rest of Ionna's story had taken on a new urgency. Someone wanted the manuscript enough to break in to Kairos, and now

Theo Bossard was flying halfway around the world to tell her something that couldn't be said over the phone.

She needed to get out of New York for a few days so she could finish reading and figure out what to do.

She needed to go home.

Even though she hadn't spoken to her mother in months, suddenly home was the only place she wanted to be.

⌁

She headed to Brooklyn to pack a bag, sure that a five-minute stop at her place would be safe. But when she got off the train, a sense of foreboding enveloped her.

The black BMW parked in front of her building looked out of place.

Semele walked several more feet toward her apartment, but every instinct told her to stop moving. She ducked inside a nearby café and waited, looking out the glass window. Minutes passed.

Then she saw him. The man from the library was running out of her building.

He jumped into the passenger seat of the BMW.

Semele stood frozen inside the café, her world in free fall. Her paranoia had been justified. That man *was* watching her at the library. Ionna had really warned her.

God only knew what he had been doing at her apartment. Hysteria gripped her: *Who the hell was he?*

As the car drove past, Semele watched through the window. What she saw completely paralyzed her.

Raina was driving the car.

Message to VS—

We lost her.

From VS—

Watch the apartment.

Message to VS—

Theo Bossard is coming to NY.

From VS—

Of course he is.

History does not remember Hayl's or Rinalto's stories. But you should. Then you will start to understand.

Rinalto was not the most physical man. He usually spent his days hunched over a worktable painting miniatures. But his height and lean frame stood in his favor: the boy he was chasing couldn't be more than six years old and shouldn't be this hard to catch.

"*Mi scusi, mi scusi. . . .*" Rinalto pushed through the crowd apologetically. The market was busy today.

Rinalto had been browsing the items on display at one of the stalls when he saw two small, dirt-covered hands reach out and snatch a necklace off the shelf. Then the boy dashed off. Rinalto had no idea if the necklace had any value, but he knew the seller, Hayl, was too old to chase him.

Rinalto lost sight of the boy for a few seconds, then spotted him heading toward the piazza. There was a special mass at the Duomo today, and all of Milan had converged on the city square. Rinalto forced himself to run faster. He lunged forward and grabbed the boy's shirt right before the little rat tried to dash between a man's legs.

"That's enough," Rinalto gasped, catching his breath.

"Let me go!" The boy kicked and spit and tried to wriggle away, but Rinalto anchored him with a firm grip.

"Give me what you took and I will."

People began to stare.

"If you don't," he threatened, "there's a priest over there I'm sure you're dying to confess to."

The boy stopped fighting. He reached into his pocket and pulled out the necklace. As soon as Rinalto had it in hand, the boy stomped on his foot with such force that Rinalto let go of him. He disappeared within seconds. Rinalto limped back to the market with a rueful grin. At least he had the necklace. It looked expensive; he was glad he had made the effort.

When Rinalto reached the stall, Hayl saw what he had recovered. For a moment the old trader looked too stunned to speak. He turned to the shelf and realized the display that had held the necklace was empty.

"The boy had a good eye!" Hayl bellowed as he took the necklace back, but his laughter rang false. "Thank you, Rinalto. Thank you." The old man slapped Rinalto on the back.

"It's very beautiful." Rinalto had never seen firestones like those before. The iridescent red looked like a field of poppies lit on fire.

"From Edessa," Hayl said.

Rinalto watched the old man gently trace the stones with his fingers and Rinalto wondered at the sadness behind Hayl's smile.

Perhaps the necklace had belonged to a woman he once knew. Rinalto and his family had bought goods from Hayl for years, but he was always alone, unlike the other traders who were often assisted by a wife or child.

Hayl was a Saracen who came from a village near the Caspian Sea. He loved to boast that he'd traveled most of the world, as far north as Kvenland and as far south as Syene—even down the Nile River in Egypt. The trader enjoyed telling tales, and every item he sold came with a story.

"What are you looking for today?" Hayl asked, still holding the necklace.

"The Book of Optics." Rinalto's eyes scanned the shelves.

"Ah, a popular one." Hayl surveyed his stock. He had already sold several copies on this trip.

Every artist in Italy was buying the book to understand dimensional mastery, "the Del Aspect" as they called it. *The Book of Optics* demonstrated how to create two-dimensional pictorial representations of three-dimensional space.

"Written by Alhazen, an Arab physicist and mathematician," Hayl said as he searched his books, "born in Basra, educated in Baghdad, and lived most of his life in Cairo, four hundred years ago!" he bellowed again in his jovial way. "I'm sure I have one left."

Rinalto smiled, grateful. "I haven't had a commission in months. I was hoping reading it might help. . . ." He trailed off, distracted by a young woman on the other side of the aisle. Every young man in the market seemed to be watching her. She was browsing the stalls and holding a petite white-haired dog in her arms.

Rinalto took off his cap.

Hayl looked over at the girl and smiled. "A rose in perfect blossom. Why don't you go gardening, Rinalto?" He winked.

"Viviana Orsini will never notice me."

"Bah!" Hayl wrapped up the book. "You're young with a heart waiting to be broken."

"She's from a noble family. And I . . ." Rinalto motioned to his clothes, which bore stains from paint. He watched Viviana move farther down the aisle. "If I had my own studio, she might. If I had commissions like Ghiberti, her family might consider me a suitor."

Hayl understood the poor boy's predicament. "Unrequited love is one of life's worst afflictions. Trust me, I know." He picked up the firestone necklace. "I tried to give this necklace to a girl once. She did not accept."

Rinalto looked over at Hayl, hoping the trader would say more. He sensed there was a story behind the necklace.

Hayl held up the firestones and watched them catch the sunlight. He had not thought of Kalinka in years. Only the necklace knew their history, a story he would never tell.

He placed the jewels high on a shelf where no hand could reach them. Then turned his attention back to Rinalto. "So. How does one get showered with commissions?"

"One piece of art for the right patron." Rinalto continued to watch Viviana. She was an angelic vision with pouted lips and hair that shone like pale amber.

"One of your miniatures?" Hayl asked.

Despondent, Rinalto shook his head. "Something grander. Like a deck of cards."

A winter breeze whipped through the market, and Rinalto watched Viviana hand her little dog to her maid so she could put on her gloves. They were a striking red that matched the print of her cape.

How he would love to paint her.

"Ah, I see." Hayl nodded, understanding. He'd been trading in the peninsula for thirty years and had seen playing cards take root. Noble families had begun commissioning famous artists to create their own decks, a sign of prestige. The cards were crafted with the finest parchment or wood and usually painted with gold.

Over the years Hayl had looked for interesting and unusual cards to bring to Italy and sell for a high price. On his last trip, he traveled as far as the Zagros Mountains, where he found an old trader looking to sell his wares. He ended up buying an unusual deck from the old man, unlike any he had seen before.

"Why are there only twenty-two?" Hayl had asked.

"These are very special," the old man said, "from the time of the pharaohs. They've been in my family for many generations."

Hayl doubted it, knowing firsthand that traders made up all kinds of stories to sell their goods. Yellow tin and fake gems were often passed off as gold and precious jewels in the markets. He was certain he could make up an even better story and sell the cards to a wealthy nobleman in Milan for a pretty florin.

Hayl didn't know what made him to do it. Perhaps it was the

longing on Rinalto's face as he watched Viviana, a girl as lovely as his Kalinka long ago. Maybe it was the look in Rinalto's eyes that said he didn't believe he would ever obtain his dreams. Or maybe it was because Kalinka's memory still had yet to fade. Whatever the reason, Hayl pulled out the special deck of cards.

"Perhaps you can gain attention with these," he said and handed them to Rinalto.

Rinalto took the cards and looked at each one closely. "Magnificent. The paintings . . ." His finger traced one design. "What kind of game do you play with these?" he wondered, studying the unusual pictures.

"Any game." Hayl shrugged. "They're cards."

Rinalto went to hand them back. "I could never afford them, but thank you." They were painted with the purest gold, and the parchment was of a quality he had never seen.

"Consider them a gift," Hayl said. "For bringing me back my necklace." He folded Rinalto's hands around the cards. "I too was young and in love once."

Rinalto looked down, unable to believe his good fortune. The nobility sought only the best artists to paint unusual decks for their salons, with each patron trying to outdo the other. With these cards his circumstances could change.

"Hayl, how can I ever thank you?" Rinalto laughed, feeling more hopeful than he had in years.

Viviana glanced over from across the market upon hearing the confident ring of his laughter. She met Rinalto's eyes and gave him a shy smile before turning away to continue shopping.

Hayl winked at him. "Win her heart. That will be thanks enough."

⁓

For two months Rinalto painted an entirely new deck of cards. He used all of his savings to pay for the endeavor. Working in secrecy, he moved his table into his bedroom, away from the studio he shared with a group of other miniaturists. He even turned down a small commission to paint a client's newborn child. A sense of urgency filled him and he made the cards quickly. For he knew exactly whom he would present them to.

He studied Hayl's enigmatic cards for days to figure out how to paint the images. Never had he seen such designs. Their symbology felt magical, and he sensed that, all together, the symbols told a story.

He decided to adapt the figures to a more Milanese sensibility by adding beautiful crosses, chalices, cherubs, and angels to the cards, hoping the embellishments would please the church. For *The Lovers* card, he gave the woman a gown that resembled Viviana's red-and-gold cape, but with red sleeves instead of gloves; he even grew so bold as to paint a little white dog at her feet. If Viviana ever saw these cards, she would realize he had painted her.

With painstaking precision, he created a new twenty-two-card set using gold leaf and silver foil. Then he painted a matching Mamluk deck of fifty-two cards, the most popular cards in Milan, and combined both decks into one. The Mamluk deck had four kings, each holding a different sign—coin, baton, cup, and sword. The kings were each accompanied by two viceroys and four sets of ten pip cards.

Rinalto made one other alteration for his new deck. He created four queens to pair with each of the kings, which had never been done before. It was a bold idea because he was planning to deliver this deck to the duke of Milan's mistress as a gift.

Duke Filippo Maria Visconti was the foremost card collector in Milan and also the wealthiest man in Italy. Only the Medicis in Florence rivaled him. Giving the cards to the duke's mistress at the ball, a ball being held in her honor, was the only way Rinalto could think to gain his notice without requesting an official audience. Rinalto could never give the duke the cards directly; to do so would be overstepping his place. But if the duke's mistress

showed him the cards in front of the crowd, it might win Rinalto his attention.

When he was finished, the seventy-eight cards glittered on his
worktable like his own firestone necklace.

The time had come to unveil his masterpiece. The duke of
Milan was holding a ball to honor his mistress and the birth of
their new daughter the next week. It would be the perfect event.

He used his last coins to buy presentable clothes. The market
seller assured him the outfit was the height of Florentine fashion. The voluminous cape had thick pleats made of ornate brocade, fully lined. He paired it with blue hose, parti-colored
boots, and a matching hat. They were among the finest clothes
he'd ever owned.

He managed to secure an invitation to the ball from one of
his studio mates. By now they had all seen Rinalto's finished
work, and rumors were spreading throughout Milan that a special deck of cards would be presented to the duke's mistress.
Rinalto was taking his first step into high society and had little
time to prepare. In Milan, every mannerism was an art. He practiced throwing back the sleeve of his cape all week.

The city was ready for a celebration. The duke had recently be-
headed his latest wife, and the people hoped the birth of his
mistress's child would improve his mood. Most of the attendees
had never seen the tyrant. He was a suspicious and paranoid man
who distrusted people so much that he changed beds several
times a night for safety. Rinalto was not the only one curious
to see the duke in person.

Rinalto's curiosity quickly turned to horror when he caught
a glimpse of the surly fat toad hobbling around on deformed feet.
The duke's protruding eyes surveyed the room. He looked ready
to order someone's execution, which was disheartening since his
advisors had assured the people in attendance that his lordship
was in high spirits. Rinalto almost lost his courage.

All the nobles were deep in their cups, pretending the fear in the room did not exist. Rinalto's mother had always warned him to be wary when approaching the seat of power. If she were still alive, she would have advised him to keep his cards, return to his studio, and cherish his modest life. But when Rinalto saw that Viviana was watching him from across the room, the warmth in her eyes steeled his nerves. Without giving himself another moment to doubt his actions, he approached the duke's mistress.

"If I may be so bold to present this token in honor of your celebration tonight." He knelt before her and opened the wooden box of cards with a bow of his head. "A gift for you, my lady."

His heart thundered in his chest as he waited for her to look inside the box. She gasped with pleasure when she pulled out the deck. "Who made these?"

He dared to raise his eyes to her. "I did, my lady."

With great excitement, she called the duke over. Soon a whole crowd had gathered, and the duke's inner circle began to pass around the cards. Rinalto could hardly believe that Michelino da Besozzo, the most celebrated artist of the day, was holding his work in his hands.

"Exquisite." Besozzo gave him an assessing look.

The duke seemed thrilled. "Ingenious! Think of the trick games we can play." He turned to Besozzo. "I must have one like it!"

Besozzo bowed meekly. "Of course."

The duke held out a card and squinted. "See how he's painted my coat of arms and mottos. . . . He's even made the coins in my currency." He looked back at Rinalto. "Well done," he praised. "Well done!"

With those two words, said not once but twice, Rinalto was granted a seat at Milan's table. Before the end of the night, he received a dozen commissions for identical decks.

Throughout the evening he caught Viviana staring at him.

As the ball neared its end, he steeled his nerves and finally approached. He bowed low with a flourish.

"Your playing cards have made quite an impression," she said.

The praise and the ever-flowing wine made him bold. "I painted them to win your notice," he confessed with bright eyes and flushed cheeks.

Viviana looked astonished, then gave a tinkling laugh.

"As an acceptable suitor, of course . . . ," he bumbled. He realized that he was saying too much with little aplomb. He tried to throw back the sleeve of his cape and failed miserably. Viviana giggled again.

"And now I must leave before I make a bigger fool of myself," he said and turned to escape.

"Wait!" She placed her hand on his arm. "Is it true her gown has red sleeves and there's a white dog?"

In response Rinalto plucked a rare striped rose of scarlet and gold from a nearby vase. "She also has your hair." He handed her the flower and hurried away.

Viviana held the flower to her lips and watched Rinalto head to the door, where he was waylaid by the crowd.

Tonight Rinalto was a shining star. Although he did not know it, he had completely endeared himself to the one person he had hoped to impress.

⌒

Viviana and Rinalto married with her parents' blessing within the year. On their wedding night Rinalto gave Viviana an exquisite handmade wooden card box made of rosewood, which was crafted with inlaid floral designs. Inside lay Hayl's original deck, along with a set of Mamluk cards he had painted to match. But Viviana never played the Tarocchi card games that were popular in the salons. She kept her treasured cards in Rinalto's engraved wooden box instead.

This new type of deck, with its seventy-eight cards, made its way from Milan to Ferrara, Venice to Bologna and Florence, and then throughout Europe. No one ever questioned the cards' origins. So they stayed hidden, like most symbols do, in plain sight, until one man in France recognized them for what they were.

Justice

Semele's mouth dropped open in a silent "Oh."

She had been translating for the past two hours on the train to New Haven when she recognized the name Filippo Maria Visconti. He had been the duke of Milan and had commissioned the Visconti Tarot Decks, the oldest-known tarot decks in existence. They were even named after him. Semele knew this because the Beinecke Rare Book & Manuscript Library housed one of the decks—her father, Joseph Cavnow, had been a curator there. On several occasions she had seen the library's Visconti Tarot Deck, also called the Cary-Yale Tarot Deck after the collector who donated them. *Were Ionna's cards tarot cards?*

Here she was heading right toward the Visconti Deck, and she was beginning to sense that it wasn't an accident.

When the train arrived, she decided not to tell her mother she was in town just yet. First she needed to stop by the library to see the duke's cards.

The Beinecke Library's unusual architecture gave the illusion that it hovered in the air. Strategically placed pyramid columns raised the building off the ground, and instead of windows, opaque marble shielded the sunlight, changing colors throughout the day. The effect always made the library seem alive. Growing up, Semele had called it "the magic square."

When she walked inside, the marble was glowing like citrine

clouds. The towering walls of books rose six stories like a benevolent giant, greeting her like an old friend.

A rush of emotions hit her and tears prickled her eyes. She hadn't been in this building for years, and still it felt like home. Of all the libraries she visited through the years—and she had been to many—Beinecke remained the most special. Her childhood was wrapped around this building. One of her first memories was of playing with her mother in the courtyard while they waited for her father to be done for the day.

She couldn't help noticing the parallels between her life and Ionna's. They were both daughters of librarians, men deeply read in history, literature, and philosophy, who oversaw the largest ancient manuscript libraries in the world. Librarians had served as guardians of the written word throughout the ages, and Semele grew up witnessing her father's devotion. To her, he was as noble as a knight. Like Ionna's, her childhood was filled with countless hours in the library, where she would look at the exhibits while her father worked. She had gotten her undergraduate degree in Classics at Yale and she had spent many an hour researching papers in the Beinecke's reading room. Ionna and her story had brought her back.

Semele approached the information desk, hoping Thomas was in today. She needed a favor. Thomas was the head conservator and the only staff member she could ask. He had worked with her father for years and been a pallbearer at his funeral.

The person behind the desk called his office, and Semele was relieved to learn that he was there. A guard directed her to the lockers and coatracks, where she checked her personal belongings. No bags were allowed.

When Thomas arrived, the sight of him without her father brought a lump to her throat.

"Well, well. If this isn't the best surprise." He greeted her with a hug. "You in town to see your mom?"

Semele nodded, although she had yet to tell her mother she was in New Haven. "I need to ask a favor. A client has some really old tarot cards we're handling, and I was hoping to take a look at the deck." She didn't need to tell Thomas what deck she was talking about.

He glanced at his watch; he was most likely busy, but she could tell he didn't want to say no. "Sure, sure. Let me see if I can have it brought to a meeting room."

Semele understood the enormous favor she was asking. Usually visiting conservators had to book an appointment with a curator several days in advance to study items from the archives. Mini-microscopes, UV lamps, and other tools were often brought out to assist them.

"Do you need any equipment?" he asked her, ushering her downstairs to the first lower level, the "court level," where a periphery of meeting rooms and classrooms were located.

"No, just a visual. I only need a few minutes."

They stopped at the Reader Services desk right outside the reading room. Thomas spoke with the staff member on duty. "I need to request the Cary cards, call number ITA one-oh-nine."

Thomas led Semele to one of the meeting rooms while Reader Services paged someone to have the item brought from storage.

"I was actually planning to give you a call soon," he told her. "We've been waiting for your mother to come clear out Joe's office. I've called her a few times, left some messages. . . ."

"I'm so sorry." Semele couldn't believe her mother had been such a flake. "I thought she took care of that months ago."

But she hadn't. Her mother needed her help to do it, and Semele had abandoned her. She was flooded with guilt.

"I started putting things in boxes," Thomas said. "Maybe after you're done taking a look at the deck you can pack up a bit more."

"Of course," she quickly agreed, embarrassed. If her father were still alive he'd sit her and her mother down and lecture them both. "I died and you forgot about my office?" She could just hear him. His beloved office. He had two, one at the Beinecke and one at home, and not a day passed when he hadn't been in either.

But Semele understood why her mother hadn't come yet—she'd been avoiding the office for the same reason. Neither of them was ready to say good-bye.

⁓

When Thomas showed her the Visconti Deck it felt as if Ionna was standing beside her, whispering Rinalto's story into her ear. A shiver flowed through her.

Her eyes went to *The Lovers* card, which showed a couple reaching out to embrace. The woman had blond hair and was wearing a red-sleeved gown. She had a little dog at her feet, exactly as Ionna had described.

Semele took a step back from the table. There was no doubt that the duke of Milan had modeled his cards after Rinalto's deck. If the duke's cards had survived, then Rinalto's original cards—the ones that contained Ionna's twenty-two—may have survived as well. They could still be out there somewhere sitting on a collector's shelf. And if they were, perhaps she could find them.

"How many other decks are there as old as this one?" she asked Thomas.

"This old? Only a handful. The Morgan has another Visconti Deck, which you must have seen."

Semele nodded. She had seen their deck when she had interned at the Morgan Library one summer during college. How was it that she had such intimate ties to two of the places that housed the oldest tarot decks in the world? Somehow they were connected.

⁓

Thomas led her out of the meeting room to her father's office, and they both grew quiet. He understood how hard this must be. When he unlocked the office door and turned on the lights, Semele felt her father's presence for a moment. But, just as quickly, the feeling was gone.

"Well, I'll give you some privacy," Thomas said. He was already backing away. "Take your time."

Semele walked farther into the room and heard Thomas shut the door behind him. She had not been expecting to face her father's memory today—at least not like this. She sat down at his desk and stared at all his things.

He's been waiting for me to come. She could feel him all around her.

Remnants of him were everywhere . . . remnants she did not want to lose. She looked at the family photos he had framed and knew she couldn't pack them away yet. She couldn't pack anything away.

She ignored the empty boxes on the floor and instead turned on her father's computer. After seeing the Visconti Deck, she knew Ionna's cards were out there.

Her father's password was still active. She logged in to his databases and spent the next hour cross-checking collectors' information, news sources, and international auction listings. Nothing remotely resembling the cards turned up.

Frustrated, she leaned back in the chair and closed her eyes, spinning around, much like she had when she was a child.

If Thomas walked in on her now, he'd think she was worse than her mother. She hadn't boxed up a thing, she'd hacked into her father's computer, and she was twirling in his chair like a six-year-old. The thought made her smile.

Then she stopped and opened her eyes.

The chair was turned away from the desk, facing the back table, where her father's appointment book rested in the center. She picked up the leather-bound notebook and flipped it open.

Her chest tightened when she saw his handwriting. Her father's penmanship had always been graceful with its forward and upward slant, his *t*'s crossed high and long, and open end-marks— traits of a high achiever who loved his work and the people around him. "A scholar and a gentleman" is how he had been described at the service.

The week he died, his writing looked robust and healthy, and this made Semele frown. When someone was sick, usually the illness showed in their writing. Graphologists believed writing revealed every aspect of a person—their mental and emotional states, their physical well-being, even their level of intelligence—and Semele had done enough analysis to agree. Studying someone's handwriting was like reading their diary.

She checked all the entries in her father's calendar, looking for clues that pointed toward a looming stroke, but she could find no abnormalities. Her father had died in April. Nothing he wrote that month, or in the months before, indicated he was near the end of his life.

She flipped forward to May. What she saw made her stop.

There, in the first week, her father had marked an appointment:

Marcel Bossard, 1 P.M.

Semele couldn't stop staring at the entry. The way her father had scribbled the words seemed rushed and agitated, unlike the others. She struggled to grasp the implications. Why had her father made an appointment with Marcel Bossard? How long had they known each other?

Did Theo know?

The questions consumed her. Part of her wanted to call Theo right then and ask if he knew about the meeting. Was this what he had been holding back from her?

She wasn't sure if she could trust him. She wasn't sure about anything at this point except that she needed to finish Ionna's story.

Simza was a seventh daughter and a powerful cohalyi, *a witch-wife trained since birth in all things magic.* The Rom believed all their people were gifted with supernatural powers, but a seventh daughter possessed the ability to become a great seer.

Every Rom woman was taught to read fortunes from an early age. Their ancestors came from the Far East in India, a motherland of ancient mysticism steeped in Vedic magic, and the Rom carried on this tradition through their travels.

To tell a fortune they would read a person's palm or gaze into a crystal. The crystal gazers preferred to hold the crystal ball in their hands. They would stare into its depths, opening their minds to truths waiting to be told. Quartz crystals with little to no imperfections were always best. The balls were made of stone that had been washed on the full moon and charged with its light. Palm readers examined the lines of a person's left palm to determine their innate gifts, and the right hand showed what he or she would make of them. Every etched line had meaning and created the map of that person's life.

The Rom also practiced the art of reading tea leaves. Tea readings required a special ritual. The tea was steeped, never with any milk or sugar, and then poured into a white teacup. The cup always had to be white or light colored so each pattern could be discerned. The deeper one read into the cup, the deeper one read into the future.

A Rom seer could use anything to see the future—sticks,

water, fire, dice, even playing cards. Every seer had a favorite medium, and Simza's was seashells. She would throw her shells into the air, let them land, and read the pattern. Then she would pick up her favorite shell and hold it to her ear.

"What do you hear, Grandmother?" Aishe, her granddaughter, would always ask.

"The ocean, telling me its secrets. Here, its song sings forever." She would pass the shell to Aishe so she could listen. No matter how long and hard she did, Aishe was sure her grandmother could hear more.

Simza was also skilled in the art of finding missing people: she would track them down using an object they had owned. People marveled at her ability. Sometimes a child would purposefully hide in the forest and others would run to get Simza. They'd place the missing child's favorite toy in Simza's hand, and off she would go to find them, the other children chasing after her skirt.

Simza said possessions were filled with the owner's spirit, and if she listened closely enough they would whisper in her ear just like the shells. Each time Simza found the missing child without fail.

Aishe would beg her to explain how she did it, but Simza would only say, "The wind is the wild hunter. I follow it."

Simza practiced all the old ways. She believed power resided in her hair and refused to cut it. She believed every day was special. On Tuesdays spinning fabric was forbidden. On Wednesdays no one was allowed to use a needle or scissors or bake bread. Thursdays were considered unlucky. On Fridays no one could bargain. And on Saturdays no one could wash a thing.

Simza also believed garlic was a powerful charm for protecting against evil spirits, storms, and bad weather. She hung ropes of garlic bulbs outside her family's tent and wagon. She rarely spoke during the day, but when she did, she would usually go around yelling "Garlic! Garlic! Garlic!" Just saying the word, she believed, was enough to ward off evil.

Nightfall was the only time Simza talked at length; she would join the other elders, telling stories by the fire. The campfire was the center of their lives, where they passed down their history, and in this way, the flame never died.

She always told Aishe she was lucky, for Aishe had red hair. The Rom called it sun-hair and considered it a mark of good fortune. Aishe had gotten her red hair from one of her ancestors, who was not a Rom, but a wandering Sufi woman. She had joined their tribe when they crossed the desert hundreds of years ago. The woman had been near death from thirst, and Simza and Aishe's ancestors had revived and welcomed her into their band. The story had become a legend in their family, and was one of Aishe's favorites. She would beg Simza to tell it again and again.

Simza was full of stories, especially stories about their family's past. She had a special treasure chest, colorfully painted, that had belonged to her own grandmother, Dinka, and had been passed down to her. It was filled with jewelry, silver spoons, delicate scarves, music boxes, and handmade dolls. Dinka had been the band's best scavenger and had amassed a large collection of trinkets over her lifetime. Aishe loved to take out all the objects and ask Simza the story behind each one.

One day Aishe pulled out a wooden box filled with strange picture cards that had always fascinated her. "Where did Dinka find this one?" she asked her grandmother.

Simza looked up from the evening meal she was preparing over the fire, a rabbit stew in the big iron pot. "In Milan when she was just a girl," Simza said. Then she dropped her voice dramatically, as she loved to do when telling a story. "A curse had spread over all of the city, killing almost everyone. The stench of rotting bodies traveled for hundreds of miles."

Aishe put the wooden box back quickly, afraid to touch it now. Ghostly homes and decaying bodies could only have stemmed from evil spirits.

"Our band had been heading south when they heard the Black Death had taken thousands of lives. Empty houses meant treasure! So they came to Milan to search the cordoned-off areas."

Aishe gasped. "They searched the houses?" Simza nodded solemnly, but Aishe caught the twinkle in her eye. She knew how much her grandmother loved a rapt audience.

"Every day they were in Milan, the *phuri dai,* the elder women, would whisper prayers for protection to the four winds and drape the children with charmed amulets to shield them from the bad spirits. Then the children would go off to scavenge what they could. Thousands of *gadjos* in Milan had fallen dead! It was their bad luck, their *prikaza,* that a little grandmother had come and killed them all," she whispered.

The fire under the iron pot crackled and danced in agreement.

Aishe shivered, chilled by the wind, and wrapped herself up in her blanket. Little grandmother was the Rom's name for a bad spirit. *Gadjos* were city-dwellers, and the Rom thought them impure and polluted.

"For three days Dinka searched the houses in the abandoned neighborhoods, no easy task with dead people rotting around you!" Simza bulged her eyes for effect and waved the rabbit's legs, making Aishe squeal. "Dinka was now convinced all the ghost-eyes were watching her. She searched the last house in a panic and rooted out all the treasure. She had turned to leave when the wooden box caught her eye."

"Then what happened?" Aishe whispered, her eyes flitting to the box again.

"She stuffed it into her bag and hurried out. On her way back to camp, she stopped at the river and offered prayers to the water." Simza stood and reenacted the story to Aishe's giggles. "She stomped on the ground and spun in a circle three times, commanding any fever that may have entered her body to flow out and into the earth. And she shook a tree—" She paused and pointed to Aishe.

"Four times," Aishe answered like a dutiful student.

Simza nodded, pleased at Aishe's memory. "Just like her grandmother had taught her. When she arrived back at camp, she opened her sack for her parents. They allowed Dinka to choose one treasure to keep. Instead of picking one of the fine dolls, she surprised them by choosing the wooden box."

Aishe listened, wanting to remember every word of her grandmother's story so she could store it deep inside. One day she would be the old woman by the fire with stories to tell and memories that should not be forgotten.

Simza smiled a toothless smile, her eyes sparkling again. "Maybe one day the box will belong to you."

Aishe doubted anything in the chest would belong to her. Her parents, aunts, and uncles would inherit Dinka's treasures first. And she had countless cousins.

Aishe didn't agree with her grandmother's opinion of the *gadjos,* that the people who lived in cities were always ill. She found cities exciting and dreamed of one day living in such a place, instead of always on the outskirts, by a river with their livestock.

Usually they would enter a town for just a day, their long caravan a chain of colorful moving houses on wheels. Their wagons' exteriors were intricately painted, with artful trim and decorative embellishments. Their wooden cabins had shuttered windows, and the interiors had built-in seats, cabinets, wardrobes, and beds. The band would only stay in a town to trade and entertain. Then they would head to the forest to camp in a clearing, their wagons ringed together in a circle. By morning they would be on the road again, never to return to the same town.

Whenever Aishe asked why they had to leave, her parents explained that they needed to protect their spiritual energy, their *dji,* which they believed became drained when they spent too much time in *jado,* the non-Romani world. Aishe's ancestors had left their homeland hundreds of years ago to become nomads, traveling the *lungo drom,* "the endless road with no destination." Because of this, outsiders called them gypsies, though they despised the name.

Aishe closed up Dinka's chest and put it back in the wagon in its special spot. She kissed her grandmother's forehead and went off to meet her two cousins for their special outing. Every Eve of Saint George, the elder girls would let Aishe join in their secret ritual.

The ritual was quite simple. They carried fried fish and brandy to a place where two roads crossed. They would lay their offerings out and sit in the middle of the crossroad and wait for the apparitions of their future husbands to appear. Legend said that if a male figure appeared and ate the fish, it was a sign for a good marriage. If he drank the brandy, that was a very bad sign. And if he touched neither, then the bride and groom would both die within the year. The cousins never saw any apparitions, but every year they continued to try.

Sometimes they would strip naked at midnight by the nearest body of water—a lake or a river—and stare into its pool to see the reflection of their future husbands. When that didn't work, they stood naked on top of a dunghill at midnight with a piece of cake in their mouths and waited for a dog to bark. The direction the sound came from was supposedly the direction where their future husband lived.

While her cousins were busy, Aishe would lie back in the grass with her eyes closed and dream about what her husband would look like. She never imagined him as a Rom, but she kept that secret to herself.

⌣

Only in winter did Simza and Aishe's band quit their travels. Every year they settled in Styria, a small town in Austria, where they made their living in a variety of trades: metalworking, carpentry, basket weaving, and blacksmithing. Many of the men were also musicians—masters of the violin, flute, and zimbles—and often played for money. Aishe was a gifted harp player. She was also quite clever, which is how all the trouble began.

Aishe befriended a sweet Austrian girl named Kitti, whose family owned a small farm. Aishe wanted nothing more than to learn how to read like Kitti, who always had storybooks with her. Aishe had never seen books up close, for no Rom knew how to read or write. Her people carried their history through songs and the stories the elders told every night around the fire. When Aishe offered Kitti a necklace to teach her to read and speak German, Kitti agreed.

Aishe snuck into her family's wagon to retrieve it; the necklace she found in Dinka's chest was one of countless others. She assured herself no one would notice if it went missing. Her grandmother could barely see anymore and there were plenty left.

The girls met almost every day for several winters, and by the end of the past winter, Aishe had mastered the language. She and Kitti had also become friends.

Kitti began to lend her books, which Aishe took special care to hide. If she was ever caught with a book she would be beaten. The Rom were not allowed to pollute their mind with the *gadjes'* words.

One day Aishe came home from Kitti's and found the camp in an uproar. Her father had found the books.

"What are these?" He threw Kitti's books at her feet and stomped on them. Then he grabbed Aishe by the hair and dragged her to the campfire.

"Papa, no! I'm sorry!"

Enraged, he took a leather cord and whipped her back repeatedly. "You! Are! Not! My! Daughter!" he yelled. With each word he cracked the strap harder.

Deaf to her screams, he reached for the branding iron in the fire.

Her mother grabbed his arm, "Stop! Stop it!"

She barely managed to keep him from maiming their daughter's face. He took the rod to Aishe's hand instead and held it until it seared off her skin.

Aishe shrieked and fell back, clutching her hand.

"So you'll never forget." He raised the rod, ready to burn her again.

Hysterical, her mother screamed to Aishe's eldest cousin. "Take her! Niko! Take her!"

By now Simza and all the elders in the camp were yelling the same. Niko picked Aishe up and ran off with her into the forest. They found a faraway place to hide, and Niko brought Aishe water from a nearby stream to soak her hand.

"What were you thinking?" he scoffed. "Reading words. Bringing books here. Everyone knows they're tainted."

"They're not. They're beautiful." Aishe wept, cradling her maimed hand. "One day we will have our own books."

"That's absurd," Niko said, turning his back on her.

That evening Simza came to find them. She appeared beside Aishe in the dark and lifted her chin. Aishe stared back at her with tears glistening in her eyes.

"It is done" was all Simza said. Then she led her back to camp.

Her father had gone off to drink away his anger. Aishe lay down in her family's wagon and let Simza tend her wound with one of her special salves. All the while Simza sang a song Aishe had never heard before, a sad melody about a daughter leaving her family and never seeing them again.

"What is that song, Grandmother?" Aishe whispered.

"One you know well," Simza said.

Before Aishe could ask Simza to explain, her mother came inside.

Her mother hesitated, something she never did. Aishe had never her seen her look so solemn.

"You must marry," she finally said.

Aishe could not believe it. "Who?"

"Milosh Badi."

Tears sprang to Aishe's eyes. "But Milosh Badi is Grandmother's age."

"You will marry him," her mother said. "You're sixteen."

"He's as old and weathered as a tree!"

"He is a musician," her mother reminded her. "A good one."

"He's ancient!" Aishe began to sob. She could not believe her parents would marry her off to him.

"Milosh Badi will die soon and you will be a widow," her mother said in her pragmatic way. "Your father has willed it so."

"He is punishing me for the books."

"You are never to speak of them or I will disown you my-self!" her mother hissed. Then she left.

Aishe curled up on her blanket and felt her grandmother's frail hand stroke her hair. Simza began to sing the same song again. Aishe closed her eyes and pretended to sleep, but her mind was full of wild thoughts. She must leave. She had to. Like the girl in the song, she would run away and start anew.

Simza was right. Aishe did know the song. She had known it all her life.

～

While everyone slept, Aishe gathered her things with the stealth of a thief. She moved to the edge of the tent and saw that her grandmother was watching her.

Simza sat up with the eeriness of a phantom. Aishe froze, not knowing what to do. Simza had the power to decide her fate. If her grandmother woke her father, no one would be able to spare Aishe from his retribution.

The two women locked eyes. Simza's held the full weight of the *cohalyi* that she was. She picked up an object in the darkness and offered it to Aishe.

Through the faint streams of moonlight, Aishe saw that her grandmother was holding out Dinka's chest.

Aishe took the gift. Then Simza draped two amulets around her neck and placed her favorite seashell in Aishe's hand as a blessing. She motioned Aishe toward the wagon's open door with a look that said, *Go and live. I will always be with you.*

The Hanged Man

Semele knew exactly the year that Simza had described in Dinka's story. The plague had hit Northern Italy in 1629 and wiped out half of Milan's population by 1630. Somehow Ionna had foretold those events over a thousand years before. It was just too incredible.

Semele closed her computer. She had been in the Beinecke reading room for hours and her eyes needed a rest. The day was winding down and she couldn't put off calling her mother any longer. She gathered her things and left the building.

The brisk air hit her when she stepped outside. She buttoned her coat and walked over to Blue State Coffee to get an espresso. Depending on how fast she worked, she might be able to translate several more pages before heading to her mother's. She wanted to find out what happened to Aishe and the cards.

She knew with striking certainty she needed to figure out how to locate them, and quickly, and she realized there was one person she could call: Sebastian Abbes, a card historian in the Netherlands. She had worked with him earlier in the year while dismantling a collection for a Dutch client who had several valuable decks. If anyone knew about Ionna's deck, he would.

She checked her watch and quickly calculated the time difference. The Netherlands was six hours ahead. It was evening there now, but Sebastian wouldn't mind. The man was a night owl and crazy to boot.

She fished her cell phone from her purse and saw she had four missed calls and three voice mails from Bren. She stared at the phone with a sinking heart, unable to listen to the messages and call him back—not yet, not when she didn't know how to say what needed to be said. It felt like swimming upstream. Instead she sent him a text: *At Mom's dealing with some things. Will call you when I get back.* She clicked send, feeling like a jerk, but she had to focus.

She forced Bren from her mind and called Sebastian. He answered on the second ring. "Madame Cavnow! Please tell me you are in Amsterdam."

Even in her dismal state, Semele couldn't help laughing. Sebastian was a terrible flirt and had asked her out on more than one occasion. "No, still in the States. Listen, I need to ask a favor for one of my clients. They're interested in acquiring an antique tarot deck, fifteenth century or earlier. Have there been any finds?"

"We've had some exciting sixteenth-century finds, but not many cards older than that have survived."

"I was curious . . ." She hesitated. "Where did tarot cards originate? Was it Egypt?"

Sebastian laughed so heartily, she felt embarrassed. "Semele. Don't tell me you've been reading French Enlightenment manuscripts. No, the Egyptian notion is a complete myth," he assured her. "A whimsical idea someone dreamed up in a Parisian salon."

"Oh." What else could she say? *I'm reading an ancient seer's memoir and I'll get back to you?*

"Playing cards came from the East and exploded on the scene in Europe during the 1400s. Think of them as the video games of the time. People were obsessed. The priests were up in arms."

Sebastian was always animated whenever he talked about his favorite subject. Semele sipped her coffee while she listened.

"Cards went from being incredibly expensive works of art to being mass-produced on paper. Games usually involved gambling, which is why the church set laws, tried to ban them, burn them. It's where the idea that cards were evil came from. No one wanted to do anything but play."

"But where did the tarot come from?" Semele returned to her original question, the one he hadn't answered. "Who was the first to make them?"

"That, unfortunately, we don't know. The tarot literally popped out of nowhere in Italy a short time after playing cards arrived."

Semele tried to clarify. "So tarot came after playing cards, and they were used in a card game?"

"Basically, yes, like bridge. There were also funny little parlor games people played too. Then in the late 1700s, a group of Parisians claimed the tarot was a set of ancient Egyptian divination symbols. That theory was widely publicized by a man named Antoine Court de Gébelin."

"And who was he?" Semele wrote down the name so she wouldn't forget. She wondered if he'd show up in Ionna's story.

"A Protestant pastor who was attempting to prove that there was a universal root for all languages and religions. He believed all cultures were schisms derived from an ancient golden age of humanity."

"Sounds pretty utopian."

"Well, his writings were quite popular with both commoners and the king's court. He wrote a large volume of essays called *Le Monde Primitif.*"

Semele jotted that down as well. "Then what happened?"

"Within a few years Eteilla, France's first professional cartomancer, began to publish whole tarot-card-reading systems. Through the years he trained over five hundred card readers. Then Eliphas Levi came along and said the tarot was a system of high magic that gave us a glimpse of the inner workings of the universe. Levi believed the tarot would allow anyone to acquire universal knowledge."

Semele's eyebrows rose. That seemed a little far-fetched.

"By the end of the 1800s there was a fortune teller on every street corner. These so-called 'founders' of the tarot tradition never said where they got their theories. They claimed it came from intuition." Sebastian stopped talking. "Does that help?"

"Yes, actually, thank you. Could you let me know if a tarot deck like this surfaces?"

"Believe me, if tarot cards dating back farther than the fifteenth century surface, everyone will know. So when are you coming back to Amsterdam? I'm lonely over here."

"Sebastian, you're horrible," she teased. "Talk to Mikhail."

After she hung up she thought about what Sebastian had said. She didn't have any new leads. He hadn't given her anything to go on, but she still believed Ionna's cards were out there. She would just have to keep looking.

She grabbed a table and logged into her computer. Since her return from Switzerland she'd forgone her daily routine of checking e-mail and scanning auction news. Usually she would jump online throughout the day to keep abreast of every sale and discovery, every "first found" and "only known" announcement. It felt like checking the pulse of history, but lately she just didn't care. The more entrenched she became in Ionna's story, the more it seemed like the world was spinning without her. Still, she needed to review the information on her Beijing trip and also let Mikhail know she'd be out for a few days. She had been procrastinating looking at the new account, but she couldn't put if off any longer.

With a pained sigh, she opened the file to see what lay in store for her next assignment. At least reading English would be a welcome distraction.

She scanned the client overview. One of China's top restaurateurs had recently passed away and Semele's new clients were the heirs. The family owned a string of Hong Kong's most expensive restaurants—the kind where a simple club sandwich, laced with caviar and Wagyu beef, cost five hundred dollars. The restaurateur had died at the ripe age of ninety-five, and during his long life had built the largest collection of autographed menus from around the world.

He had every menu imaginable: menus signed by countless composers, including Rossini, Puccini, and Strauss, with handwritten musical notations next to their signatures; menus autographed by stars like Frank Sinatra, John Lennon, Marilyn Monroe, and Charlie Chaplin, and others like Nikola Tesla, Thomas Edison, and Einstein. He even had a collection of menus signed by various presidents and had several official coronation menus. There would be several thousand for her to sort through.

Semele had to admit that if she weren't so upset about the theft and losing the Bossard account, the assignment would be fun. She was sure to be seriously wined and dined. The trip would be a once-in-a-lifetime gastronomic adventure, in the name of work, no less. Maybe a thousand-dollar piece of chocolate ganache cake would help her forget Bren, Theo, and the disaster her life had become.

She quickly typed an e-mail to Mikhail, letting him know she had reviewed the file, and gave him her initial thoughts. Then she slid in a line about how they could go over the details on Friday, because she needed to take the next few days off.

The e-mail sounded apologetic enough. What could he do, fire her? She was his best appraiser, a consistent workhorse who hadn't taken a day off in over a year except to attend her father's funeral. Mikhail would get over it. She hit send.

Death

Six months ago her mother had called in the middle of the night crying hysterically that he was gone. Her parents had been to a gala at the Beinecke that evening, and Semele could hear the champagne-slur in her mother's voice.

They screamed over each other, Semele yelling that she needed to call an ambulance and her mother trying to explain that she already had.

"He's gone. He's gone" was all she could say.

Semele had launched out of bed and driven straight to New Haven with a coat over her pajamas. When she arrived the police were there. Her mother couldn't stop sobbing until Semele finally got something to calm her down.

The coroners had already taken her father away.

Semele had missed him—missed his last breath, his last moments. She had just talked to him the day before, having no idea it would be their last exchange. She barely managed to get through that first week, to make the funeral arrangements, to medicate her mother and put her to bed. No one, not even his internist, had seen her father's stroke coming. He was gone without warning, and her mother was comatose, barely able to attend the service.

Semele found the adoption papers three days later. She had been working all day in her father's home office, going through his bills and bank accounts, and looking at insurance policies.

Her father had always taken care of those things, and now Semele had to help her mother manage life without him.

The papers were in his bottom drawer.

At first she didn't understand what she was looking at. She saw her name alongside her parents' names on a certificate issued the year she was born. Then she realized. It wasn't a birth certificate. Her parents were *not* her real parents.

The words on that page shattered her. She had grown up as Daddy's little girl, his faithful shadow, and knowing he died carrying this secret felt like losing him not once, but twice. Now, in some ways, she didn't feel like she had a mother either. She didn't have anyone.

That night Semele had wanted to march into her parents' bedroom, wake her mother up, and scream until she told her the adoption was a lie. But her mother was asleep, thanks to the Ambien.

The discovery was too much. She was already in a fragile state. So she set the adoption papers in the center of her father's desk, next to the checkbook and credit cards, the safe-deposit-box key and all the other important papers. Then she went to her bedroom and packed.

Her mother's younger sister was staying with them for the month. Semele assured herself that her aunt could take care of her mother without her. When she was certain her aunt was asleep, Semele left. The eighty-mile drive to Manhattan passed in a blur of anger and tears. Looking back now, she realized she was lucky she hadn't gotten into an accident.

The subsequent phone calls from her mother were both maddening and heartbreaking—the sobs, the begging, the long voice mails asking Semele to come home so that she could explain. Semele told her she would come when she was ready. She was too raw from the loss of her father and really didn't want to know. Whatever her mother had to say would only make the pain worse.

So they went months without speaking at all. Occasionally her mother would break down and call, begging her to come home so they could finally talk. Usually she would phone on a Friday after dinner and drinks with girlfriends. Semele always used work as an excuse to ignore the calls. Her first assignment after the funeral was in Amsterdam, the trip where she met Sebastian.

In Amsterdam she was a recluse. She threw herself into her work to mask her hurt. Sebastian managed to drag her away every once in a while to show her the sights. One of those trips was to an exhibit of playing cards at a local museum. Inside the minimalist space, rows of glass boxes showcased eighteenth-century playing cards under pin lights. She would never forget their story.

At that time, women who were too poor to care for their children would leave the baby on the doorsteps of churches, or at the houses of good townsmen, where they knew the child would be cared for. Often the mothers couldn't afford stationery, so they would tuck a playing card into the baby's swaddling with a message, usually with the child's name and their reason for leaving the baby. The mother always begged the stranger to save the baby's life.

Semele read each card in the exhibit:

Please, I cannot afford to feed him. He has not eaten in three days.

My son must live. His name is Jan.

Save her.

Feed him.

Help him live.

Please open your hearts.

The messages were all similar.

Halfway through the exhibit Semele gave up on hiding her

tears. What broke her heart the most was the story behind the cards that were cut in half. A halved card meant the mother had kept the other half as a way of telling the caretakers she would try to come back for her child one day.

The exhibit had hit Semele hard. Her real mother had abandoned her at birth. Would her card have been cut in half or left whole?

The question haunted her for months afterward. She thought of all the children who faced the world without their mother or father, and now she was one of them. Suddenly her whole childhood, her whole life, didn't make sense. Who was she really? Now she was ready to find out.

She decided to send her mother a text instead of calling her; it was cowardly but easier:

Hi Mom, decided to come home. Have a few days off from work. Will see you tonight.

Within two minutes her mother texted back with an upbeat reply:

Wonderful news. Usual time?

Semele could feel her emotions churning. She used to take the train to New Haven once a month to visit her parents, always the 5:22 with the 7:07 arrival. Her dad would pick her up and her mother would have dinner ready. Joseph would uncork his favorite wine and they would talk for hours.

She texted back: *Yes.*

Why she didn't tell her mom she was already in town, only ten minutes away, was because ten minutes felt too soon.

With a new city comes a new life. Aishe began hers in Paris.

On the road outside of Styria she met a nice German family traveling to France and they offered to let her accompany them. Aishe helped cook and clean at the campfire and take care of the small children in return for safe passage. When they arrived in Paris, Aishe said good-bye to her friends and declined their invitation to continue north. Paris was the only place she wanted to be.

The first year she squatted in the forest, on the edge of the city, with all the other beggars. Every day she would walk to the markets to play her harp or sell wooden flowers she had made from fallen branches. Some days she would earn a coin and other days she would not. When too much time went by with nothing, she would dig into Dinka's chest and find a trinket to trade for bread.

She befriended other squatters at her encampment who taught her to speak French. "Wandering Angel" became her nickname because she always had the harp in her arms and Dinka's colorful chest strapped to her back like a pair of boxed wings.

One day, while playing on a street corner near the market, Aishe looked down and noticed two coins in her basket. She was giddy that she would eat for the first time all week. Just then, a woman nearby dropped her purchases, spilling oranges and pears on the ground.

Aishe rushed to help her. With nimble hands, she put all the fruit back in the woman's basket. Aishe accepted the woman's thanks but was secretly wishing for a pear.

She turned back and saw a young boy snatching her two coins. *"Arrête!"* she screamed. The boy dashed off, disappearing into the market stalls. Aishe returned to Dinka's chest, which she often used as a stool, and sat down. She could not keep her tears at bay.

Patrice Brevard was keen enough to know the girl had lost the coins on account of her. She also knew from her matted hair and filthy clothes that this waif needed more than two coins. She had heard Aishe strumming the harp and thought how well the girl played. Her employer, Mme Helvétius, enjoyed having unusual entertainment in her salon. Perhaps if the girl bathed and was given a proper dress, she could play for their guests.

Before Patrice could question her judgment, she approached Aishe. "I'm afraid you lost your coins because of me."

"Do not worry, Madame, I will earn more," Aishe said bravely, wiping her eyes.

Patrice could hear the accent in her voice. "Do you have family?" she asked.

"No, I am alone." Aishe eyed the fruit and her stomach rumbled.

Patrice held out a pear, which Aishe grabbed, barely able to utter a "thank you" before shoving it into her mouth.

Patrice watched her devour the fruit. "Your playing is quite lovely. I could offer you a few days' work if you would like."

Aishe's eyes grew round, as pear juice dribbled down her chin.

"I am the housekeeper at a salon in Auteuil, a village not far from here. I could give you a maid's dress and a proper bath, and you could stay for a few days until we see how you get on."

Aishe jumped up. "Oh yes, Madame. Thank you! I will do whatever you wish."

Patrice stepped back to allow more air to come between her and Aishe. That dress would need to be burned. "You will assist me and my maids and play music for our guests in exchange for room and board." Aishe nodded vigorously as Patrice turned away. "Now come along before I change my mind."

With the pear stuck in her mouth, Aishe gathered Dinka's chest and her harp and hurried to follow.

And so it was. If life was a game of chance, Chance had just offered itself up to her.

—

Aishe played the harp in the salon for one hour in the afternoon and one hour in the evening. She had no idea who the people were or why they came and went.

In the evenings the voices became loud and hearty; there was talk of a revolution in some place called America and that France would perhaps undergo the same. The afternoons were less boisterous: a poet would recite his work, or a playwright would come with a troupe of actors. On quiet days the guests would gather around gaming tables to play cards.

The salon's owner, Mme Helvétius, was a striking beauty, even in her sixties, and easily commanded the room. She dressed in the exaggerated fashion of the day—wide panniers with a cinched waist, and a tall wig adorned with gaudy feathers—with the wise wink of a woman who understood that sometimes it was necessary to look foolish.

All the great minds of the day attended her salon. Auteuil was a charming resort village, and Parisian elite flocked there to escape the stench of Versailles. The palace had fallen into severe decline, becoming an odorous cesspool where aristocrats and servants alike often took to relieving themselves in the stairs and corners. Much of the court no longer wanted to attend.

Philosophers, writers, artists, astronomers, and physicists all mingled in Mme Helvétius' blue-and-white parlor. Many days the salon held as many as fifty people, each eager to connect with like minds. Paris was entering its Age of Enlightenment, a new order in which brilliant ideas reigned supreme, and the conversations happening in Mme Helvétius' salon could cut through the powder on any man's face.

The men who gathered there were Freemasons, a fraternity dedicated to deciphering the order of nature and humanity's place within it. At present, they were studying the priests and philosophers of ancient Egypt, Greece, and Rome to understand the knowledge of the ancient world.

A pastor and Freemason named Antoine Court de Gébelin loved to air his thoughts at the salon. On this particular day, however, he sat in quiet repose and enjoyed Aishe's playing.

Aishe was stationed near the door with her harp. The sunlight streamed through the window behind her, and her fingers flew over the strings with easy grace. When two young gentlemen entered the room, she almost played a wrong chord.

She tried not to stare, but her eyes kept wandering to the taller of the two men. She couldn't help it. He looked just like the husband she'd conjured in her dreams all those nights with her cousins. Now here he stood in the flesh.

When they locked eyes she did play the wrong chord. She quickly covered her mistake but caught him smiling. He seemed to know he had been the cause.

He was introduced around the room, and Aishe overheard that he was from Russia and his name was Andrej Cernik. A thick accent laced his French. Andrej continued to stare at Aishe the whole time he spoke. His attention made her blush. When his gaze drifted to her hand, she knew he was wondering how she'd gotten such a horrible scar. She wished she could cover it. Every day, the scar reminded her how alone she was, how her family was lost forever.

She closed her eyes and played faster, imagining Simza dancing and twirling like a dervish as she had loved to whenever Aishe let her music fly.

Court de Gébelin stood up and hovered at the table where a small group had gathered to play cards. He stared at the deck spread out before Mme Helvétius' hands.

Mme Helvétius glanced up with an inquisitive smile. "You wish to play?"

"These cards," he said.

"Aren't they intriguing? I bought them on my last trip to Germany. They're called the tarot."

Court de Gébelin picked up one of the painted cards and read the words under the image. "The Hermit." It showed an old man holding a lantern in the dark. Then he picked up another of a magician. "The Magician," he murmured.

Court de Gébelin had never seen these cards before. To the average eye they looked exotic.

"May I?" He derailed the game, taking all twenty-two face cards and laying them out together. By now everyone was crowded around the table; even Aishe had stopped playing.

Court de Gébelin grew convinced that the cards were symbols, and that hidden within them was a secret wisdom from remote antiquity, from Egypt. He shared his belief with such conviction that soon he had everyone in the room convinced of his hypothesis.

Mme Helvétius looked at her cards with newfound curiosity. "How did such cards come to Europe in the first place?"

"Must have been the gypsies," Andrej's friend proposed.

Aishe smiled at that but remained silent.

Andrej noticed. "You find that idea amusing?" He stepped closer to her.

Turning pink, Aishe demurred but said nothing. Her people had not traded these exotic cards. She had seen only one of these decks in her life, the one in Dinka's chest.

Andrej's gaze swept over her red hair and delicate features. "Would you play for me once more? I have never heard such beautiful music."

Aishe nodded shyly and began to play a soulful Rom melody, one of Simza's favorites, a tune called "Find Me in the Wind."

As Aishe played, Court de Gébelin became even more certain

he'd made a miraculous discovery, and he announced that he would write about the cards in his next volume of essays. The essays would start a wildfire that would soon burn through Paris and into Europe and beyond.

That day in Mme Helvétius' salon, two stars collided. Antoine Court de Gébelin met my descendent, and the future of fortune telling was born.

Message to VS—

Interesting call from Beinecke.

Reply from VS—

Excellent. Notify me when back in NY.
She should have them by then.

Temperance

Semele could almost hear the harp playing, the scene was so vivid in her mind. She had rushed to translate Aishe's story but was unable to finish before it was time to head to her mother's. As she rode in the cab, she wondered what happened to Aishe after Mme Helvétius' salon. Had she stayed in Paris? And what happened to the cards in Dinka's chest?

The cab turned down her street, interrupting her thoughts. They arrived at a two-story turn-of-the-century classic New England home in East Rock near Yale. The house had been a constant in Semele's life. Over the years, her parents had lovingly renovated every room and painted the outside powder blue. The color only made the house, with its wraparound porch and original woodwork, more picturesque.

The porch light turned on and Helen came outside.

Semele couldn't help the sinking feeling in her chest. She still wasn't ready.

Her mother hurried to the curb before Semele could shut the door. "It's so good to see you," she said, giving Semele a hesitant squeeze, unsure if her embrace would be welcome.

Semele hugged her back. "You too," she said automatically.

Like Semele, Helen was petite in stature and wore her hair pixie short. She always dressed in linen pants and flowing batik blouses that made her look as if she were on vacation somewhere fabulous like Morocco. But tonight her colorful blouse and pristine makeup couldn't hide the strain in her eyes. She looked thinner and more fragile than the last time Semele had seen her, which made Semele's guilt return tenfold. She had abandoned her mother in her most desperate time of need.

Helen watched the cab drive off. "What, no bags?"

"I figured I'd wear whatever is here," Semele lied. She had no clue what clothes she had in her old room.

Her mother assessed her. "You look exhausted."

"Just a little tired."

They headed up the brick walkway. Once inside, Helen made a beeline for the kitchen. "I hope you don't mind chicken," she said, as if Semele had come home for their usual dinner and they hadn't been estranged for months.

"Sounds great." Semele grimaced internally. Baked lemon chicken was her mother's go-to. She always paired it with warmed spinach salad and quinoa.

"I invited Macy to join us," Helen called out.

"Oh." Semele wasn't sure how she felt about that. Macy was one of her oldest friends. It wasn't that she didn't want to see her, but now the whole dynamic would change. Macy knew all about the drama with her mother and had been urging Semele to patch things up.

"I thought it'd make tonight more festive, a real homecoming." Helen flitted into the dining room to light a votive candle. Semele noticed that the old wooden high chair had been brought down from the attic; apparently Macy's toddler would be here tonight too. Forester would probably be as cranky as last time, which meant dinner would involve a lot of buttered noodles on the floor.

Semele went to open a bottle of wine.

"Not that one, honey." Helen took the bottle away and handed her another. "I thought tonight we could open this one."

Semele saw the label. It was her father's favorite sauvignon blanc from a boutique winery in Napa. They'd bought a case on their last trip, and Semele knew this was the last bottle. "We don't have to open it," she said quickly, trying not to get emotional.

"No, I want to." Helen uncorked the wine with nervous hands and poured them each a glass. They stood at the dining nook like strangers at a cocktail party. "How's work?" Helen smiled.

"Busy. I've been dealing with a special collection from Switzerland." She didn't say that she'd been taken off the account or that the prize manuscript had been stolen. "I may go to Beijing next."

"Ooh, that sounds fun." Helen headed off to the kitchen again. "Let me check on the chicken."

"I'm translating a manuscript from Greek," Semele called out, not wanting to follow her.

"That's wonderful!" Helen's reply sounded overly cheerful.

Semele rolled her eyes, now completely regretting this visit. She didn't know where to put her anger. Nothing had changed.

The doorbell rang. Semele barely had time to open it before Macy blew inside, juggling a diaper bag full of toys and a bottle of wine. Forester was almost two now and sat perched on her hip like a koala bear. Somehow Macy made it all look effortless.

"Oh my God! I'm so glad you're here." Macy managed to give her a huge hug.

Her long hair was wrapped and knotted in a scarf that matched her peasant skirt. She smelled like sandalwood oil, and a dozen more freckles had appeared on her face since the last time Semele had seen her.

Macy lowered her voice. "Sorry. Your mom wanted me to be here. I think she was really stressed out about tonight."

Semele nodded as if she understood. It was surreal to think that her mother needed the moral support of her best friend in order to see her again.

"Is that Macy?"

Within seconds Helen had the baby blanket spread out on the living room floor and Forester playing with his toys, while Macy helped herself to a glass of wine. Semele felt a tug of jealousy.

She couldn't help wondering if Macy and Forester came over here a lot.

"How are you?" Macy asked. "How's Bren? I haven't talked to you in ages!"

"I know. I've been busy on the road." Before Semele could say more, Helen shuttled them to the table and started bringing out the dishes.

Semele and Macy looked at each other and smiled. How many nights had they eaten at each other's houses? Growing up, the two had been inseparable.

Helen sat down at the table with a martini in hand. She had already moved on from the wine. Semele frowned, unable to withhold her judgment. Whenever her mother was in a stressful situation, she drank more than usual. It had been that way all her life and had only gotten worse. Even Macy would probably still remember when all the mothers quietly discouraged Helen from driving the kids to French club in high school, because they were worried she would have one too many at the "cultural" dinners. Semele dropped out of the club soon after and never told her mother why.

The three ate in uncomfortable silence. Occasionally Helen called out to Forester, to see if he wanted to join them at the table. Macy assured her he had already eaten.

"So, how have you been, Mom?" Semele knew it was a clumsy attempt at a first step.

"Good! So busy!" She launched into an upbeat spiel about her social calendar, throwing words about like Band-Aids as though they could somehow mend the rift between them. Instead the chatter was just awkward as Helen went on about her bridge group, her book club, and the "marvelous" show she just saw at Yale Repertory Theatre.

When her mother started describing the upcoming Botanical Society tea party she was invited to, Semele poured more wine. She figured she might as well top herself off too at this point.

Helen finally petered out and there was a lull around the table.

Semele decided to broach a new subject. "Have you given any more thought to selling the house?"

Helen gave her a sharp look. "Now why would I do that?"

Semele tried to placate her, realizing she had stepped on a hot spot. "Mom, the place is huge. The upkeep . . . the stairs. It's a lot of work."

"I'm not that old yet."

"You don't need to be close to the university anymore."

"This is our home. Why are you so eager for me to sell it?" Helen didn't try to hide the edge in her voice.

"I didn't mean it like that. I just don't want you to think I'll be upset if you wanted to move. I worry about you here all by yourself."

"Well you could've fooled me," Helen snapped.

Semele rose to the challenge. "You really want to do this now?"

Macy looked from one to the other, afraid to say anything.

"Macy, as you're well aware, things have been quite strained between me and my daughter lately," Helen said, finishing her martini and obviously feeling fortified.

"Yes, it seems like you've been inviting my friends over a lot to talk about how strained things are."

"Sem—" Macy hedged.

"Because I'm feeling set up here."

"I just thought having Macy would be a nice way to make tonight more festive."

"So you keep saying! And no, you didn't. You just didn't want to talk about why I left," Semele challenged. "You still don't."

"Talk? All I've been trying to do is talk and you won't return my calls!" Helen tried to defend herself. "You left without a word, skulking off in the middle of the night. . . ."

"Skulking! I left because I didn't want to scream at you right after Dad died!"

"So you abandoned me!"

They were both yelling now. Forester had begun to fuss and Macy went over to distract him.

"You were so high on pills I'm surprised you even noticed."

"Of course I was on pills! I'd just lost your father!" Helen's voice broke and tears filled her eyes.

Semele glared at her, a savage part of her satisfied that she was making her mother hurt. "And I didn't?" she yelled back. "Did you even hear him call out in pain? Or were you too drunk to wake up and dial 911?" Semele was screaming. A volcano had erupted inside her.

Helen broke down and started to sob.

"Sem—" Macy returned to the table, imploring her to take it easy.

Semele ignored her and stared down at her mother. "Did you hear him?" she bellowed, slamming her hands down on the table.

Forester began to wail. No one said a word.

This was the question that festered beneath the hurt of finding the adoption papers, the open wound that would not heal: the thought that her mother could have prevented her father's death, that her weakness was the reason he didn't survive.

"I did! I did hear him!" Helen cried. "I heard his first gasp of pain. I sat up. His body was rigid. He couldn't answer me. I held him while he was convulsing. I reached for the phone. . . . I dropped it once, but I called 911 right away. I swear to God I called right away."

Semele began to cry too.

"The doctors said there was nothing I could have done. No one could have saved him. I tried. I swear I tried." Helen wept.

Semele whispered, "I'm sorry," and left the room.

She went into the kitchen and put her head on the counter. She tried to breathe through the pain. The well of anger and heartbreak had risen to the surface again.

A minute later she felt a warm hand on her back. "Hey," Macy said gently.

Semele wiped her eyes. "Mace, I'm so sorry. I don't know what happened. I lost it."

Macy had tears in her eyes too. She handed Semele a tissue box and led her to the breakfast table in the corner. They sat down.

Semele looked at the garden outside the window. "Shit." She sighed. "Is she okay?"

"She's playing with Forester."

Semele shook her head. "I'm so sorry I yelled in front of him."

Macy shrugged. "He's one. He'll get over it."

Semele put her head in her hands. "God, I'm the most horrible daughter on the planet."

"You're angry and you have a right to be. Want to tell me why Bren isn't here helping you get through this?" Leave it to Macy to zero in on the other hole in her life. Semele's silence said it all. "Holy crap. I knew it." Macy sat back.

"What? That we'd break up?" Semele looked at her, surprised.

Macy held up her hands in surrender. "He's a great guy, don't get me wrong. You just didn't seem matched."

"Why didn't you tell me?" Semele asked, though she already knew the answer. She had been over the moon about Bren. Macy wouldn't have wanted to take away her happiness, so she kept her feelings to herself.

"What happened?" Macy asked.

Semele debated telling the truth. Macy was the only person who could possibly understand. "I had a premonition."

Semele let out a deep breath. *There. I said it.*

Macy's eyes widened and she sat forward with excitement. She knew Semele had had premonitions when she was younger— and that they'd all come true. She was the only person Semele had confided in.

As a child Semele had been incredibly intuitive, always knowing things before they happened. Helen brushed it off, and her father would just laugh until Semele felt silly for even telling him. So she began to keep her foresights a secret. Only Macy knew her struggle.

The turning point had come the summer she was twelve, when she had a vision of one of her classmates drowning. She never told anyone, not even Macy, and convinced herself the dream couldn't come true. But the girl had died, and Semele always wondered what would have happened if she had said something, warned her. Maybe she could have saved her life. Semele carried that guilt for years, and over time, trained herself not to remember her dreams. Eventually they stopped.

As she got older she continued to experience déjà vu—the kind that rained down and flooded a moment, like she was actually reliving it again. She told herself everyone had these experiences, and then she started to ignore the sensation until she no longer experienced this either.

Now her talent seemed to be resurfacing.

"Do you want to talk about it?" Macy asked gently. She knew how Semele had shunned her abilities as a child, how much she had tried to bury her visions. Macy was the complete opposite, the kind of person who embraced intuition and strived to stay in tune. She saw synchronicity in everything and "The Universe" was always talking to her, which was why Semele felt able to open up to her in the first place. Never once had Macy thought Semele was crazy. "I'm always here. You know that."

"I know, thanks." Semele gave her a faint smile.

"Oh, I almost forgot," Macy said. "I have a present for you."

She ran to get her purse and came back with a heavy object that she plunked in Semele's hand.

Semele looked down at the smooth rock and laughed. "Um, thank you?" Then she turned it over and saw the beautiful mandala painted on the front. "Oh, Macy." She gasped. "It's beautiful."

"It's called a dream stone. You're supposed to keep it on your nightstand for good dreams." She waved a hand in the air. "I saw it in a boutique and thought of you."

Semele smiled, touched. Macy was her oldest friend. Semele had been maid of honor at her wedding, had thrown her baby shower, and had been at the hospital for Forester's birth. Of course Macy was here tonight, helping her get through this. Helen hadn't asked Macy over for her sake—she had asked her for Semele's. Her mother had known how hard this would be.

They said their good-byes outside. Helen helped buckle Forester into his car seat. Macy hugged Semele and whispered, "Talk to her. She misses you."

Semele nodded and hugged her back. "Thanks for coming." She stood on the curb with her mother and watched Macy and Forester drive off.

Semele was about to head inside when she glanced across the street. Her heart did a double flip.

The black BMW turned on its headlights and the car took off.

Semele could tell the driver was a man. She tried to convince herself the car was a neighbor's. But it was him. She was sure.

She didn't know what to do. If she told her mother what was going on, Helen would become hysterical and never let Semele go back to New York.

"Come on, Mom. Let's go in."

She quickly led her mother back into the house and double-checked to make sure all the doors and windows were locked.

"I'm setting the alarm," she announced. She tried to tell herself that, if the man was planning to do anything, he would have already made a move.

Helen watched her, unsure of what to say. Unspoken apologies hung in the air as they cleared away the remaining dishes. Neither could muster the strength to push past the silence so they could meet each other in the middle.

After they were done in the kitchen Semele headed upstairs. "I think I'll go to bed."

"All right, darling. Good night." Helen sounded hesitant but said nothing more.

On the way up the stairs, Semele walked past the large portrait of her mother's family tree. Helen's aunt had commissioned the project when Helen was a young girl and given a print to each of her children, nieces, and nephews as a wedding gift, adding their spouses' names. Semele always loved to find her mother's and father's names together side by side.

The framed chart made her Semele Cavnow, and it was a stark reminder that her own family tree was missing.

Eight of Cups

Semele placed Macy's dream stone on the nightstand and looked around her old bedroom. At some point she really did need to go through everything. Her parents had kept all her things from childhood. She stared at the family pictures, mementoes, and treasured books on the shelves. These walls held the girl she once was, all her hopes and fears. Love filled this room.

She found a pair of pajamas from high school in the dresser. The pants fit like weird capris and the top was now a mid-rise, but they would do. She turned off the light and snuggled under the comforter. As she lay in the dark she debated whether or not to read more of the manuscript. But her eyes were heavy with exhaustion.

Semele heard her mother come up the stairs.

A moment later her bedroom door whispered open and Helen appeared, a lonely silhouette in the hallway. She came into the room and sat on the edge of the bed without asking Semele if she was awake; her mother could always tell if she was asleep or not. The most important talks of Semele's life had always seemed to happen at her bedside, in the dark, a time when facades were laid to rest.

"We didn't want to tell you because we always considered you ours," Helen said softly.

Semele waited for her to say more. Her anger toward her mother had begun to dissipate. She knew her mother had been suffering with the lie for years. "I need to know, Mom."

Helen took a deep breath. "We were still in New York. Your father had just been offered the curatorship and we were about to move."

Semele's father had worked at Columbia before coming to Yale. It was where he became a central figure in the International Federation of Library Associations. But Semele knew that history. *Go on,* her silence prompted.

"We had been trying to have a baby for years. The doctors, the tests said we couldn't. So we registered with an adoption agency—all very private. They said it might take a while. Then we got a call one day. A woman had requested us. . . ." Helen swallowed. "Your grandmother."

Semele sat up and hugged her knees to her chest.

"She was in failing health and couldn't care for you. She wanted you to have a good home, a loving family—"

"But why you? Why did she request you? And what about my birth mother? Where was she?" The questions tumbled out from her.

"I don't know," her mother said, knowing it wasn't a satisfying answer. "But we were overjoyed."

"Did you ever meet her? My grandmother?"

"Once." Helen hesitated. "She was there when we . . . first met you."

Semele's voice grew smaller. "What was she like?"

"Frail . . . very intense. She was ill." Helen's eyes grew distant, trying to remember. "She had an accent, Eastern European I think . . . and beautiful eyes. Your eyes." Helen brushed a strand of hair from Semele's cheek. "She said your name was Semele and made us promise we wouldn't change it." Helen seemed to remember something else and frowned.

"What?" Semele asked.

"She gave us a package and asked that we give it to you when you were older. Your father took it and promised her we would." Helen's eyes watered and she shook her head, more to herself with shame, confessing, "I don't even know what it was—maybe

I didn't want to know, to acknowledge you had a past that didn't include me." Semele was about to interject, but Helen kept on. "Please understand, we meant to tell you one day, but after we had you, it was as if our lives had started over. We couldn't remember ever not having you. You became a part of us." Helen choked back her tears.

Semele reached out and took her hand, letting her continue.

"As the years went by, we wondered if maybe it was better not to tell you. No one knew you were adopted except my sister. We came to New Haven with a clean slate, a new job, new house, new friends . . . and a newborn everyone thought I had given birth to. I wanted so much for that to be true. So it became our truth."

"You should have told me."

Helen wiped her cheeks. "We were planning to. You know your father. He thought he had all the time in the world."

Semele could feel tears slipping down her face. "I don't want to be mad at him anymore." She broke down and her mother gathered her in her arms. "I've been so mad at him. At both of you."

"I know, baby, I know." Helen cried with her. "I'm so sorry. But you're my daughter. You've always been my daughter."

Semele pulled back to look at her. "But who are my real parents?" She saw the pain the question inflicted, but she had to ask. "What happened to them? I feel like there's this big hole inside me."

Helen didn't say anything. She only nodded and reached for the box of Kleenex. "We can try to find the answers."

"And the package?"

"Tomorrow, we'll look. I promise."

Semele nodded, though her heart didn't feel any lighter. Her mother kissed her forehead as if she were five again and left the room. Semele waited until she heard her mother's bedroom door shut. Then she turned on the light and opened her computer to read the last of the manuscript.

Fortune telling had become the rage all over Europe, and Russia followed suit. At Sytny Market in St. Petersburg, a fortune teller had a stall. Kezia would always beg her parents to go, but they would only laugh. Then Kezia would look over and catch her grandmother's smile as she sat knitting in her rocking chair.

Kezia remembered all the lessons her grandmother Marina had shared with her, how symbols and patterns existed everywhere in nature—in rocks, leaves, and crystals—waiting to be seen. These mystical ideas had always fascinated her.

Her grandmother would tease that this was her gypsy blood shining through.

Kezia's great-grandmother Aishe had been a Rom. She had run away from her band to Paris with nothing but her musical skills, which led her to a grand salon where she played the harp, and met her future husband, Andrej Cernik.

Andrej came from one of Russia's wealthiest families and had been sent to Paris as a diplomat. When his post ended, the couple left for Russia, relieved to escape the growing dangers in Paris. France's great revolution, the one so hotly debated in Mme Helvétius' salon, had finally erupted.

In St. Petersburg Andrej hired the best tutor to help Aishe learn Russian and fitted her in gowns suitable for Catherine's court. The Cernik family was a favorite of the empress and often dined at the Winter Palace, where the elaborate banquets exceeded even those of Versailles. The people saw Aishe as exotic at a time when Russia could not get enough of the West.

Kezia loved to hear stories about her great-grandmother's arrival in St. Petersburg. Marina described the beautiful harp Andrej bought her as a wedding gift, and recounted the time Aishe played for Catherine the Great.

Marina was Aishe and Andrej's only child. As an adult, she became fascinated with genealogy and preserving the family's history. She went to great lengths to chart both sides of her parents' lineage. She loved the stories about Aishe's childhood as a wandering gypsy, and how her grandmother, Simza, had helped her escape. Marina wrote down the stories behind every object in Aishe's keepsake chest—Dinka's chest—in a diary. She became the memory keeper.

Once Kezia learned to read, Marina's diary was her favorite book. She would steal away under her favorite tree for hours and read the incredible tales about Simza finding missing children and foretelling the future with seashells. Kezia yearned to do the same. She often tried to read her palm or stare into the bottom of a teacup. She was like a student without a teacher. The urge ran deep inside her to grasp the future's unknown.

So one day, without permission, she snuck off to see the fortune teller at Sytny Market. She had saved all her kopeks to pay for the adventure, but it became one of the major disappointments of her young life.

"Madame Zazouska" was a charlatan, a pretender who spouted vague musings, fortunes that could apply to anyone. The woman took Kezia's money and lavished her with praise and promises of prosperity.

"You will find love, a husband, and have three children."

Kezia had heard her give the same fortune to another girl while she was standing outside the stall.

Although Kezia was disappointed by Madame Zazouska, she was entranced by the woman's mysterious cards. The madame had used tarot cards, and Kezia had felt a rush of excitement as she watched her study them. But too quickly the Madame's hands swished the deck back into a neat pile and the reading was over.

When Kezia returned home, her grandmother called her over to her rocking chair.

"You do not need anyone else to tell you what you already know," Marina said. Then she opened up the family's keepsake chest and took out an intricately carved Italian box. "I always wondered why we kept these. Now I know they were meant for you."

Kezia opened the box and found the most exquisite tarot deck she had ever seen. She moved her fingertips over the cards in awe. With each stroke she could feel the spirit of her ancestor like a living force. Kezia met her grandmother's eyes, and understanding passed between them.

"She must have been a great seer," Kezia whispered.

"Yes, she must have," Marina said and returned to knitting.

From that day on, Kezia was never without her cards. She even slept with them, wrapping them in silk and tucking them under her pillow. She would often study the cards one by one, writing down what she thought each image meant. Her notebook filled with ideas. She may not have had a teacher, but she had powerful intuition. For Kezia, the two became one and the same.

Every morning she picked a card and used it to interpret how the day would go. Sometimes when she asked a question she had to lay out several cards until she saw her answer. She had no idea if what she was doing was right. She had no books to learn from, but it didn't matter. Soon she was performing readings for her grandmother and parents, and then her friends. By the time she was a young woman, her intuition had flowered into powerful foresight.

When Madame Zazouska died, Kezia lit a candle for the old woman. The Madame may not have been a seer, but she had never physically harmed a soul. And she had been right about one aspect of Kezia's future. Kezia did marry—a young writer named Sergei Leykin.

Sergei came from a merchant family and over time became an accomplished playwright. He had productions mounted at the Alexandrinsky Theatre and was a part of a ring of artists with voracious intellects. Sergei found Kezia's card reading fascinating, and he loved her all the more for her gift. For several years they lived a happy life together.

Kezia had always known she would have a daughter one day. So when she lost a child midway through her first pregnancy, she was devastated. Again, she got pregnant, and again, the pregnancy failed. For the first time, Kezia's faith in her sight was shaken. The doctors told her she wasn't able to become a mother, but Kezia had seen her daughter's spirit. She had seen her live.

＿

For years Kezia waited. Sergei had long given up hope of having a child. Then, in the year of Kezia's thirty-fourth birthday, she conceived. As the child grew in her womb, Kezia's powers amplified, and she began to see future events with certainty.

Russia was in a state of violent upheaval. A revolution had occurred in the past year, triggered by the war with Japan. The entire country went on strike, grinding everything to a halt. When it ended, daily life barely returned to normal. But Kezia knew the worst was yet to come. In a little more than ten years, there would be a revolution that would change the face of the country forever.

Two months into her pregnancy, she attended a tea hosted by one of St. Petersburg's most prominent families. She rarely went to such functions but she had heard the infamous mystic Rasputin would be there. He had arrived in the city the month before, and everyone wanted to meet the renowned prophet and healer. Kezia had come to judge the man's abilities for herself.

She sat quietly in a corner sipping tea and watched the ladies flock around him. Rasputin was the only man in the room. He cut a dramatic figure with his long black hair and beard, but his body emitted the odor of one who never bathed. This "holy man," a peasant from Siberia, had somehow gained entry to the highest levels of St. Petersburg society by preaching that people should sin as much as possible to find their path to God. He fully embodied his mantra by drinking to excess and hosting orgies at his home.

Squeals of laughter erupted from the women in the parlor as Rasputin squeezed their breasts. "I can measure your spirit this way," he explained.

When he started unbuttoning the blouse of a grand duchess, Kezia burst into laughter before she could stop herself and caught his attention. With a sinking heart, she watched him excuse himself from the red-faced ladies and approach her.

"Grigori Rasputin at your service," he said in a rich voice.

Kezia acknowledged him with a polite nod, but did not offer him her hand.

His gaze swept her body with open lust. "Would you like me to measure your spirit also?" He cocked an eyebrow.

"I'm afraid it is heavier than you think," Kezia said with a confidence she didn't feel.

He laughed and took two glasses of vodka off the tray of a nearby servant. He sat down and handed her one. "Then we must drink together." He raised his glass.

"Only tea for me," she said, wishing he would shower his attentions elsewhere.

"Because of the child in your belly?" Kezia looked at him in surprise and he shrugged. "Haven't you heard I can read minds?"

"And see the future," she added, wanting to see his reaction. He smiled without humor. "Yes, I'm a very lucky man."

As he downed his drink, she continued her appraisal. Was he truly a seer or just a drunk, sex-crazed farmer? She wasn't sure what to make of him. He seemed quite mad.

When his hand moved to her leg and slid up her skirt, Kezia was too shocked to react at first.

"I think we have many things to talk about, you and I," he whispered.

She grabbed his hand to stop him and their fingers locked. A shudder passed through her before she could wrench her hand from his, and she stood up, almost overturning the chair.

He chuckled. "Most women do not run away from me," he said, touching her arm.

Kezia pulled away, about to be sick. "Excuse me, I must go."

All eyes were on them, with a dozen women ready to take her place. As Kezia rushed toward the door, Rasputin called after her, "Many good blessings on the health of your daughter!"

He raised the vodka glass.

Kezia did not question how he knew the baby was a girl. She turned and nodded to him in acknowledgment, but she could not offer him a similar blessing. For when their hands had touched, she caught a glimpse of Rasputin's future. He would be murdered in ten years' time, his body brutally defiled by the family he was drinking with today.

Kezia could tell by the way his eyes surveyed the room that Rasputin knew it too.

⁓

When Kezia's daughter, Galina, came into the world, the years of her life were measured not by the inches her body grew but by the violent changes happening around her.

When Galina was eight, Russia possessed the largest army in the world and went to war with Germany. When she was ten, Rasputin—who had made his way into the private circle of the tsar—was murdered, just as Kezia had portended.

Rasputin too had foreseen his future. He had told the tsar that if he died, and if Russia went to war with Germany, there would be "grief and no light . . . the war would bring an ocean of tears and there would be no counting them."

By the time Galina reached eleven, the First War ended, leading to the country's great revolution. Imperial Russia collapsed and gave rise to Communism and the Soviet Union. The new leadership wiped out the old regime. They had the tsar and tsarina, their five children, and their physician all killed in the same room.

Sergei quit the theater, fearful that any involvement in political art would bring their family unwelcome notice. Anything that was not propaganda went underground. Plays that contained social commentary were no longer performed in the glittering halls of established theaters but by candlelight in the basements of private homes. At Kezia's urging Sergei joined the Communist Party. She had seen what would happen to those who didn't.

Fashion became an important symbol in the Communist era, and Galina embraced this new idea of materialism for the working class. She wanted to design clothes. She found work apprenticing with a popular designer who was fixated on creating the attire of the future. The government wanted to promote new fashions distinct from Western styles to show a better life was possible under Communism.

Kezia didn't know what to think of the strange, minimalist garments her daughter now wore. She was relieved when Galina married and she convinced the young couple to live in the family apartment so they could all stay together. To Kezia, nothing was as important.

⌣

There was an old folk saying in Russia: if you speak against the wolf, then speak against him well. Two years into the birth of the Soviet Union, a new leader emerged. He was a wolf named Stalin and no one could speak against him. His rise to power was accompanied by a storm that upended every sense of normal life.

First he stole the farms and shipped 15 million peasants to prisons across the Taiga. Their rights would not be recognized. The only record of their suffering was written in the sky by the steam from the trains as they were taken away. A famine unlike any seen before decimated the country. Compassion became unthinkable.

Galina's daughter, Nadenka, came into the world three years after Stalin rose to power. Kezia lovingly called her granddaughter Nettie, and soon everyone else did too.

Nettie was a solemn, thoughtful girl who grew up listening to her grandmother tell the fortunes of those who quietly came to seek her counsel. With Communism, any occult or esoteric practice had become a part of the underground culture, hidden yet still alive.

Nettie would often frown when she listened to a card reading, as if Kezia had said the wrong thing. Kezia would catch the criticism in her granddaughter's eyes and tease, "So the egg thinks it's smarter than the chicken?"

Then they would share a secret smile. Kezia knew Nettie had the sight, perhaps even more than she did.

Kezia still studied her grandmother's diary, and Marina had taken care to note Simza's knowledge of the body. According to Simza, the body was a portent of the future, and Kezia became concerned about Nettie's moles. The marks either signified great prosperity or adversity, and Kezia felt certain the two large moles on the back of Nettie's neck implied the latter. Kezia would often examine the moles and shake her head. "These signal not one, but two misfortunes. And these . . ." She would turn her focus to the moles beneath Nettie's shoulder blades. "You will have a hard life, my child, and face many disappointments."

"I know, Grandmother" was all Nettie would say.

They had this conversation many times. Kezia felt Nettie needed to know what life had in store if she was to survive it. She was only fourteen.

Nettie didn't tell her grandmother that she had already seen what would come to pass. The government had begun rounding up citizens and shipping them to gulags, labor camps, where every door to life was closed. Stalin's henchmen targeted the educated: professors who taught the wrong subject, writers who wrote the wrong words, and politicians who did not clap long enough for speeches. Quotas for filling the camps were established and had to be met. As a playwright and a fashion designer, Sergei and Galina were surely sympathizers with the West. The government put them on the list. The entire family was marked. Her mother would be sent to one of the worst gulags in the Taiga Forest, far to the north in Siberia. She would labor for three years before dying of starvation. Nettie's father would survive two years longer and be shot in a field with other prisoners. Her grandfather would die much sooner, unable to survive the initial interrogation. And her grandmother . . . Kezia would die first. She would pass away the day after saving a young girl from being beaten and taking the punishment herself.

Nettie would have given anything to erase the knowledge burned into her mind. She had had premonitions all her life, and they had always come true. But her worst visions still had not come to pass, and she prayed every day they never would.

⁓

As the months passed, Kezia felt a growing urgency and encouraged Nettie to use her cards.

"Always remember, they are only symbols on cards allowing you to see into your own mind. Divination is a mirror, reflecting what is here and here," Kezia would tell her, pointing to Nettie's heart and head. Nettie nodded like a solemn student.

"Whatever the cards show you, always trust the words that well inside you. The truth is waiting to be heard. Never doubt it."

Nettie held the cards in her hands. They felt smooth and pulsed with energy.

"People want to hear about their lives. They are afraid. They want to know what is in store for them. Speak the truth as the words come. Now draw," Kezia commanded.

Nettie drew the top card. *The Hanged Man.*

"What do you see? Quickly, without thinking," Kezia demanded.

"All of life's trappings stripped away," Nettie answered.

"And what does it mean?" Kezia asked with impatience.

"A second war."

"And?" Kezia sounded harsh. "What is in your mind? Say it!"

"They are going to take us away. I hope you die in your sleep before they come here." Nettie gasped, appalled that she had said such a thing.

"But I won't," her grandmother said softly.

They stared at each other in a moment of deep understanding. The raids were going to happen. Soon the country would go to war—the Second World War. St. Petersburg, their beloved city, now called Leningrad, would come under a siege that would claim the lives of over a million people. But they wouldn't be there.

Nettie wondered how much her grandmother knew. Perhaps she knew just as much.

⁓

The night before they came, Nettie helped her mother bathe and brush her hair dry. Galina sang along to a favorite song on the radio. Nettie could sense the change in the air: it was as though they were stealing this moment of joy. Soon they would no longer have these simple comforts. A black maw was descending on them.

The next morning the family sat down at the table and had breakfast. Galina puttered around the kitchen, humming the same tune. When Nettie's father left for work, she ran to the door and hugged him longer than usual.

"What's this, *Solnyshko*?" He laughed. "I'm not going on a trip. I'll see you at supper."

"Yes, Papa." Still, she squeezed him harder and tried not to cry. *Solnyshko,* Little Sun, was his nickname for her. She would never hear it again.

After he had gone, she returned to the table and sat down to wait. Sergei read the paper over coffee. Kezia sat quietly, holding her cards on the table.

Nettie watched her grandmother's fingers twitch; it was the only sign that Kezia was bothered. A sliver of sunlight pushed through the blinds and illuminated them in a golden light.

To know when a moment will become the last is a painful burden. Nettie bathed in those final seconds, feeling her family's love and wishing she could stop time forever. Then she blinked and life continued its tick forward. The moment had ceased.

A sharp knock came at the door.

Suddenly half a dozen state security men were swarming the room. They spoke in a chaotic rush of words, each one a cataclysm.

"Come with us!" "You are arrested!" "You don't need anything!"

Galina screamed as a man dragged Sergei out of the room like a sack. They took her next, kicking hysterically. She reached out for Nettie. "My daughter!"

"Mama!" Nettie cried. But Kezia held on to her, placing her cards in Nettie's hand.

"What about the girl?" one of the men asked, motioning to Nettie.

"Too old for the orphanage. Bring her."

"That would be a mistake," Kezia said in a strong voice. She maneuvered Nettie in front of her and anchored her there. "My granddaughter is a psychic, even more powerful than Messing! She can tell anyone their future—even Stalin!"

The name Messing had the desired effect. Wolf Messing was considered the most powerful psychic in the world. He had escaped Germany, where Hitler had put a price on his head for predicting the outcome of the war. Messing had sought refuge in the Soviet Union, even though Stalin publicly condemned psychics to bolster the country's new atheism. But in reality the government continued to study psychic events. They simply moved their paranormal research underground, where it was conducted in secret and controlled by the KGB. Wolf Messing was the only psychic Stalin acknowledged openly, while he searched the four corners of the country to find others just as powerful.

Kezia had just made Nettie valuable in their captors' eyes.

"Wait here," the man ordered. He left to talk to the commanding officer.

Kezia brought Nettie's hands to her lips and kissed them. The time they had both foreseen had come.

"I don't want to leave you," Nettie cried.

"But you must." Kezia held firm and gathered enough strength for both of them. "Don't cry. Don't call out. Do as they say." She squeezed Nettie tightly. "We are in the devil's den now. But you shall live through it. You will."

Nettie held on to her until the officer returned.

"Come with me." He forced them apart, yanking Nettie down the stairs. Another guard led Kezia behind them.

Outside, Nettie saw her family standing in line behind an army truck. She could hear her mother's cries. Nettie climbed into the back of a different truck, and the guard ordered her to wait. She watched an officer place her grandmother and grandfather in one line and her mother in another.

Nettie's truck shifted into gear and lurched forward, driving away. She furiously blinked back tears to keep her vision clear. She had to see them.

Her family kept their eyes on her, never wavering, as if they could stay connected forever. Nettie watched the distance extend between them, like a ribbon about to be cut.

The Devil

The manuscript ended there.

Semele wiped the tears from her eyes, unable to believe that was it. There had to be more pages missing. There had to be.

Someone had defiled the manuscript. Someone had cut out the ending.

She felt bereft. The culprit could have been anyone over thousands of years of history: a copyist with an opinion, a religious clergyman intent on editing works, a government official from a new empire whose job it was to censure—the possibilities were endless. She shook her head in frustration. It could even have been whoever broke into her hotel room.

Now she understood why someone would break into Kairos to steal this manuscript. Ionna had predicted the rise of Stalin and both world wars with the detail of a historian looking forward instead of back. This memoir was truly a journey through time, spanning two thousand years.

A deep shiver ran down her spine as she thought back to Kezia and Nettie's story. The whole family must have died. Where had the guard taken Nettie? Now she would never know. Finishing Ionna's manuscript had only burdened her with more questions. There was no resolution.

Semele rubbed both of her temples, feeling a splitting headache coming on. She thought about the package her parents had received when they adopted her. She needed to find it tomorrow.

Her eyes grew heavy, and she was unable to escape sleep any longer. She reached over to turn out the light and looked at the dream stone on the nightstand, struck by the timing of Macy's gift. It sat there like a message, a reminder. Dreaming was the one thing she had always tried to avoid—because her dreams always brought answers, answers she didn't necessarily want. But she needed them desperately now.

As her consciousness began to slip through the sieve into the realm of dreams, for the first time she yearned for her grandmother.

Ace of Cups

The countryside whizzed by like a windmill spinning too fast.

Semele sat in the back of the car, just a young girl. She rolled down the window and leaned her head out, letting the air whip her face.

"Darling, we're going in circles," Helen said to her husband as she turned the map in her hands upside down.

"What's this?" Joseph stepped on the brake and the car slowed with the rest of the traffic. "Some kind of accident?" He tried to see ahead.

They inched forward and soon had a clear view from the left windows. Up ahead a man lay in a pool of blood with a mangled bicycle beside him. His broken body was bent at the wrong angles, and his open gaze held the empty stillness of death. Semele had never seen anything so graphic. Their car passed inches from the wreck; the door was the only barrier between her and the man's body.

Then the dream took over. Semele was no longer on the ground. She was staring down at the accident from a bird's-eye view. The moment merged into another time and place: now she was in a helicopter.

She was older and Theo sat beside her. She looked out the window at a sprawling city, knowing a monster waited somewhere on the ground. She turned back to Theo, then leaned across the seat and kissed him, as if this moment together might be their last.

Theo whispered something in her ear and kissed her back. The roar of the helicopter filled her ears, and the world tipped beneath the blades. They wrapped their arms around each other, reveling in their need and the hunger of being alive.

Then the helicopter descended into the future and the dream caved in.

King of Wands

When Semele awoke the next morning, fragments of the dream stayed with her. She remembered the car ride and the bike accident—those were real memories her subconscious had served up. When she was nine her family had gone on vacation to Austria and she had seen an accident on the side of the road. She hadn't thought about that trip in years.

Then there was the helicopter ride with Theo—and that kiss. What had that been about? Her thoughts returned to the moment she'd shared with Theo in the gallery. She had replayed their stolen kiss a thousand times.

A heady sense of anticipation filled her. Theo would be here soon. They had a lot to discuss. But first, she had something very important to find.

⁓

She looked all day, in every drawer and cabinet, in every inch of closet space. She was growing more frustrated by the minute. It was Wednesday and she had to return to New York tomorrow. Mikhail expected to meet with her Friday morning to discuss Beijing, but she couldn't leave New Haven without finding what her grandmother had left her.

For the first time since her father's death she entered her parents' bedroom. Her mother had already given up on the search and had gone downstairs to make dinner. Semele could hear her singing something terribly off-key, possibly with a glass of wine in hand.

Semele grimaced. "God, please help me."

She lay back on her parents' bed and closed her eyes. For a moment, she felt herself drifting off. Then she looked over at her father's nightstand. All his things were still there: *Fahrenheit 451,* his favorite book, the earplugs he wore at night because "his beloved wife snored," and the Geiger wristwatch he took off right before bed.

He had bought the watch on that same trip to Austria so many years ago and had refused to get a new one. Helen could only talk him into replacing the leather band.

Semele picked up the watch and laid it across her chest. Closing her eyes, she felt her body become heavy and, for a moment, it felt as though her wrist had become his. Her mind emptied, floating untethered. Suspended in this limbo, her mind brought forth the answer she was seeking. With a gasp she opened her eyes and sat up. She knew where her father had put the package.

The Tower

The bank opened at eight the next morning. Semele and Helen arrived at 7:55 with the key to her father's safe-deposit box. Semele had to bribe her mother with a venti-macchiato-something to get her out of the house: Helen was not a morning person. She wore oversized sunglasses and sipped her coffee stoically.

"Why haven't you looked in it yet?" Semele asked again. It had been six months since her father died, and her mother had yet to open the safe-deposit box.

"Because everything I need is in the house. I have no idea why we even have one."

Semele had thought it odd too when she came across the key.

Inside they both presented their IDs, her father's death certificate, and the will. The manager escorted them into the back. He took out the box and led them into a small private room and told them to take their time.

Semele looked at her mother. "Do you want to do it?"

"No, you go ahead."

Before she lost her courage, Semele gave the lock a decisive turn and opened the lid.

Inside was a legal-size envelope thick with papers. On the front her father had written:

For Semele Cavnow

A square box wrapped in old postal paper rested on top of the envelope. The paper had been opened and taped back up.

Semele motioned to the box. "That's it, isn't it?"

Helen nodded.

Semele already knew what was inside, but she still couldn't allow herself to believe.

Her heart pounded in her ears like the ocean in a shell. She unwrapped the paper with shaky hands to find Rinalto's wooden box, the one so perfectly described in the manuscript.

When Semele opened the lid she felt like a part of her was no longer in the room. Her world and Ionna's had finally collided.

"My word," Helen said. "What are those?"

Semele placed the cards on the table.

Time had preserved their brilliance. The twenty-two cards—Ionna's originals—looked more weathered than Rinalto's matching fifty-six. But together they created the oldest tarot deck in existence.

There was a photo tucked inside the box. It was a small black-and-white of two women: a mother who looked about forty-five and a young girl, no more than fourteen or fifteen. Semele knew exactly who they were.

There was no mistaking the dark-haired girl, posed with a hand on her hip and a dare in her eyes—Semele's real mother when she was young. Her grandmother looked just as Semele had imagined, except for the sorrow in her eyes.

Nettie was staring straight into the camera lens, as if she knew the picture was meant for Semele. Semele turned the photo over.

Semele,
I cannot cut the card in half
*   and come back for you.*
Forgive me.
We are always yours,
Nettie

Semele took a seat at the table, unable to speak.

Nettie had foreseen Semele's question from the card exhibit in Amsterdam, the one she had carried inside her heart every day afterward.

Her grandmother had written the answer before Semele had even asked the question.

Semele could feel her reality shifting. Her grandmother was *the* Nettie in the story. These cards had been kept for *her*, entrusted to her father, who had known their worth and hidden them in the safest place he knew. As curator of the Beinecke, he had recognized their incredible significance.

Her mother hovered beside her, looking concerned.

"Do you want to open the other package?" she asked gently.

"No," Semele whispered. "You do it."

While her mother opened the envelope, Semele studied Nettie's handwriting, analyzing every line and curve. Nettie had been left-handed. Her hands had been shaking with nerves—or illness—when she wrote the message. The script slanted downward with sadness, yet the lines showed strong conviction.

"Oh, I'd wondered what happened to this," Helen said as she pulled the pages from the envelope. "Why is this here?"

When Semele saw what her mother was holding her whole body went rigid. She had been prepared for the cards, but not this.

Reaching out, she took the pages. It was a photocopy of Ionna's writing alongside her father's handwritten translation.

"How did Dad get this?" Semele asked, her voice now barely a whisper.

"Some collector in Europe asked for his help earlier this year. I don't remember his name. Your father was shut up in his office for weeks translating it."

Marcel Bossard.

Her mother had no idea what these pages were. Semele flipped to the back and found the place where she had stopped reading the night before. *Here were the lost pages.* Marcel had given her father a complete copy of Ionna's manuscript, and her father had translated every last word.

King of Pentacles

Semele looked out the train window on her way to New York. The scenery passed by in a muted blur, like an impressionistic painting she was no longer a part of. She now had Ionna's cards along with her father's copy of the manuscript.

This must have been why Marcel and her father were going to meet.

Semele shook her head, her mind spinning at the implications. She tried to center her thoughts. First she needed to authenticate and date the cards. She had to be sure they were real, and there was only one person in the world she could trust with that project.

She had called Cabe right before getting on the train. He agreed to meet at their favorite coffeehouse. He would run the tests today and then get the cards back to her after her morning meeting with Mikhail. Her only problem was how to broach the subject of Raina with Cabe. He needed to know she couldn't be trusted.

Semele's hands instinctively tightened around her purse. Rinalto's rosewood box was nestled inside, bundled in some of Helen's old scarves for protection. She was afraid to even look at the cards. Her father's translation was tucked next to them.

Why was her father's version complete, while hers had missing pages? She could have taken out the remaining pages and read them on the train, but she was worried about what she would find at the conclusion of Nettie's story. Someone else didn't want her to see that part either, or they wouldn't have hidden the pages from her.

Theo—he was at the heart of all this. He had to have known about their fathers' connection, that Marcel had given Joseph the manuscript. She had so many questions for him. Tomorrow couldn't come fast enough.

As soon as she got back to Manhattan she backed up her hard drive on an external. Then, borrowing a page from her father, she opened a safe-deposit box and locked away the hard drive. If her computer was stolen, she would still have a copy of the manuscript. That alleviated some of her fear. She kept her father's translated copy with her. No one knew about that—she hoped.

She hurried to the café to meet Cabe but slowed down in horror as soon as she walked through the door.

Cabe was sitting in the back booth with Bren.

Bren. She had never called him back. She gave them a meek wave and a smile. Bren glared back; he was furious.

Cabe hurried over and gave her a hug, whispering into her ear, "Sorry."

"You could have warned me," she muttered under her breath.

Cabe pulled up a chair, leaving her and Bren to face off on opposite sides of the booth. Cabe tried to lighten the mood by poking fun at her outfit. "Looking good, Catgirl."

She shot him a withering glance. She had raided her old closet at her parents' house and the pickings had been slim. The black turtleneck sweaterdress looked sixties mod with her winter boots. The last time she had worn this dress was in college.

"Listen, guys, I can't stay long." Cabe made a show of checking his watch. "But you two feel free to hang."

Bren ignored Cabe's attempt at normalcy and kept his attention on Semele. "Are you in some kind of trouble?" He leaned forward. "I've been calling you all week." He stressed every word, clearly livid.

She studied her hands. "I'm fine. I'm in the middle of a work crisis—"

"And you can't return one phone call?"

She couldn't meet his eyes. It felt like they were strangers now. "I've had my phone off so I could deal with this translation thing I'm doing." She glanced up. "I'm really sorry," she added, knowing it wouldn't help.

Bren glared at her until Cabe finally spoke. "Well, you should have called or texted . . . even e-mailed."

Semele shot Cabe an annoyed look.

"And what's this about you being followed?" Bren demanded.

Semele gave Cabe another look. She couldn't believe he'd told him.

"Everything's fine."

"No, you need to go to the police," Bren insisted.

"And say what?"

"That you're being followed!" Bren raised his voice.

"And you think it's connected to the theft at Kairos," Cabe added.

"I'll be fine," she said again, wanting to believe it, even though she was debating whether it was safe to go back to her apartment.

Bren drummed his fingers on the table. She had never seen him so upset. The silence was downright painful.

Cabe decided to step in. "Why don't you give me whatever you called me here for?" He checked his watch. "I need to get back to the office."

Semele welcomed the veer in conversation. She pulled the wooden box from her purse, suddenly nervous to part with it. "My grandmother left this for me—my real grandmother. You could say it's a family heirloom." She didn't tell him the cards inside were connected to the Bossard manuscript. That would take hours to explain. "Can you run the specs today?"

"Of course. Because I'm awesome." Cabe put the box in his backpack without opening it and stood up to escape. He gave them both a salute. "Later."

Semele jumped up too. "I'll be right back," she told Bren and followed Cabe outside. When they reached the sidewalk she said, "You really snowballed me in there."

"Come on, Sem. The guy is tortured. You have to talk to him."

"I will. I am."

Cabe gave her a stern look.

"I will," she said, and she meant it. She knew they couldn't go on like this. She had to face what she was doing to Bren—to both of them. "Can I stay at your place for a couple of nights?"

He handed her his keys with a pointed look. "Tonight I want to know what's going on. Including the story behind these." He patted his backpack and got ready to hop on his bike.

"Deal." Semele pocketed his keys and hesitated. "Listen, I need you to keep everything between us—including dating these cards—confidential. Especially from Raina."

He looked annoyed. "Why?"

"I know this sounds crazy . . . but I saw her with that guy."

"What guy?"

"From the library. The guy following me. They were in his car together right outside my apartment."

Cabe looked at her like she'd sprouted a second head.

"Cabe, I'm not making this up. She was outside my apartment . . . with him."

"Why?" he demanded, as if it were her fault. "That's crazy!"

"I don't know! But they were there!" Now she was yelling too. "All I'm asking is for you to not talk to her about any of this until I know more. What if she's involved in the theft?"

"Or what if that guy is security for Kairos?" he shot back. "Ever thought of that?"

Semele hesitated. She hadn't, but she quickly dismissed the possibility. That made absolutely no sense. Kairos wouldn't have had someone following her from Switzerland. No, somehow Raina was involved, but Cabe obviously wasn't ready to hear it, so she relented.

"Fine. Maybe he is. We just don't know. But for now, please

keep everything between you and me confidential. I really need you to have my back on this."

They stared at each other, ten years of friendship and trust hanging in the balance.

Cabe expelled a long breath. "Okay, for now. But"—he pointed his finger at her—"you're telling me everything tonight. Everything."

Her eyes teared up and she nodded. "I will. I promise." She gave him a tight hug. "Thank you."

Cabe hugged her back and got on his bike. "Just go talk to Bren. You two can fix whatever is broken."

All she could do was nod, her tears falling freely. It felt like everything in her life was breaking and she didn't know if any of it could be fixed.

As she watched Cabe bike away, she began to wonder if she'd made a mistake by letting him take the cards. She almost called him back, but he was too far away. Then he turned the corner and was gone.

She stared at the spot where he had been seconds before; it was now just an empty stretch of sidewalk on a gray day in New York.

A feeling of déjà vu descended on her.

Somehow the image already existed in her mind, like a postcard she would never forget. The wind whipped around her, making her turn toward the shelter of the café. She wiped her eyes and forced herself to go back and face Bren.

⌒

Semele approached the table and slid into the booth. "Sorry about that," she said. He didn't answer. She looked down, avoiding his eyes.

"Why are you doing this?" Bren finally asked, his voice breaking. "I thought we were happy."

"We were happy." She was quick to agree, bracing herself for the impending avalanche.

"Was it meeting my parents? Moving in together? What?"

Semele shook her head.

"Because as far as I'm concerned that is just the beginning. I'm crazy about you. Want to know how crazy?" He reached into his pocket and put a box on the table.

Semele stared at the ring she had already foreseen. There it was.

That little black box said everything. *I love you. Whatever you're going through, I love you. We can get through this together.* Four velvet walls full of forgiveness. All she had to do was take it.

"I bought it while you were in Switzerland," he admitted. "I thought maybe this Christmas I'd put it in your stocking." He stopped talking, becoming emotional again. "I can't believe this is happening. Please, Sem. Don't do this."

Her silence seemed to be causing him physical pain. He grew pale and let out a deep breath. Seeing him suffering like this was unbearable. She didn't care about protecting her secret anymore. She only knew she had to explain herself, to relieve him from this pain she was inflicting.

"I'm going to tell you the truth, even though you won't believe it," she said before she lost her nerve. "Sometimes I have visions of the future. I've had them all my life. I trained myself not to over time, but they've started coming back." She risked a glance at him.

He was looking at her dumbfounded.

"I had one of you. A strong one." Her voice wavered. "You were married and very much in love with someone. And it wasn't me."

Bren stared at her, hurt etched into his face.

"Say something. Please," she begged. But he wouldn't. She grew desperate and blurted, "You're going to have two kids together!"

"God, you're cruel."

He thought she was joking. Semele put her head in her hands and let out a sound between a laugh and a cry. And for a split

second she thought maybe he was right. Maybe the premonition was an excuse not to deal with her feelings. She had so
many things going on in her life. . . . But then she saw what she
saw, and if she were honest with herself, she had sensed the truth
of their relationship from the start. Her father's death earlier in
the year was just the catalyst that made her to start to pull away.

"Are you on something?"

Semele shook her head, her heart aching at the anger emanating from him.

"You're breaking up with me over a premonition?" He spit it
out like a dirty word. "That's insane!" He folded his arms and
leaned back against the booth. "And you believe it?" His voice
rose in outrage. "I don't know what to say. What do you want
me to say, Semele?"

"Nothing," she said, unable to defend herself.

"Unbelievable," he muttered. "You're unbelievable. I never
thought you would do something like this." He stared at her,
his eyes cold and hard. "I thought I knew you. But I guess I
don't." He stood and swiped the ring off of the table. Then he
stormed out.

Semele could feel fresh tears stinging her eyes. In one conversation she had lost a lover and a friend, forever. Her whole
life she had denied her intuition because facing it came at such
a high price. Now all the memories rushed back. She remembered the feeling of knowing what she shouldn't, and why she'd
tried so hard to rid herself of her ability—because in the end no
one understood. She was alone.

Message to VS—

Back in NY. Friend meeting her.

Reply from VS—

Does she have them?

Message to VS—

I'll know soon.

The Star

Semele made her way to Cabe's apartment, where she planned to camp out for the rest of the day. Her thoughts felt more weighted with every step. In her purse she had Macy's dream stone, a picture of Nettie and her birth mother, and her father's translation. That's all she had.

She walked past The Third Eye, a bookstore in Brooklyn that also offered psychic readings. She had passed by it countless times but had never been inside. Without giving herself time to change her mind she went in.

Near the door, there was a bulletin board with the name and a short bio of each psychic that was available to give readings that day. Below their bios, the psychics had listed their expertise—if they specialized in palmistry, tarot, astrology charts, channeling, or past-life regression, or if they were clairaudient or clairvoyant.

Semele read the roster with raised eyebrows, about to lose her nerve. She chose a psychic named Doreen, who specialized primarily in tarot readings, and paid thirty dollars at the register for a thirty-minute consultation.

In the glass case by the register were over fifty different kinds of tarot decks with varying artwork. Semele leaned down to read some of the titles: the Crystal Tarot, the Mythic Tarot, the Fairytale Deck. There was also a Renaissance deck depicting Greek and Roman deities, and one designed to look like stained-glass windows. There were even steampunk and *The Lord of the Rings*

decks—too many to choose from. She saw that they had a replica of the Visconti Deck, right next to the Tarot de Marseilles.

The shop clerk noticed her interest. "Rider-Waite is the perfect deck to start with. It's the ABCs of tarot. A classic."

Semele gave her a faint smile.

A plump woman in her sixties sat at a table for two in a room
smaller than a walk-in closet. Doreen had on a bright floral
blouse and was sipping a tumbler of iced tea with a big straw. All
she was missing was a sun visor and the cruise ship to go with it.
She stood up with a warm smile when Semele entered and motioned to the other chair in the tiny space. "Welcome. Please have
a seat."

Semele sat down and watched Doreen dim the lights and light
a candle. Soft celestial-sounding music played in the background.
She looked at Doreen's tarot cards with open curiosity and saw
they were the same cards the shop clerk had recommended.
"What kind of deck is that?"

Doreen seemed surprised by the question. "I use the Rider-
Waite Deck."

"What century is it from?"

Doreen's eyebrows shot up. "These originated in the early
1900s."

"In Italy?"

"In England." Doreen smiled, thinking Semele must be nervous. "May we hold hands?"

The question surprised her, but Semele nodded and Doreen
folded her hands into her soft palms. The woman closed her eyes
and took a deep breath. Then she exhaled and took another.

Semele watched her, not sure what was happening. This was
not how she thought the reading would go. Wasn't Doreen supposed to deal out the tarot cards? Semele tried hard to sit still,
not wanting to distract her.

The celestial music created a hypnotic calm, and Semele's eyes settled on the burning candle. The room began to take on a dreamlike quality as she watched the wax melt.

"You've lost someone close to you," Doreen said, her voice sad and distant.

Semele's chest seized with emotion.

"He died too soon. He's worried for you. His presence is strong. He wants to tell you he's sorry. . . . So sorry."

Semele's grief returned with a power that was physically painful. She could feel her father. She could feel him behind the words. She waited breathlessly to hear more.

Instead Doreen opened her eyes and said gently, "I'm sorry, that's all I see." She let go of Semele's hands, then picked up the tarot cards and began to shuffle. "Why don't we begin?"

Semele wasn't ready to move on to the cards. In a sharp instant she had felt her father. She wanted to call the moment back, to live there and speak with him.

Doreen held the cards out to her. "Please shuffle the deck," she instructed. "Think about what you want to know."

Semele had difficulty focusing on the task. She ended up shuffling the cards, her mind blank, and handed them back.

Doreen laid a series of cards out facedown in a crosslike pattern. She turned over the first card. *The Hanged Man.*

"You are in a place of great confusion . . . questioning everything about your life. You're starting to see the world differently."

Semele was still in a daze but thought that seemed pretty on the mark.

The next card was *The Chariot.* "I see a time of fast movement, travel. You will leave your work, your job. This will happen suddenly."

Semele's eyes met Doreen's. "What do you mean 'leave'?" Was she getting fired?

Doreen didn't answer. She was too caught up in the reading. She turned over the next card.

The Devil. This one was upside down.

"Every aspect of your life is challenging you. You must break free from your attachments to discover your true self."

What attachments? She had just dumped her almost-fiancé at a cáfe. Semele wished Doreen would slow down. The woman was turning over cards with remarkable speed, and Semele was still reeling from being told her father was trying to reach her from the grave.

The Hermit. "You must walk your path alone, but you are afraid of the knowledge that exists inside you. You must leave the world you know to find the one that waits for you."

Leave the world? Semele frowned. That didn't sound good.

Doreen studied the next card with thoughtful eyes. *The Hierophant.* "You have a teacher in your life. A woman. She has been guiding you. She has much to tell you, but you are not yet ready to listen."

Semele raised her eyebrows. Did she mean Ionna?

"You are tied to one man. The tie is strong. Trust your heart. Together you will grow stronger." Doreen pointed to *The Lovers* card.

Semele stared at it, thinking Doreen had made an error. She wasn't tied to anyone, not anymore. An image of someone did appear in her mind, but Theo was a client and an enigma—

The Tower. "You will lose something precious." Doreen stared at the cards for a long moment. She looked confounded.

"What?" Semele leaned forward.

"I'm sorry. It's just you've only drawn Major Arcana cards and nothing else." She studied the spread, bewildered. "The odds of that are highly unlikely."

Semele wasn't entirely sure what that meant, but she was becoming more unnerved as the minutes passed. She was beginning to question her sanity for even coming here.

Doreen turned over another card, *Strength.* This one faced upside down too.

"Aren't upside-down cards bad?" Semele had to ask.

"Not in the way that you think," Doreen said, trying to continue. "You are full of self-doubt and afraid to embrace your true self. You must have faith. Gather your strength."

Okay, this woman is going off the grid. This was starting to sound fifty shades of weird. Semele checked her watch, ready for this whole experience to be over with.

Wheel of Fortune. Upside down again. What was it with the upside-down cards?

"There are negative forces surrounding you. . . ." Doreen trailed off.

Semele watched Doreen turn over the next card.

Death.

Now she began to stress. Could a reading get any worse?

"You are undergoing a transformation," Doreen said, sounding vague. She pulled another card. *Judgement.* Doreen stayed silent.

"What is it?" Semele was almost afraid to ask.

"Despair," Doreen whispered, looking shaken. "I'm sorry. I try not to focus on the negative when I give a reading, but you . . ."

"Are filled up to the wazoo with it?" Semele tried to joke, but she was starting to panic.

Something was incredibly wrong. It was the same feeling that had gripped her outside the café.

"Pick a card," Doreen commanded with a sense of urgency, as if trying to gain control of the reading again.

Semele drew one from the deck. *The High Priestess*—another Major Arcana card.

Doreen stared at it, speechless. She looked at the spread of cards, then at Semele, and then back to the spread.

"What does this one mean?" Semele prompted her.

Doreen held the card up. A bead of sweat had formed on her lip. "What do you see?"

Semele studied the card, not sure what she was supposed to see. It depicted a queenlike woman sitting on a throne between two pillars. She was holding a scroll in her hands.

"*This* is your card. *The High Priestess.*" Doreen placed it on top. "She symbolizes our intuition. She guards the Tree of Life at the gate of the conscious mind, wearing the blue robe of knowledge and the crown of Isis." Her finger tapped the image. "Whatever challenges are ahead, never forget you have an inner strength and your own compass. You drew these cards for a reason. I've never seen a spread like it."

The candle on the table flickered, and Doreen swept all the cards back into one pile. The session was over.

Semele stood up, more than ready to leave. She was unnerved, but she also couldn't shake the feeling that something significant had happened here.

Doreen took Semele's hands and clasped them firmly in her own. "I'm here almost every day. You can call too." Her smile was warm and genuine, her eyes bright with awareness.

Semele felt the urge to confide in her. No one knew what she was going through. She felt trapped in an alternate reality. An ancient seer was talking to her through a manuscript, and now Semele had her tarot cards.

What did Ionna want? For her to learn how to use them? Just the thought of it made her shake her head.

Queen of Wands

"It's bad luck to buy your own tarot deck," Semele read in *Tarot for Dummies.*

She looked at the bag on Cabe's coffee table. She had purchased not one, but two decks at the bookstore, the Rider-Waite Deck and the replica of the Visconti Deck, and brought them back to his apartment. *More bad luck. Lovely.*

But as she continued reading the how-to book, the author clarified her position. It was the tarot's wisdom that couldn't be bought, not the cards themselves. So people could, in the author's opinion, disregard this belief. Semele grimaced. *At least that was something.*

She moved on to the next chapter. Within an hour she had covered many of the highlights, including the history of the cards and their meanings, some of which she already knew from Sebastian.

A typical tarot deck was comprised of seventy-eight cards. Twenty-two of those cards were called the Major Arcana, a group of symbolic cards starting with *The Fool* and ending with *The World*. "Arcana" meant "mystery of the mysteries, the ultimate secret." The Major Arcana was the backbone of the tarot.

Semele got out her new deck and studied each card. There were also sixteen court cards, consisting of four groups made up of a king, a queen, a knight, and a page, each in a suit of cups, pentacles, swords, or wands.

In a sense, the suits were similar to astrological signs: cups signified water or the emotions, pentacles were the earth and the material world, swords represented air and the mind, and wands symbolized fire and spiritual energy. The numbered cards were organized into four sets of ten cards that ranged from ace to ten. These were also grouped by suit. Every card had a meaning, and together the deck formed a system that allowed the tarot reader to see life's progression, reflected through symbols and archetypes. A trained reader could use his or her psyche to interpret the answer to any question being asked.

There was a chapter that discussed the "freak-out cards." That made her laugh. Yes, she had definitely been alarmed by some of the cards that came up in her reading. But the book explained how *Death, The Devil,* and *The Tower* cards, for instance, were nothing to fear. They meant different things at different moments: it all depended on where you were.

Another chapter explained how to find your soul card by adding up the day, month, and year in your birth date and then adding those digits to arrive at a single number. Semele quickly grabbed a pen and did the math. Her number was two.

She flipped to the chapter entitled "Pick a Card, Any Card" and was stunned to find that card number two was *The High Priestess,* the same card she had drawn at the bookstore.

Semele couldn't help shivering. She closed the book and put it back in the bag. That was enough card reading for her. She wasn't ready to attempt a tarot spread, no matter how simple *Tarot for Dummies* made it sound. Maybe she never would be.

After Cabe dated Ionna's cards, she would store them in the safe-deposit box, along with the USB and her father's translation of the manuscript. This weekend she would read the rest of Nettie's story and then go to Beijing and get on with her life. She couldn't do any more than that.

As if to prove her wrong, her cell phone rang. She answered, trying to keep her voice steady. "Hello?"

"Semele? It's Theo."

"I know," she said before she could help herself. Even the sound of his voice affected her.

"I want to schedule our meeting tomorrow. I'm about to get on the plane."

There was so much she needed to ask him, but she wanted to see his face when she did. "I'll be at the office until noon. I could meet you then?"

"Let me take you to lunch." He suggested The Garden at the Four Seasons, where he was staying.

Semele agreed to meet him there at 12:30 P.M. and hung up.

Anticipation built inside her, and her imagination began to conjure fantasies about tomorrow, of another kiss on another table. To take her mind off Theo, she jumped on the Kairos server and caught up on the latest industry news. It was the quickest way for her to refocus.

She smiled when she saw that Christie's had sold one of George Washington's personal ledgers for two hundred thousand dollars. She bet the letters Cabe was restoring would do nicely when they went to auction.

Scanning the rest of the week's highlights, she noted that Christie's had also sold a letter written to Beethoven, the original copy of a poem that had influenced van Gogh, and a map of the Siege of Louisbourg. As she read over the auction details, she was amazed at how many custodians and janitors were credited with making these finds while cleaning out old closets and basements. There was so much buried treasure out there in the world, waiting to be discovered, which was why her favorite assignments sent her to the mustiest spaces.

The next auction she read about made her sit up. J. A. Stargardt in Germany was selling the original handwritten manuscript of *Mirabilis Liber,* an infamous compilation of prophecies from Christian saints and religious men published in France in 1522. The book was quite popular in its day. Nostradamus had relied heavily on the *Mirabilis* when composing his prophecies, and there was even speculation that Nostradamus' father, Jaume de Nostradame, was the anonymous compiler.

A flurry of articles about ancient manuscripts and prophecies was circulating because of the auction. As Semele clicked on them, her despondency over the theft grew. These articles should be focusing on Ionna's manuscript, not the *Mirabilis,* which had been read and analyzed around the globe countless times. She had imagined the manuscript's announcement would be met with this same kind of excitement, if not more. Now no one would even know it existed.

She wondered about who was behind the theft, and rage filled her. Again she questioned Raina's involvement. Were others at Kairos involved too? She had a hard time believing it. Nothing made sense.

With angry pecks at the keyboard, she logged into her office e-mail to see if any progress had been made on the investigation. There was no news. She had no idea how to talk to Mikhail about Raina, but he needed to know.

Mikhail had replied to her last e-mail. He was expecting her tomorrow morning at nine. They would finalize Beijing, and he had carved out an hour for them to go over specifics.

From his curt reply, she could tell he wasn't happy that she'd taken additional days off. Her flight to China left at noon on Sunday, which didn't give her much time. Raina had already forwarded her itinerary. Semele was scheduled to be away for a month with the possibility of an extension.

Raina's reaction to her new assignment was beginning to make sense. Raina wanted her out of the way. At the time Semele had thought she was jealous of her relationship with Cabe, but now she was certain it was because of the manuscript. Semele would have to talk to Mikhail tomorrow. That would be her only opportunity.

She was about to reply when out of nowhere a wave of nausea hit her. It was so intense she had to close her eyes.

Once the worst had passed, she went to the kitchen and drank a glass of water, hoping it would help. Then she checked the time and saw it was already seven. She hadn't eaten all day. Maybe she'd duck out and pick up some Thai takeout. Cabe should be here soon.

She grabbed her phone to order the food and noticed that she had a missed a call from him. He had left a voice mail too. Her stomach fluttered again and she had to sit back down.

How had she missed that? She was about to listen when her phone rang.

Raina was calling her.

Just seeing her number made Semele's nausea worsen. She answered the call, knowing that, whatever this was, it had to be bad.

"Semele?" Raina's voice was thick with emotion. She didn't sound like herself. "Cabe's been in an accident."

The Moon

It felt like all the oxygen in the room was gone. Semele couldn't breathe. She sat in shock in the waiting room of Lenox Hill Hospital. Raina was trying to tell her what she knew.

No one saw the plates. Cabe was outside Kairos when the car had come up right behind his bike. Witnesses said a man wearing a hoodie had taken Cabe's backpack and run off during the commotion.

Semele closed her eyes. *They wanted the cards.* She covered her mouth, about to be sick.

Raina was an absolute mess. Mascara ran from her eyes and her hands shook as she crumpled and uncrumpled a ball of Kleenex. "I can't believe. . . ." She trailed off.

Semele sat beside her, rigid. Raina seemed truly upset, but Semele could barely look at her. Wild thoughts were filling her head.

Had the man from the library done this?

What if Raina had been the driver?

Just who the hell was this person sitting beside her?

"How did you find out?" she asked Raina in a dull voice. "Were you with him?"

Raina shook her head. "He stopped by my office on his way out. The guard on duty at the front desk heard the accident and ran outside. . . ." Raina wiped her eyes, unable to continue. Her face was red and blotchy. "He said he was going to see you."

Raina looked her in the eye. "Did Cabe call you before he left the office? Did he say anything?"

Cabe had called her, but Semele had yet to listen to the message. She wasn't about to tell Raina that.

"Why?" Semele folded her arms. "Why do you want to know?" she asked, unable to keep the anger from her voice. She looked hard at Raina, trying to see past her weepy exterior and glimpse the truth.

Raina was involved.

Semele could feel it in her core. She saw the guilt in Raina's eyes, along with something that looked like shame. Semele was done pretending. "I saw you outside my apartment that day—with the man who's been following me."

Raina locked eyes with Semele, and for a moment, there was a bridge between them.

"Were you a part of this?" Semele gritted out the words.

It looked like Raina was about to answer when her phone beeped and she glanced down at a text. Semele watched her face go hard.

Raina shut off her phone. "I have to go." She stood up. "I'll let Mikhail know what's happened."

Semele grabbed her arm. "Wait." Raina turned back, her expression now turned to ice. Semele held her ground, her body quivering with fury and helplessness. "I know you know what's going on."

Raina laughed without any humor. "All I *know* is that someone has taken a personal interest in the Bossard Collection—and doesn't care who he destroys. Why do you think Mikhail wants you in China?" Raina looked haunted. "I didn't do this to Cabe. *You did.* You involved him and he's paying the price. Now"—Raina wiped her eyes, looking in control again—"I hate you as much as you hate me," she said and walked off.

Semele sat down in a daze. She listened to the clicking of Raina's heels and then the sound of the elevator doors as they closed. Raina was gone but her words lingered.

Semele stared at her phone, her mind barely able to function. She called Bren.

He answered on the first ring, a faint sound of hope in his voice. "Semele?"

"Cabe's been in an accident. We're at Lenox Hill." She completely broke down. "They don't . . ." She couldn't finish.

"I'll be right there." He hung up.

She needed to let Cabe's brother know. She had to search her e-mail to find his number. Her hands shook and tears blinded her vision, but she finally found it and got him on the phone. She could hear the panic in Oliver's voice. He was jumping in his car right away—it would take him two hours to get there from the Hamptons. She promised to call him if anything changed.

Depleted, she made her way to the ladies' room. She sat inside one of the stalls and bawled her eyes out. When she was finally able, she listened to Cabe's voice mail. She had to restart the message twice until she could stop crying long enough to hear what he was saying.

His voice bubbled with excitement. "Semcat, you're not going to believe this. This little family heirloom of yours is from about 45 B.C. And that's not even the most mind-blowing part. Remember how I ran your DNA? My computer matched your sample to the cards. It's in the paint! I double-checked the hypervariable control regions, and your DNA matches." He laughed. "Holy shit, right?" She could hear him getting on his bike. "This is amazing. My mind is blown. I'll explain everything when I see you."

She listened to the message again, feeling light-headed.

Her DNA matched the paint?

That didn't make sense. What was in the paint? Ancient DNA?

God, she needed to talk to Cabe. She never should have let him take the cards.

Thirty minutes later Bren found her in the waiting room. All the awkwardness between them evaporated as they embraced. Semele couldn't explain what happened without crying again. They sat together for hours holding hands.

"He's going to be okay," Bren would say every now and then. They both knew it was more like a prayer.

Semele wanted to believe. She wanted to take all the thoughts running in her head and annihilate them. The surgeries were still under way. Cabe could still pull through. She needed to think positively.

Around 11 P.M. Oliver walked in and Semele hurried over. "We don't know yet," she said and gave him a tight hug.

Oliver squeezed her back. "That damn bike of his." He broke down. "I told him not in New York."

His words were like a cold shower on her skin. Semele thought back to that day at the lab when she had noticed the bike. She had begun to sense the accident then but had repressed the thought, just like she had all her life.

And the dream. She'd pulled the dream of the bicycle accident from the recesses of her memory, but she hadn't understood the message. Then the real question came with punishing force: Why hadn't she allowed herself to foresee what would happen to Cabe? If she had, could she have saved him?

She put her head in her hands, unable to bear the truth. Because in the deepest chamber of her heart, in the darkest shadow, she knew her friend wasn't going to make it.

He wasn't going to live, because of her.

The Sun

Cabe remained in critical condition. He had survived the first round of operations, but he still had several more to go. The surgeons had to wait for the swelling in his brain to recede, and his doctors placed him in a medically induced coma for the time being.

Semele gasped when she saw him hooked up to so many instruments. She couldn't bring herself to sit beside him, afraid that, just by being near, she might make him worse. She didn't deserve a place by his side.

The accident had been intentional. There was no doubt in her mind. Someone had wanted the cards.

She needed to go to the police, but first she had to talk to Theo. She had a feeling he knew who was behind this. Her sense of helplessness was driving her mad.

She hovered in the doorway while Oliver sat beside Cabe and held his hand. Semele and Bren spent the early morning hours trying to comfort Oliver as best they could, bringing him water and coffee and Kleenex. There was nothing else they could do.

Then Cabe and Oliver's parents finally arrived from Santa Cruz, looking travel-worn and teary-eyed.

Semele felt like an interloper, or maybe the guilt was driving her away. She needed to leave before she completely broke down. She told them she was going home to shower. The excuses tumbled out of her mouth.

"Do you want me to come with you?" Bren offered. She saw

a glimmer of hope in his eyes, as if the night together had repaired the damage she had inflicted. He seemed willing to forgive her.

"No, I'll be fine." She watched his face fall.

"I'll call you at the first sign of change," Oliver promised.

Semele nodded and left, unable to fathom what that meant.

The minute she stepped out of the hospital she was hit by the sunlight. It woke her up and her mind burned with questions. Who had done this? What should she do? Ionna's cards were now missing—no doubt taken by the same person who'd stolen the manuscript.

She thought back to what Raina had said at the hospital. Mikhail's decision to pull her off the Bossard account was beginning to take on new meaning. He might be involved too. She didn't want to believe it, but she wouldn't know unless she confronted him.

For the first time Semele truly understood Marcel's message. *You can trust no one now.* There was perhaps one person left, but first he had to answer one pivotal question.

⌣

Theo was waiting for her when she arrived at the Four Seasons. He stood up when she entered the restaurant. The concerned look on his face almost did her in. He left the table and hurried over to her.

"Are you all right?" He touched her arm.

Semele shook her head, realizing she must look a mess. She hadn't slept in over twenty-four hours, and her face was surely streaked with mascara from her tears.

"We'll be dining in my room instead," Theo told the hostess, and guided Semele out of the restaurant by the arm.

The private elevator whisked them up to the thirty-second floor. The Royal Suite had two bedrooms, three and a half bathrooms, and a living room with an adjoining den. Semele glanced up at the ceiling and was momentarily trapped by a sense of surrealism. The chandelier was made of mother-of-pearl. What the hell was she doing standing under it?

She turned to Theo and saw his faced lined with worry. Clearly his actions were speaking for him now. He had come all this way to confide in her. Now she decided to do the same.

"Have you read the manuscript?" she asked him point-blank.

"Yes." His eyes said more than that. Semele could tell he had read it many times.

"Did you know my name was in it? That it was meant for me?"

"Yes," he said, searching her face. "There was a risk letting you take it back to New York, but the manuscript is yours. It's always been yours."

"But you were going to sell it."

Theo shook his head. "I was planning to pull it from the auction. I was trying to give you time to read it. The theft changed everything."

"Your father left me a note inside it." She could see the shock on his face. So Theo hadn't known.

She began to pace as the words spilled out of her. "I made a copy in secret. The night before I flew home, someone broke into my hotel and found the file. Then a man followed me back to New York." She turned to him. "I saw him at the library the *exact* moment Ionna warned me. It was like she knew, she saw me, and now . . ." She fought to retain control.

"Have you read it all?" Theo asked, taking a step toward her.

"Everything but the missing pages. You took them out, didn't you?"

"I had to," he admitted.

Semele stared at him in disbelief, unable to stop herself from erupting. "Why? It's a priceless manuscript!" She waved her hands around and yelled, "You don't just take a surgical knife to two-thousand-year-old parchment!"

"I had to!" Theo raised his voice too, matching her passion. "I couldn't risk anyone else reading those pages but you." He tried to explain. "I was planning to give you the rest before the auction. I wanted to give you time to come to terms with what Ionna had written. But I can see now that wasn't the best course." He rubbed his eyes, clearly tortured.

Just hearing him say Ionna's name, as if he knew her, made Semele's anger dissipate. She sat down on the couch and tried to calm down. "Your father gave my father a copy of the manuscript."

He appeared momentarily stunned. It seemed Marcel had kept secrets too.

"My father translated it." She pulled out Joseph's copy from her purse and showed it to him. "They were planning to meet the week he died."

Theo digested the news. It was clear he hadn't known. "I think it's best if you read the rest of the pages first," he said. "Then I'll explain everything."

Semele wondered what the pages contained that made him feel he had to defile the manuscript. She needed to tell him everything. "I have Ionna's cards . . . had them," she amended.

"You found the cards?" He looked taken aback.

"My grandmother left them for me. I gave them to a friend yesterday so he could examine them." Her voice began to quiver, but she had to let him know. "He was in an accident last night and the cards were stolen. He . . ." She couldn't go on.

Theo blanched at the news. He pulled out a handkerchief from his pocket and offered it to her. The simple gesture was so thoughtful it made her cry more.

"I don't know what to do," she said. "Should I go to the police?"

Theo seemed to be measuring his words. "I'm afraid these people are beyond the police."

"Who?" A heady rush of fear hit her. "Who are they?"

Theo walked to the metal attaché case on the table. He unlocked both electronic locks, scanning his fingerprint on a built-in thumb-pad. The case clicked open and he took out a folder and handed it to her. "I'll order up lunch and coffee while you read. The table is cleared for you in the den."

He had prepared the table for her, which meant he had already planned to bring her up here. What else had Theo Bossard been planning?

Semele felt as though she were being whiplashed, unsure of anything except that she had to read the pages. Without a word she went into the den and shut the door.

Her eyes stung from exhaustion and she couldn't fathom the idea of having to decipher more Greek, but sleep wasn't an option. She ducked into the bathroom to wash her hands so she could handle the parchment. Then she sat down on the couch and opened the folder.

Touching the leaves of the original manuscript again revived her and helped to bring her thoughts into focus. She hadn't read from the actual pages since she was in Switzerland.

Ionna's handwriting leaped from the page; every brushstroke was a living memory in motion. Semele traced her finger over the symbols with a feather-light touch and imagined Ionna at her desk, writing this to her—because Semele knew that Ionna *had* written this to her. And why Theo felt these pages had to be protected above all else was a mystery she was about to solve.

She opened her father's copy to the same page. He had translated Ionna's story word for word, and she could feel him with her. She wasn't sure she would have had the courage to know what happened to Nettie without him.

∞

From Leningrad Nettie went to Gorky by train with other prisoners. She had special papers tagged to her coat like a package. Her final destination paralyzed her with fear. She heard murmurs among the officers that Germany had broken their treaty and invaded Russia. Gorky was the country's military center. Why were they sending her there?

On the journey no one offered her food or water or a word of explanation. The other prisoners were too afraid to speak. There was a silent consensus among them: if everyone followed orders, this misunderstanding would be rectified and life could return to normal, because none of them deserved to be arrested.

At the train station in Gorky, a cluster of KGB and military personnel waited to take the prisoners that had been assigned to them. A KGB officer looked at Nettie's papers and gave her a sharp appraisal. She moved to fall in line with the others, but he put a hand on her shoulder.

"Not you," he said and led her to an army truck. He ordered her to climb into the back.

As the truck drove away, she could only see through a small slit of canvas. They crossed the Volga and headed down the riverbank through the open countryside. Nettie watched the sun set. The trip felt like an eternity, although they must have been driving less than two hours. They passed through a stone entryway with castlelike towers at the corners and into an enormous inner courtyard where the truck parked.

A soldier banged on the side of the car. "Out!"

Nettie parted the canvas and climbed down to find herself surrounded by clusters of old church buildings illuminated by industrial lighting. Soldiers scurried past in a den of activity. This old monastery had been converted into some kind of military complex. She saw rows of medical trucks parked next to a makeshift armory.

The driver led her to the nearest building. Rowdy songs and lewd jokes were coming from one of the rooms.

"Delivery." The driver stood in the doorway.

Inside a group of officers was eating dinner. Bottles of vodka littered the table. Nettie hovered behind the driver, trying not to be seen.

"Oh, look, the dessert has come," a drunken officer said, his glassy eyes fixed on her.

The driver waved the papers. "One of Evanoff's. She's off-limits."

The officer gave Nettie a cool assessment. "Pity." He turned to the most junior officer in the room. "You take her."

The young man got up from the table and took the papers from the driver.

"Come on." He led Nettie down an endless hallway and unlocked the last door, then motioned her inside.

Nettie stepped into the cell-like room. The door locked shut behind her. Inside it was nearly pitch black. Only a sliver of moonlight illuminated the shadows.

After a minute her eyes adjusted and she saw children sleeping on an assortment of old mattresses. There was no food or water, only a bucket in the far corner that seemed like it was being used as a toilet.

She made her way to the corner farthest from the door and curled into a ball on the floor. She hugged her knees to her chest and tried not to think of her family, of her life that was forever gone.

For years she had prepared for this day, ever since her first vision. She had replayed what she saw over and over in her mind so she could withstand the reality of it when the time came. Now here she was, living it out.

A girl's voice whispered in the dark. "You can share my mattress."

Nettie squinted. She saw a figure sitting up two mattresses over and felt her way toward her in the dark. She found the girl and lay down beside her, relieved to be near someone who meant her no harm.

"Thank you," she whispered back.

"I cried my first month here. There's no shame," the girl said.

Even so, Nettie vowed tonight would be the only time she would give in to her grief. She promised herself she would do what her grandmother said. Whatever happened, she must survive.

"My name's Liliya. What's yours?" the girl asked.

"Nettie," she said in a hushed voice.

"Why have they brought you here?"

Nettie hesitated, unsure how to explain and too numb to try. "I've no idea," she said instead. "Where are we?"

"Makaryev Monastery, but it's not a monastery anymore. After they kicked the nuns out, this place became an orphanage for a few years. I came here then."

"Why did they keep you here and not send you to another orphanage?"

"The experiments" was all Liliya said. "You'll find out soon enough. We should sleep." Before Liliya closed her eyes, she added, "Impress them and they'll let you live."

Nettie tried to sleep, but her mind couldn't rest. She was already trying to feel her way into the future. She would have to give up her secrets, to expose her gift in order to stay alive.

She had already seen Dr. Evanoff many times in her visions. He would stand before her tomorrow, giving her sweets to gain her trust. Soon he would take a keen and singular interest in her.

The next morning sunlight forced its way through the grime-covered windows. Nettie opened her eyes and met her fellow cellmates, all raggedy children with gazes that ranged from inquisitive to dull and apathetic. There were twelve of them. Liliya was the oldest, maybe sixteen or seventeen, and the youngest no older than five. Her tattered gown and shaved head made her look like a doll that had been stripped bare and forgotten.

The doors opened and a guard placed thirteen bowls inside, each with a piece of black bread, and thirteen cups of coffee. Liliya passed them out to the children who sat, surprisingly docile. Or perhaps they were just too weak to stand. Liliya handed Nettie her bowl.

"We get a boiled potato for dinner."

Nettie ate the bread and drank the tarlike coffee. She wished for water, but at least it was liquid. An hour later the young officer opened the door. It was the same man who'd escorted her to the room last night. He seemed to steel himself to appear authoritative.

He motioned to Nettie. "You. The new one."

Nettie stood to follow him, then looked back to Liliya for support.

"Impress them," Liliya reminded her softly.

The officer led her down the hallway and up the stairs. "You'll be meeting Dr. Evanoff today," he told her, as if that somehow made her captivity more tolerable.

Nettie didn't answer, but she knew this man from her visions too. His name was Lev.

Their footsteps echoed as he led them past a stretch of abandoned rooms, as if even God had turned his eye from this place. They stopped at an imposing door. Lev knocked twice, and a nurse in a crisp uniform stepped out.

"I brought the new one," Lev said.

The nurse's eyes raked Nettie up and down. "Good. That will

be all," she said in a clipped tone and moved aside for Nettie to enter. "Come, girl."

Nettie fought to keep her panic from rising. Her grandmother always used to tell her that no matter what happened, no one could ever break her spirit. "Pity your enemy," Kezia would say, "for hating him will bring only hatred in return." She would put her hands on Nettie's cheeks and look directly into her eyes. "And you know too much to hate."

Nettie held on to her grandmother's wisdom and carried it with her into the room.

The enormous space was once a gathering hall but had now been converted into a medical clinic. The nurse led her through a maze of partitions. Nettie spotted an operating table with surgical equipment to her left, and on the right, an unusual-looking dentist's chair with limb restraints and an overhead light attached.

The last partition had been sectioned into an office. Bookshelves lined the entire back wall. A row of wooden filing cabinets took up one side, and the other had a small table.

"Welcome, Nadenka," Dr. Evanoff said, calling her by her birth name. He stood up from the reading desk in the corner. He was wearing a doctor's robe with stains all over it, and his wild black hair sat like a crow's nest atop his thin frame. His eyes flared with excitement behind black-rimmed spectacles as he studied his newest ward.

"Turn around," he instructed, motioning his finger like a puppeteer.

Nettie did as she was told.

The nurse sniffed. "I'll get her a patient's robe."

Nettie looked down at her dress. It was the only thing left from her life before. Her mother had made it and she didn't want to take it off, but she was too terrified to speak.

"Come. Sit." Evanoff motioned to the chair near his desk.

Nettie passed by an open bowl of sweet pastilles and raspberry lollies perched on the corner of the table, and her mouth watered.

"Would you like one?" He held the bowl out.

She nodded and took one. "Thank you," she murmured.

"Manners. Good." He sat down across from her and waited while she sucked on the candy.

Nettie's eyes kept straying toward his, but then she would catch herself and look away. She could sense the threat behind the doctor's penetrating stare and soft-spoken voice.

"Do you know where you are?" he asked.

"An old monastery?"

He gave her a patronizing smile. "This is now part of a military research center, a very secret one. Do you know about secrets?" She nodded and he leaned forward, dropping his veneer of civility. "You are never to speak to anyone, not even the guards, about what goes on in here, or you will be punished."

"Yes," she whispered.

"Have you heard of psychic energy?" He started to pace, not expecting an answer. "It is the hidden force in the world, a force that the human mind can harness." He stressed his next words, rapping his hand on his desk with each one. "Equal. In. Importance. To. Atomic. Energy." He resumed his pacing. "With this force we can control the body and the mind, achieve telepathic or telekinetic power. See the past and the future."

He pivoted to her. "Few people are born with the ability to access the source—and those who can are most capable in childhood. You are one of my children now, yes?" He picked up the candy bowl and offered her another.

Nettie nodded, knowing she could do nothing but acquiesce. She took a candy, feeling sick to her stomach.

"Mathematicians deal with space, physicists deal with atoms, and I study the connection between the two, the human psyche."

He bent forward, as if to retrieve something, and what he pulled from his desk drawer made her entire body lurch. He had her grandmother's cards.

"These cards are quite interesting. I've been told that you use them. Yes?"

Nettie nodded again, unable to speak.

"I'm fascinated with any system of divination that helps us transcend the mind. Tarot cards, the *I Ching,* runes . . . they are all codes and we are the code breakers." He picked out a random card from the deck, *The Emperor,* and smiled. He obviously thought the card represented him. He showed it to Nettie to prove his point. He was the one in control.

"All symbols have power. They are the doorways that enable us to see beyond the illusion of time." He looked through each card as he spoke. "Predicting the future is a wondrous thing. Nature has its irreversible processes—an egg cracks and it is broken—which makes time seem to point only in one direction, ahead. While in fact, outside the physical laws of gravity and thermodynamics, time does not move at all."

Nettie forced herself to look away from the cards. She would not give him the satisfaction of seeing how much she wanted them.

"We have already discovered that quantum physics is predictive. On the subatomic level, effect can happen before cause." He placed the cards on the edge of his desk, as if extending an invitation. "People who see the future can engage their minds at the quantum level. What I want to know is *how.* How do you do it?" He motioned to the cards, offering them to her. "By helping me in my studies, you will avoid the gulag. Your family has not been so lucky. Yes?"

With shaky hands, Nettie reached out and took the cards. An immediate feeling of calm washed over her when she held them, as if her grandmother were there, and Nettie felt like she could breathe again. Fighting back the tears pooling in her eyes, she held the cards in her lap like a schoolgirl sitting at attention. She had to figure out how to keep the cards. She couldn't give them back.

The nurse entered with a tray. Evanoff picked up a large syringe and smiled. "You can keep your gypsy cards. They do not matter to me. What matters is the precious sight they inspire." He came toward her. "We must find out all about it."

Nettie quivered with terror. "Please," she whimpered.

"Hold still or it will hurt worse."

She watched the needle go into her arm. What scared her most wasn't the drug, but the fact he looked at her as if she weren't human.

For more than three years life was hopeless.

Every day the walls closed in tighter and the light grew dimmer. The children who shared the room with Nettie were all test subjects tethered together for the same reason. Like many scientists across Europe, Dr. Evanoff was attempting to grasp the para sciences—telekinesis, telepathy, precognition, and mediumship—in an effort to win the war. They were all mad dogs chasing the scent of something divine, because in this day, it seemed like nothing was.

From that first night on, Nettie shared Liliya's mattress. The two slept side by side with their backs against each other, as if to protect one another in their sleep.

"Are you awake?" Liliya asked one night. When Nettie answered yes, she asked, "Do you remember Harry Houdini?"

"Of course," Nettie whispered back. Though the magician had died the year she was born, everyone knew Harry Houdini.

"Don't you find it odd that he was obsessed with all things mystical, yet he didn't believe in mysticism? He spent most of his life trying to prove everything was a fraud."

Nettie waited for Liliya to explain. Liliya rarely spoke of such things—she rarely spoke at all. So Nettie knew whatever was on her mind had to be significant.

"Even though he said he didn't believe, he had his wife memorize a code with him. He said whoever died first was to communicate the code from the other side, to prove that life after death existed. All he wanted was the proof." Nettie remembered hearing about this story. Liliya went on. "A year later, a medium said he was in touch with Houdini—that his spirit could not move on and be at rest. Houdini was desperately trying to get the code to his wife. The man presented the code to her and it was correct. 'Tell all those who lost faith because of my mistake to grab hold of hope again, and to live with the knowledge that life is continuous. There is no death.'" Liliya hesitated. "He supposedly said that from beyond the grave. Houdini's code was ultimately declared a hoax, even though his wife had written a public letter defending it. People didn't want to believe. But I do," she admitted softly.

Nettie lay in the dark, oddly comforted by the story. Nettie didn't need a code. She didn't need proof. She could feel her grandmother watching over her now. Kezia had been the first to die. Soon all of her family would be with her. Nettie would be the only one left to carry their memories.

"What is your ability?" Nettie finally asked.

Liliya hesitated. "It's hard to explain."

"Try."

"When I close my eyes and focus, I can move out of the room with my mind's eye and see other things."

"What things?" Nettie propped herself up on her elbows, astonished. "You mean you can see through walls?"

"In a way. It's like I'm traveling without my body. But I can't go far." When she saw the look on Nettie's face she added, "Why are you so amazed? You're the one who can see the future."

"I didn't know that was possible. How far can you go?"

"I've never been able to see past the monastery."

"But you can go anywhere on the grounds?"

Liliya nodded. A dark look came over her eyes. "I've found it's best not to." They had heard the sounds at night, the screams of other prisoners. Evanoff and his team of scientists were not just experimenting on children. Nettie had caught glimpses of men and women undergoing brutal procedures.

"Will you follow me, when they take me?" Nettie asked. When Liliya hesitated, Nettie said, "It will make me feel better, knowing you're there."

"Will you tell me my future then?"

Nettie agreed and a pact was made. She pulled her cards from her pocket. It was her first time using them since arriving at Makaryev. Soon Evanoff would have her use them repeatedly.

Liliya looked on in fascination. "Is that how you do it? With fortune cards?"

"Sometimes," she said, although she didn't actually need them.

The future simply came to Nettie as knowledge. But the cards helped her focus her thoughts, and touching them made her feel closer to her grandmother. The parchment felt alive in her hands. Nettie believed that Kezia's stories about Aishe, Simza, and Dinka lived within the cards, that they carried their spirits. These cards had saved her life.

"They've been in my family forever." She held them out to Liliya.

Liliya gently took the cards. "They're so beautiful." She handled them like priceless treasures as she mixed the deck.

Nettie laid them out in a crosslike pattern, like she had seen Kezia do so many times before. The faces of the cards were faint shadows in the moonlight, reaching out like a hand to guide her.

When Nettie finished telling Liliya what she saw, Liliya looked at her with tears in her eyes.

"Did you lie to me?" she asked in a timorous voice.

Nettie shook her head, at first not understanding. "I told you what I saw."

"But does everything come true?"

"So far," Nettie said without any pride.

Liliya bowed her head and covered her face as she wept. For Nettie had not only told her she would survive this place, she had told her the names of her children and grandchildren. She said the next chapter of Liliya's life would be filled with love and beauty—two things Liliya had thought she would never know again. Her heart was filled with hope for the first time in years.

"Promise me you'll stay with me," Nettie insisted again.

Liliya could see the terror in her eyes and understood. Nettie had seen her own future. "What's going to happen?" Liliya whispered. Nettie could only shake her head, unable to explain. Liliya took her hand. "I'll stay with you, no matter what."

⌣

Liliya kept her promise even in the darkest days. Evanoff was consumed with unraveling the mystery of their abilities and he had singled Nettie out. He used various aids—barbiturates, sensory deprivation, electric shock—to force her into hypnotic states. He threatened to hurt the other children if she didn't cooperate.

Most of the tests occurred in "the chamber," an electromagnetically sealed, soundproof space. He would lock Nettie inside for hours, sometimes days. Her only respite was when he would go on trips for stretches at a time—to where, she didn't know.

Beyond the monastery's walls, battles raged across the Eastern Front as war consumed the country. Nettie stayed locked inside Evanoff's madness up until the end.

Out of any country in Europe, Czechoslovakia was the most advanced in researching the paranormal, like ESP and clairvoyance, and integrating it into their military operations. They had separated psychic phenomenon from the occult and designated "psi" experiences as part of accepted science.

Evanoff was driven by a maniacal desire to take command of the Czech research facilities. He traveled to the Ukrainian front to be there when Russia liberated Czechoslovakia from the Germans and brought his most promising psychics, including Nettie and Liliya, along with him.

⌣

Nettie had imagined the moment a thousand times, seen the events unfold like fractals coming into the sharpest focus. She had shared her vision with Liliya many nights during their imprisonment. Knowing this day would arrive was the only reason they had survived their time at Makaryev, the only reason they had survived what had been done to them.

The caravan of trucks was deep in the forest making its way westward toward Prague when the explosions occurred.

They were only a mile from the offensive front. The soldiers pulled their trucks over and climbed onto the hoods to look out over the valley. Nettie and Liliya sat in the bed of a covered truck, the last in the convoy. Lev, their guard, jumped out to join the others.

Liliya stared at Nettie, terrified. "When do we go?" she whispered.

"Wait," Nettie said, her eyes closed, counting the seconds. Minutes passed. Finally she heard a cannon sound far off in the distance. "Now," she whispered, and the two girls climbed out of the truck as quietly as possible.

They were almost to the trees when Lev turned around.

"Stop or I'll shoot," he ordered. But he had not yelled loud enough to alert the others.

Nettie turned to face him without flinching. Lev had witnessed Evanoff's atrocities. Every day he had escorted her from the children's room to those malevolent doors. Nettie had gotten to know all her captors at Makaryev, and Lev was the only one she was sure would seek absolution for his crimes.

Nettie and Liliya only had moments before another soldier would discover them. Nettie stared into his eyes and said, "When you die, the only memory from the war that will give your soul any kind of peace is the knowledge that you helped us on this day. You will never speak about Makaryev to your wife or children. You will die an old man with a clear mind. You will carry the screams, the fear, the darkness, as we will."

Every word echoed like a hammer. Lev listened, his eyes bright.

"Now let us live," she commanded.

Lev said nothing. He turned his back and climbed inside the truck. Nettie and Liliya ran toward the tree line, empowered, knowing that freedom was on the other side.

When they reached the trees, the leaves kicked up under their feet and the forest enveloped them. They kept running long after the sounds of the soldiers had faded. They stopped when they found a small stream and finally rested, heaving with exhaustion as they drank their fill. Nettie began to shiver, succumbing to the shock of their escape. The two girls gripped each other tight and held one another as they cried. They had just done the impossible.

Judgement

Semele set the pages down in disbelief. She hadn't finished reading yet, but she had realized something so shocking she couldn't continue. She walked to the main room and caught Theo pacing.

"Liliya was your grandmother," she said.

His eyes filled with immense relief that she finally understood.

"But how?" Semele asked weakly, sitting down on the couch. "How did you get this manuscript?"

Theo sat beside her and tried to explain. "Right after the Gulf War, antiquities began to make their way out of Iraq—a lot of them," he stressed. "Museums and libraries were looted. When my grandmother heard that a manuscript about an ancient deck of cards had been taken from Baghdad to Jordan, she had her buyer make an anonymous offer. My family paid a fortune."

Semele was well aware of the ongoing looting in the Middle East. Countless manuscripts and artifacts had found their way to New York, London, Moscow, and Rome. Most were sold discreetly. The trade in stolen items was the ugly underbelly of her industry, but to her knowledge, Kairos had always avoided handling questionable works. "Then she translated it?"

"No." Theo shook his head. "She waited."

Semele frowned, not understanding. "For what?"

"For me."

It took her a moment to realize what he was saying. "*You* translated the manuscript?"

He nodded. "Nettie told her I would."

Semele remembered Ionna's story. Nettie had told Liliya her future. Nettie had also told her tormentor, Evanoff, countless secrets while she was drugged. Liliya would have heard all of them. Her conscious mind had been with them in the room.

"Nettie foresaw that Ionna's manuscript would find its way to Liliya," he said.

"So Liliya knew she should look for it," Semele finished. The thought made her head spin. Where did the thread begin and where did it end?

"My grandmother was adamant that I learn Greek, and my parents supported the idea. I thought they were all mad collectors, that they were trying to turn me into one of them. I hated the lessons. You should have heard the arguments—and the bribes." He smiled, remembering. "My grandmother gave me the manuscript when her health was failing. When I finished the translation, I finally understood. The story was my grandmother's story too. She read my translation days before she died."

The look in his eyes made Semele's breath catch.

"Nettie saved my grandmother's life. My grandmother made a vow to Nettie that she would safeguard the manuscript until her heir could claim it. . . ." His eyes would not let go of her. "You."

Semele couldn't find the words. What he was saying was too much.

"My grandmother made us promise we would do everything in our power to deliver the manuscript safely to your hands. But I didn't know who you were, where you were. All I knew was your first name. When my father died he had already chosen a firm to handle the collection. Our estate attorney showed me the details. That's when I saw your name. I realized my father had found you."

Semele felt goose bumps traveling down her arms. For the first time she could see the Bossards and what they meant to her family clearly. Theo Bossard was the ally she hadn't known existed.

"I've waited years to meet you, Semele."

His confession left her speechless. The powerful connection she'd felt since that first day they'd met enveloped her in the deepest warmth.

Theo reached for her hand and leaned forward. His lips brushed hers with surprising gentleness, a tender introduction. She answered back with a feather kiss. Each touch was a question and an answer. Better than their stolen moment in the gallery, here he was telling her that he was hers.

The sound of her phone brought them back. Semele pulled away. "It could be the hospital," she said.

She grabbed her cell, catching it on the last ring. "Hello?"

As she listened to Oliver, her body began to tremble. He was crying. She told him she was coming and hung up, looking wildly around the room. "I . . . I have to go—the hospital. I have to . . ."

Theo was already on the hotel phone calling for his car. "I'll drive you."

She hurried to gather her things while Theo put the manuscript pages back in the case. They took the elevator downstairs without a word. Semele clutched her arms around her middle, as if it would keep her from falling apart.

A driver waited outside in a Land Rover. Theo helped her into the back and climbed in beside her. Semele kept her mind numb, trying not to think. She didn't want to break down in the car.

They were halfway to the hospital when her cell phone rang. It was Mikhail. She answered immediately.

"Semele, I just heard the news. I'm so sorry. I know how close you two were. . . ." Mikhail let out a pained sigh, followed by a long silence. "I know this is a difficult time. Can you call me this evening? I'm afraid we've been unable to push back the review in Beijing."

"You're kidding. I'm not going to Beijing," she erupted in disbelief.

"I need you to go to Beijing. There will be repercussions if you don't go," he said with unmistakable firmness.

"That doesn't matter to me anymore. I quit."

"You don't mean that. We can talk tomorrow—"

"I've made up my mind."

"Semele, I'm trying to protect you!" Mikhail shouted. "Get on the damn plane!"

His admission stunned her into silence. There it was. He knew.

"I can't do that," she said and hung up.

Theo gave her a questioning look.

"Kairos is involved with the theft." She drew her hand to her mouth, shaking with adrenaline. Mikhail had just confirmed his guilt.

Ten of Swords

A white sheet was draped over Cabe's body, leaving his face uncovered. He looked like an empty shell, the room around him just as barren. All the beeping monitors and machines had been wheeled away, replaced by silence and a family devastated in their grief.

Cabe's mother, Cora, saw Semele hovering in the doorway and jumped up to embrace her. "Oh, Semele."

Semele felt a dam break within her as she hugged Cora back. Cabe's father began to sob and Oliver had to leave the room. Cora pulled away to grab tissues. "I can't believe he's gone." She dabbed her eyes.

Semele couldn't tear her eyes away from Cabe. Her tears ran unchecked. She didn't hear when Cabe's parents told her they were stepping outside to give her a moment, and she didn't hear the door shut behind them.

She sat down in the chair beside his bed and put her head in her hands. The pain inside her unlocked with such force that she began to break apart.

"I'm so sorry. I'm so sorry" was all she could say to her friend. The grief—she felt as though she would drown in it, and the word Doreen had whispered in her reading came back to haunt her.

Despair. This was despair. Semele closed her eyes, unable to accept the reality around her. How could she not have foreseen this? Cabe had died because of her. With that thought, a feeling of fury consumed her. She would find who did this. Whatever it took, she would find them.

━

Oliver waited in the hallway, talking quietly on the phone. "Yes, I understand. Whatever you can do." He hung up, rubbing his eyes, and turned to Semele when she joined him. "That was the police. They're done interviewing witnesses. No leads."

Semele tried to process everything. She needed to talk to Theo before going to the police. Mikhail's words were still reverberating in her mind.

"Tell them to interview everyone at Kairos," she said. "There was a high-level theft there a few days ago. Cabe had just left work—"

She stopped talking.

A vase of rare striped roses in brilliant gold and scarlet loomed from the nurses' station at the end of the hall. The flowers looked just like the ones Rinalto gave Viviana at the ball.

What were they doing there?

Semele walked down the hallway in a daze. Oliver didn't notice her leave; he was already calling the police back.

The flowers looked strange in these surroundings, like an artifact from another time and place.

A page from Ionna's manuscript had just sprung to life.

"Excuse me. Who are these for?" she asked the nurse behind the desk.

It was the same nurse who was on duty right before Semele left this morning. "Your friend," the woman said gently. "I was going to give them to his parents." The phone rang and she turned to answer it.

While the nurse had her back to her, Semele snatched the card from the flowers and hurried off.

As she walked away, she opened the envelope.

The card contained two words, written in bold black marker:

Well done.

Underneath the message was a phone number. The handwriting bombarded her with its angry back-slant and hard angles. A man had written this, a very disturbed man. Semele knew the message was meant for her.

On the verge of hysteria, she put the card in her purse and headed to the lobby, where Theo was waiting. She found him sitting in the far corner. He read the panic on her face and stood up.

"Sem?" Bren had just walked through the doors and was heading toward her. He saw Theo approaching and looked from Theo to Semele.

"Bren, this is Theo Bossard, a client of mine." She hurried to make introductions, still reeling over Cabe's death and in a frenzy about the note. She needed to leave. Now.

Bren gave Theo a measured look. "And I'm Bren, an ex-boyfriend."

A rush of anger hit her and she lowered her voice. "Really? You're going to pull this now? Now?" Cabe was gone and she didn't have it in her to deal with this. She stormed toward the doors.

Bren looked taken aback and followed her. "What? You're just leaving?"

She whipped around. "I'm dealing with an emergency."

"Something more important than your best friend dying?"

Semele stepped back as if he had struck her.

"Sem, I'm sorry—"

"Don't." She held up her hand to stop the apology. "I'm dealing with something you can't understand. Go help Oliver. I'll be back when I can."

She was holding a note from the killer. He had the cards and the manuscript. Now he wanted her to call him.

"Sem, wait!" Bren called out.

Semele didn't turn around. She got into Theo's car with Theo one step behind her.

When the doors closed, she showed Theo the note. He agreed she should call the number from the hotel.

Semele stared at the handwriting the whole drive there. The writing told her what she already knew. This was the mastermind, the monster behind it all, and now he was coming after her.

King of Swords

When Semele and Theo got back to his suite, they each picked up a phone so Theo could listen to the call.

A man answered on the first ring. "Very good. You found the flowers."

"Yes." Semele could barely get the word out.

"Speak up, dear girl. It's so lovely to finally hear your voice." His breathing sounded labored and he spoke with a slight Slavic accent. "I'm so sorry about your friend. But you see, studies have shown precognition is triggered by tragedy more than anything else. Death being the utmost one, I'm afraid I had no choice. Is Theo there with you?"

Semele couldn't speak. She was about to be sick.

Theo answered. "I'm here."

"Ah. The little ones together at last. Nettie and Liliya protected you well, but all good things must come to an end." He stopped to take several wheezing breaths, then continued on. "You've suffered a great loss, Semele. But monumental achievements require sacrifices and so far you've achieved nothing."

Semele's entire body was shaking. "What do you want?"

"I now hold several things that are quite dear to you. Two items you know about and one is a surprise. Your chances of retrieving any one of them depend on how well you do on the test."

She was too petrified to speak. An image had already formed in her mind.

"Why do you think the tarot starts with *The Fool*?" he asked.

"Because we are all fools traveling on a road with no beginning and no end. Do you have the courage to be the fool, Semele?"

"Please. Just say what you want from me."

"Every human has intuitive abilities. We see images in clouds, rocks, tea leaves . . . or cards. Symbols are the signposts, all around us if we are looking. *Pareidolia* is the ancient Greek word for this phenomenon, but you can see so much more. How good is your sight, dear girl, when there is something—or someone—depending on you?"

He hung up with a click.

Semele clutched the phone. Terror gripped her and she prayed she was wrong. In her heart she already knew what he had—who he had.

Theo didn't understand. "What did he mean?"

She turned to him, her heart full of hopelessness. "My mother."

Message to VS—

    Beijing canceled.
    Friend is dead.

Reply from VS—

    I sent flowers.

Message to VS—

    Does this not mean anything to you?

Reply from VS—

    More than you know.

Ace of Swords

On the drive to New Haven, Semele tried calling her mother's cell and the home line countless times. With every minute that passed, her panic intensified.

When they arrived, they found her front door unlocked and the lights on. Unfamiliar music was playing on the stereo. Helen's purse sat on the kitchen counter next to her keys, and her Audi was still parked in the driveway.

"Mom?" Semele cried out when she saw the dining chair on its side.

The signs of a struggle echoed through the room.

A coffee cup lay shattered on the floor, and a bowl of cereal was overturned on the table.

"Mom!" She sank to her knees.

Theo put his arms around her. "We're going to find her. Semele, listen to me. We're going to find her."

For minutes she cried gut-wrenching sobs, unable to calm down. She had reached her breaking point.

"We're going to find her." Theo kept saying the words until they registered. Slowly, she calmed and attempted several deep breaths. "That's it," he encouraged.

The house phone rang.

"It's him." She sprang for the phone. "There's another in my father's study. Hurry!"

Theo raced to the other room.

Semele snatched up the receiver and yelled, "Where is she?"

"Good." The man chuckled. "Good! You are awake now. I can hear your passion." He took a labored breath. "It's amazing what losing your friend has done for you so quickly. You knew right away to run home to Mommy. Bravo," he taunted her. "But isn't this what you wanted after you found out the truth about your birth? To give Mommy away, so that she'd know what it was like?"

"No." Semele's voice trembled.

"Intuition can be triggered by many kinds of crises, Semele. My father, in his extensive studies, found a threat to a loved one most effective. But such parameters are hard to duplicate in a laboratory. So I've got you out in the real world, where I can conduct this experiment with high confidence. And the messiness of life can do wonders. Like your father, his death was the tragedy that started you on this yellow brick road. How I've enjoyed watching."

Semele slid to the floor.

"I saw her that night at the gala—your mother. We met at the bar. Such a lovely woman, Helen. I got her and Joseph drinks. She was so talkative, never suspecting what I had done."

Semele covered her mouth to keep from crying as she listened to his confession. He went on.

"But she couldn't have saved him that night, dear girl. Yet you still blame her. I think it's because, deep down, you blame yourself for not foreseeing his death. Time to own up to the truth, because there's no hiding it from me."

Semele gripped her stomach.

"Nettie chose your parents quite carefully, knowing her granddaughter would grow up under the guidance of a brilliant scholar who would encourage her to embrace history and challenge her to learn Greek until she could read it as well as he could. Nettie wanted you to find Ionna's manuscript and recognize yourself within the pages. But I knew that Joseph Cavnow would have only gotten in the way now. His part had been played, and strokes can happen at any age."

Tears fell from Semele's eyes as she listened to him.

"You were lucky, though. The two of you shared a close bond while he was alive. I was my father's worst disappointment."

It took all her will to speak, but she had to know. "Who are you?"

"Don't you know?" When she didn't say anything, he laughed again, drawing heavily on his oxygen. "That's the shame of family secrets. You're supposedly one of the great seers, the Keeper of the Gift. Your grandmother grasped this power but did not live to pass her insights on to you. Pity, since you're the one who will need them most. For years you've been unwilling to believe. And without belief you have nothing."

He hung up again.

"Wait!" she yelled, but he was gone. She slammed down the receiver. "Dammit!"

She took the phone and threw it across the room. It hit the wall and crashed to the floor. She sank down to her knees crying, now a heaving mess.

She tried to think—she had to calm down. This psycho had her mother and God only knew what he was going to do to her—what he had already done.

Theo hurried into the room with a strange expression on his face.

She looked up, meeting his eyes. "What?" She gritted her teeth in desperation.

"What he said . . . about his father. Nettie and Liliya were always afraid Evanoff would find them, even after they created new identities for themselves in Austria."

"Now his son has found us." Semele's body tingled. She knew that was the answer.

The song playing on the stereo looped and the same music filled the room again. The melody pulled at Semele and surrounded her.

Then the harp solo began.

She stood up, feeling light-headed.

"This music . . . ," she said, approaching the stereo.

Her parents never owned music like this. And suddenly she understood. "He left this music when he took her."

She ejected the disk. The CD wasn't from a store. It was burned from a computer, and on the disk was a handwritten message.

Very good. Now find her.

Seeing his handwriting again gave her chills. Unlike the note at the hospital, this message included a lowercase y and g that showed a glaring personality trait: the letters had been written with a straight line down and an angry slash to the side instead of a loop. This was a rare occurrence that experts called the Felon's Claw, and it showed a dangerous propensity for manipulation only seen in extreme criminals.

Semele stared at the note a long minute, the music filling the silence. She turned to Theo with utter certainty.

"Aishe played this music. He wants me to go to Paris."

Page of Swords

Theo chartered a private plane out of Tweed New Haven Airport, a Challenger 300 that sat eight. They would arrive at Paris–Le Bourget Airport in less than seven hours.

Semele tried to dissuade him, but Theo insisted on taking care of their travel, explaining it was the quickest way to get there. The flight attendant gave her a glass of cabernet before takeoff, and the wine helped calm her nerves. Semele hadn't slept in over thirty-six hours and needed to rest. But before she could she needed to know what had happened to Nettie and Liliya after they escaped.

"They went to Austria?" she asked Theo, who was settled into the seat across from her.

"To a displacement camp." He nodded. "Camps were set up all over Europe. People flooded in from the Nazi concentration camps. Many survivors traveled from camp to camp looking for their families, but Nettie and Liliya didn't have anyone. They stayed at one camp and pretended to be sisters under a false name, keeping mostly to themselves. They were terrified of being discovered."

Semele couldn't begin to imagine. "How long were they there?"

"A year. Things changed when they started helping a group of nuns who ran an orphanage in Vienna. Working at the orphanage was a kind of self-imposed penance. My grandmother told me she and Nettie suffered terrible guilt from leaving the other children behind at Makaryev. It's something that stayed with them the rest of their lives."

Theo grew quiet a moment, remembering. "My grandmother never spoke of her time in Russia. I never even knew about our heritage until I translated the manuscript and my grandmother told me her story. That was days before she died."

Semele hung on to every word. Part of her was jealous that Theo had gotten to hear the story firsthand.

"When the orphanage started planning to open another location in Switzerland, Nettie urged Liliya to go and start a new life there. She moved to Lake Geneva and met my grandfather a year later."

"And what about my grandmother?" Semele asked, her voice barely audible.

"Nettie stayed in Vienna. The orphanage was right next door to an academy for the blind, where she met your grandfather, Elias."

Semele's stomach did a somersault when she heard her grandfather's name.

"He was a music professor there. He taught the children how to play instruments reading Braille. He was blind too, and an incredibly empathetic teacher."

Semele began to form a strong picture of Elias in her mind: tall and elegant, even in a simple suit. His hand held a cane with the long, graceful fingers of a pianist, and he carried himself with a quiet countenance.

"Nettie wrote to Liliya that, in many ways, Elias could see more than she could. After they married, they stayed in Vienna and had one child—your mother." Theo hesitated. "Carina."

Carina. At last her mother's name. Semele held her breath, waiting to hear more.

"My grandmother said Nettie let her run wild. When she was a teenager Carina would stay out late or not come home at all.

She had a new boyfriend every month." Theo added, "That is, according to Nettie's letters."

Semele raised her eyebrows. At least she knew who to blame for her rebellious streak. If her mother were here she would say it all made sense. "So they were in Vienna all this time?"

"No." A shadow passed over Theo's face and he looked away. "Someone pushed Elias in front of a moving train when he was on his way home from the academy one day. They never found out who did it. But Nettie believed his death was connected to her past at Makaryev—that Evanoff had found her. She went into hiding and forced Carina to come with her. Carina was two months pregnant with you, no longer with the boyfriend, and distraught over her father's death. Nettie told her they were going to the States to get away, to heal. So they came to New York."

Semele's hands gripped the armrests. She was glued to every word.

"Carina was an actress in Vienna and had ambitions of being on Broadway. She wanted to stay in New York and pursue that dream, but . . ." He hesitated. "She died giving birth to you."

Semele could feel a part of her pain release, like a breath held too long and at last expelled. Her mother hadn't abandoned her. She had died giving birth.

"I'm sorry," Theo said softly.

Semele cleared her throat, her voice husky from the emotion swimming inside her, the anguish, the guilt, the relief of knowing the truth. "You found all this out from the letters?"

"Liliya and Nettie wrote to each other for years. The last letter my grandmother received was right after Carina died. Nettie was still in New York."

"Do you still have them? The letters?" What she wouldn't give to read one, to see more of her grandmother's handwriting. She felt an ache for Carina, Elias, and Nettie—the family she would never know.

"I've never seen them," he said. "But we can look." Theo reached out and took her hand.

Semele looked down as Theo's hands joined hers. They were a "we." She knew that now. They had been long before they ever met.

Queen of Pentacles

Mme Helvétius' salon had been at 24 Grande rue d'Auteuil, but it was no longer there. Though she was originally buried in her garden as she had wished, she had been moved to a nearby cemetery years later. The village of Auteuil was in the 16th arrondissement of Paris, nicknamed "le 16e," a prestigious area filled with mansions, historic buildings, and museums.

Semele looked at the building that stood in place of the old salon and felt as if she'd time-traveled to the future.

"My mother's not here," she said.

"Are you sure?" Theo pressed.

Semele shook her head. She wasn't sure about anything. She thought the harp music had been a sign to go to Auteuil, but maybe they were meant to go to Russia instead, where Aishe and Andrej had settled.

She closed her eyes and tried to focus, her body tingling as she entered a state of hyperawareness. The stories of the past that Ionna had so vividly painted for her flashed through her consciousness, filling all her senses. The blue of the salon lived in the sky, the smell of the lime trees in Mme Helvétius' courtyard wafted down the road, and the sound of Aishe's harp echoed in the air.

The music grew louder. It sounded like the song playing at her mother's house.

Semele opened her eyes and did a full 360, trying to pinpoint where it was coming from. "Do you hear that?"

"Hear what?" Theo looked around, clearly not hearing anything.

"Listen." She began walking, following the melody. Every note beckoned her like a finger pointing the way.

A soft breeze picked up and the song intensified.

Semele realized it was Simza's song, "Find Me in the Wind."

She took off, running down several blocks, turning corners and dodging pedestrians. She didn't hear the angry swears or Theo's apologies in French as he tried to keep up.

She raced to the end of a street corner and found a lively outdoor market under a canopy of century-old buildings.

What had brought her here? Had there been music? Because she couldn't hear it anymore.

Theo caught up with her, slightly out of breath. "What is it?"

Semele shook her head, her senses still tingling. Then she looked behind her. There was a vendor with ornamental seashells for sale, including jewelry and purses made out of shells.

Semele walked over to the table, to the shell that was calling her, a spiraling conch with a blue iridescence that dazzled in the sun.

She lifted the shell up to find her mother's pearl necklace resting underneath. Her body froze in shock, and for a suspended moment she was unable to accept what she was looking at. This was the necklace her father had given her mother on their anniversary, the one with the heart locket. Now here it was under a seashell, on a table in the middle of Paris.

And she had found it. What was going on?

The vendor was a young Rastafarian preoccupied with his iPad. He finally looked over. "Mama, that necklace is brand new. I sell it to you for two hundred euros," he said in French.

Semele picked up the pearls, too distraught to speak. Theo didn't need to be told whose necklace she was holding.

"How did you get this?" he demanded in French.

The vendor shrugged. "Guy sold it to me. You want it or not?"

The man seemed oblivious; he was just a pawn. Theo quickly

paid him and guided Semele away by the arm. She was in a daze as she held the pearls in her hand, barely able to walk.

Her cell phone rang. She answered with shaking hands, already knowing it was him. "Hello?"

"Dear girl, you're not trying hard enough," he said.

"Yes, I am!" Semele couldn't stop the shrill in her voice. "I found the necklace!"

"Please don't delude yourself. You're running out of time."

Desperation, adrenaline, and fear hit her in a heady mix. She started to shake. "Then tell me where you are and we can end this game."

"Oh, this isn't a game, Semele. It's empirical evidence."

Semele had no idea how to handle this deranged man. She just didn't want him to hang up. The more he talked, she might get a clue to her mother's location. "So this is an experiment?"

"All psychic events are fifty percent coincidence and forty-five percent fraud, fabrication, and selective memory. That leaves five percent that cannot be explained. A five percent we call the 'something else.' *You* are that something else."

"I'm afraid you've got the wrong person."

He chuckled. "And yet you found the necklace," he said, throwing her words back at her. "Do you know what entelechy is? The sense the acorn has of the oak tree. Sixth sense is actually the first sense, but our conscious minds keep us separated from it. Entelechy is the first step to remembering."

She had no idea what he was talking about. Her rage and frustration got the better of her. "You crazy bastard! Where is my mother?"

"About to die."

Her breath caught. "No, please," she begged, desperate.

"Did you dream about your father before he died? Call him without knowing why? You've had dreams all your life. Make no mistake, future events cast their shadows."

"Please don't hurt her." She began to cry. This man would kill her mother if he had to. She was certain.

"That's not up to me. I'm afraid talent such as yours requires extraordinary proof."

"You don't need proof."

"Oh, the proof is not for me, Semele. It's for the world. Right now I have you under a microscope. But soon I'll be sharing you with my colleagues. There are many scientists back at the institute in Moscow who will be so fascinated to know that Nettie survived the war after her escape from Makaryev and that her granddaughter is alive. Nettie's case study is infamous. But it will be nothing compared to yours. Your life is about to change, dear girl."

Click. He hung up.

Semele looked to Theo helplessly. "He wants to experiment on me like they did to my grandmother." She put her hands on her head and sobbed. She didn't care that she was standing on a street corner in Paris having a complete meltdown. "I can't do this—oh my God."

"Semele," Theo said firmly, taking her hands. "Look at me. He's trying to get in to your head. Don't let him. You're going to find your mother. Believe that."

Semele fought the hysteria threatening to overwhelm her.

"Go over everything he said," Theo suggested.

She could barely recount the call. Evanoff had stolen Nettie's life, and now this man wanted hers. Her terror threatened to suffocate her until finally something inside her pushed back, a survival instinct, a will to live, and it turned her fear into anger. The spark that was lit at Cabe's bedside fanned into a flame. She would not let this man harm her mother.

The pearls grew warm in her hand. "He left this under a seashell for a reason," she said. Then she realized. "It's the shell that holds the message. The shell."

She and Theo looked at each other and said the answer at the same time.

"Simza."

Two of Cups

Within hours Semele and Theo were en route to Admont, Austria, the place Simza had stayed every winter and the only place during her lifetime where she could be found on the *lungo drom,* "the road with no destination."

Semele looked out the plane's window, unable to fathom that the madman who had killed her father and Cabe now had her mother. She didn't know if she could survive losing all of them.

She thought back to the day before her father died. She really had called him on a whim, just to say hi. Right before they hung up he had said, "There's something important your mother and I want to tell you when you take the train up next week."

She hadn't thought much of it at the time, but looking back she knew he had meant to tell her the truth about her adoption. He and her mother had gone to their favorite neighborhood restaurant the night before, a little Italian joint, and discussed it at length; her mother had cried as they walked home hand in hand. Semele had no idea how she knew all this, but she did. She could see the moments strung together like a movie of someone else's life.

"What are you thinking?" Theo asked her, taking her hand.

"Just thinking about my father." She looked over to him, not sure how she could explain.

"Was he the one who encouraged you to work in antiquities?" he asked.

Semele gave him a sad smile, knowing he was trying to distract her. "I was fascinated by handwriting as a teenager. I used to study it as a hobby. For a while I thought about becoming a professional graphologist after college." She shook her head at the idea. "I used to give all my friends handwriting analyses."

"I'll have to show you mine," he offered and kissed her hand.

"That's not even negotiable." She couldn't wait to analyze his handwriting, to see which way his words slanted, how sharp the angles were, how hard he pressed to impose his will on the page. Every little idiosyncrasy had meaning.

"So that led you to manuscripts?" His finger absently stroked her palm in a soothing motion.

She nodded, staring at their joined hands. "I'd request volumes of antique letters from Beinecke to study the penmanship, but over time, I became more interested in the letters themselves." This had prompted her interest in paleography, the study of ancient writing and manuscripts. Slowly, she began to find her niche. "My father was the one who suggested I learn Greek my freshman year in college."

"Funny, that . . ." Theo murmured, shaking his head.

Now she wondered if Nettie had asked Joseph to make sure she learned Greek, or if his encouragement had happened naturally. With both of them gone, she would never know for sure. He had kept her mother in the dark; had that been to protect her? How much had Nettie told her father?

Semele was surprised by how much she wanted to talk about her parents. Since her father's death and learning about her adoption, she had tried to shut them out. Now the memories were flowing freely again.

"While other kids were at the beach, we would visit libraries and tour collections on our vacations."

"Where you saw countless treasures," Theo surmised with a smile.

"The earliest known copy of the *I Ching,* Shakespeare's First Folio, the Magna Carta, the Dead Sea Scrolls. We went every-

where. The Bodleian Library, the Vatican Library, the Biblio-
thèque Nationale . . ."

"So you traveled the world and stayed home for college?"

"I moved to Michigan for graduate school, Ann Arbor," she
pointed out. Ann Arbor had the largest collection of ancient
papyrus and parchment in North America and a top conservation program. That program had launched a career in which she
handled every kind of rare book and manuscript—early printings,
maps, atlases, heirloom books, and first editions. She'd worked
with libraries, museums, and private collectors around the world.
Looking back, she could see that everything had led, one stepping-
stone at a time, to finding Ionna's manuscript, and Theo.

Strange how she and Theo barely knew each other and yet
she felt as if she'd known him forever. Now they were forty-
one thousand feet in the air, on their way to find the place where
her ancestors once lived. She had the seashell from Paris in her
purse and the necklace in her hand. Ever since she had found
her mother's pearls, she had yet to let them go.

Message from VS—

> You're angry.
> One day you'll understand.

Reply to VS—

> Flying home tomorrow. We can talk when I arrive.

Message from VS—

> No longer there.
> I love you.

Reply to VS—

> What have you done?

Ace of Wands

In Admont, Theo followed two steps behind Semele with the faith of a shadow. He never said a word except when he thought her frustration got the better of her. Then he would put a soothing hand on her back and murmur words of encouragement. She walked the streets of Admont for hours with no idea what she was looking for. The beauty of the historic town, the glistening Enns River and Ennstal Alps were all but lost on her.

They finally stopped at a café. Theo bought them coffee and a sandwich and they sat outside. She tried to eat, but the bread tasted like cardboard, the coffee like bitter water.

Theo's cell phone rang. "What did you find?"

Semele watched him as he listened intently.

"Good. We're in Admont. I'll let you know if we need anything else." He hung up and explained. "I had my IT specialist see if he could dig up anything else on Evanoff—my guy's thorough. Evanoff did have a son, Viktor Salko, born during the war. He changed his name." He noticed the color drain from her face. "What is it?"

Semele knew that name.

"He's on the board of directors at Kairos." She had never met him, though. He lived in Moscow. Now he was out there somewhere with her mother.

She scanned her surroundings, beginning to panic. Was her mother in Russia? Had they been looking in the wrong places?

She took in the family crossing the street, the little girl holding her father's hand, and the two men on bikes whizzing past her, bringing a fresh breeze in their wake. Then her eyes landed on the man reading a book at the table next to them. He was wearing a Geiger watch.

"The watch," she whispered. "That's it."

If synchronicity was life's way of sending messages, it had just delivered several. She looked down the street and found the shop right away. There was a reason this street, and this corner, looked so familiar. When she was nine, her father had bought his Geiger while they were here on vacation. Semele remembered waiting outside the shop, eating ice cream with her mother. Afterward they had toured the library at Admont Abbey.

This city was the place she had dreamed about that night back in New Haven. She and her parents had been in the car heading *here* when they saw the accident. Her heart began to race with urgency. "I need to go to the library."

Theo's eyebrows rose, but he stood up with her and they quickly left the café.

The library was only meters away. All day, she had been walking in circles around the one place she needed to be.

⸻

The Admont Abbey Library was an exquisite masterpiece of Baroque architecture and the crown jewel of the city. The moment Semele stepped through the doors, a wave of calm descended on her. Every stone and piece of marble had been laid for one purpose—knowledge. Semele could feel its light shining all around her.

She remembered her visit to the abbey as a child with crystalline clarity. She had broken away from their tour to go look at the books.

One particular book had drawn her attention, and she'd pulled it off the shelf. The text was in German so she hadn't understood the words, but the pictures of children from World

War II had mesmerized her. They were black-and-white photos; the children dressed in old-fashioned clothes that were ratty and torn. Aid workers, nuns, and nurses stood hovering in the background of each of the pictures, but it was the children whose images broke the heart. They stared straight into the camera lens with eyes that said they had suffered too much.

Her father had found her sitting on the floor next to a bookshelf.

"What are you doing?" he whispered. When he saw what she was holding, he took the book away. "Darling, this is a historical archive, very precious. We can't touch."

"What is it about, Dad?"

He glanced at the title with raised eyebrows. "Orphanages in Austria During the War." He returned the book to the shelf and led her back to the tour. Semele had thought about those pictures for weeks afterward. It was as if every image had been imprinted on her mind.

The moment returned to her with a strong feeling of déjà vu, showing her a memory carefully preserved within these walls. In that book was a picture of Nettie standing with the children in front of the Engel House Orphanage in Vienna.

Semele had found her grandmother twenty years ago, and she knew without a doubt it was the place where her mother was being kept.

Ten of Wands

They were en route to Vienna when Viktor called again.

"Semele, I grow tired."

"We're coming! We're on our way to Engel House. Is my mother all right? Let me speak to her!"

Viktor ignored her. "Your words fill me with profound relief. Your little field trip took longer than I expected. We are almost done with this phase of the experiment. Now don't let us down, dear girl. And come alone, just you two, or you will never see your mother again. You have until sunset, and then she dies."

He hung up. Semele began to shake.

Theo looked over at her in concern. "What did he say?"

"My mother's there. We don't have much time."

～

The next few hours were an intense whirlwind. Theo chartered a helicopter to take them to Vienna, brushing off Semele's lingering concerns about the cost. "Your family is my family," he insisted.

Semele was choked with gratitude and could only nod her thanks. It was true that Nettie and Liliya had become sisters at Makaryev, bonded by something stronger than blood. It was a bond that would survive well beyond their deaths.

Semele looked out the helicopter window at Vienna, a sprawling city of over a million and a half people, where her grandmother had spent her years after the war. This was where her mother was born.

Another feeling of déjà vu enveloped her.

The dream.

She knew this moment—had experienced every second before—a moment so powerful, the memory had imprinted itself in her mind before it ever took place. Just as she had in the dream, Semele leaned over and kissed Theo.

He pulled away, their lips inches apart, and whispered, "You know you're not going to get rid of me after this."

She kissed him again as her answer, for the first time understanding her gift. Her intuition had been her shadow all her life, always there, always a part of her, speaking to her in dreams and thoughts and inklings. Because of the darkness surrounding her now, she could finally see.

The Engel House orphanage and the Academy of the Blind stood side by side, and when she saw them, Semele felt like she was meeting her grandmother and grandfather for the first time.

The orphanage was boarded up and had long since shuttered its doors. Several buildings on the block had construction signs posted outside them, and the four-story building that had once housed the orphanage would likely soon be refurbished.

The heavy wooden doors resembled the entrance to a church. A bolt and chain wrapped around the wrought-iron handles like a snake. It had been cut by someone to allow them entry—an ominous welcome.

Semele felt like she'd located a needle in a haystack. She couldn't believe she had managed to find her mother in all of Europe with the sheer force of her mind. She watched Theo take the chain off, and her pulse began to race. Whoever—whatever—was waiting on the other side of those doors terrified her.

"Semele, you can do this," Theo said.

She nodded, knowing she had no choice.

Ionna had foreseen these events and had tried to prepare her: *The road must be walked whether you are ready or not.*

The World

Semele stepped inside and let her eyes adjust to the darkness. The boarded-up windows allowed in little light. She moved through a hallway filled with cobwebs and dust. Cracks riddled the walls like veins.

"Apropos. Don't you think?" Viktor's voice rang out from a room up ahead. "Nettie's sanctuary for years. The place where she tried to forget. The place where you must remember."

Semele walked toward the voice, leaving Theo to follow behind.

She found Viktor Salko in what could only have been the library, though its bookshelves were now empty. He sat on the far side of the room in a high-back chair, like a king at court waiting for an audience. An oxygen tank stood next to him and a mask covered his mouth. He had thinning hair, and a pained expression dulled the hawkish lines of his face; he wore an ivory suit with a matching shirt and tie, as though he were dressed for a wedding . . . or a funeral.

Her eyes landed on her mother.

Helen was gagged and strapped to a chair twenty feet away. Wires had been hooked up all over her body and led to a strange contraption at the center of her chest. Semele had no idea what she was looking at.

Her mother's eyes watered when she saw her, and she tried to call out through the gag. The sound brought Semele out of her stupor and she took a step forward.

"That is close enough," Viktor ordered in a sharp voice. He had taken off his oxygen mask. "Stand still and let me look at you."

Semele glared at him, her body emanating cold hatred.

"I'm quite impressed you made it in time. It seems my experiment worked." He laughed in relief. "I really wasn't sure it would."

"Why are you doing this?" she demanded, her voice unsteady.

He answered her question with a question. "What battles intuition? The haze of doubt, the fog of the mind. You have been in a fog all your life. Now it is time to step out of it if you want to live."

Semele's body quivered. Every atom within her vibrated with fear and anger.

"Your grandmother hid you away, and your intuition was buried with the help of a workaholic father and an alcoholic mother. I've been attempting to liberate you. It's been very difficult."

"We know who you are." Theo spoke up, his voice strong.

"Do you really?" Viktor gave him a condescending smile. "My father was a brilliant man. But he was also cold, with no understanding of life or the human heart. I understood why Nettie and Liliya ran away. My father spent years trying to find them."

He turned to Semele. "For him, Nettie was the key to unlocking a future world. He never stopped looking for her. I used to dream that I too would meet her someday. I so wanted to."

Viktor drew from his oxygen. "You see, you belong to that rarest group of observers—the truest of seers—who can take the full measure of life, filled with all its infinite probabilities, and see the future that has been set forth. Just look at Ionna's manuscript. She didn't write to Nettie. She wrote to you—she singled you out because you are next in line. Her heir. Your sight, your ability has even greater potential than your grandmother's."

Semele shook her head in denial.

Viktor's gaze shifted to Theo. "Tell me, did you inherit Liliya's gift?"

Theo didn't answer, but his eyes hardened.

Semele looked to Theo in surprise. She had never considered that he might possess Liliya's ability.

Viktor chuckled. "It is no matter to me if you can see through walls." His eyes searched Semele's again. "Nothing in the world is more powerful than time. It is the only thing that controls us, until we can grasp how to break free." His next words made her freeze in terror. "There is a device strapped to your mother, and the countdown has begun. I will leave it up to you to free her. Me, I am happy to watch. My greatest triumph would be to see you become your ultimate self or to die trying."

"You're crazy," she whispered.

"Am I?" Viktor shrugged. "I've gotten you this far, dear girl, when no one else could." He held up Ionna's cards and the manuscript. "Are you really going to let her down?"

Semele instinctively took a step toward him.

"For the first time since Elisa died so tragically in Gundeshapur, the cards, the manuscript, and the heir are all united. It has taken a long time for this day to come. If it wasn't for me, Ionna's legacy would have been kept hidden by both of your fathers, and you would continue to forget who you are."

Semele found her voice and hated how weepy she sounded. "Why are you doing this? What do you want from me?"

"Your best self." He motioned to her mother. "You have the power to save her."

"I don't . . . I can't. . . ."

"Yes, you can!" he erupted. "Do you know there are premonition bureaus around the world where people send letters filled with visions of the future?" He waved his arms like a conductor. "Do you know how many letters arrived before the *Titanic*? Before Kennedy was assassinated? Human consciousness *knows*. The mind *can* travel time. You have no idea how many others with the sight are out there. But you have the power to write more than a mere letter." He took a long breath from his oxygen tank and gestured to her, indicating that she could approach her mother. "Now prove me right."

Semele couldn't move. She shook her head, unable to understand what she was supposed to do.

"Go on," he said, his voice muffled behind the mask. "The bomb will explode soon. At least say your good-byes."

His words galvanized her. Semele rushed to her mother and knelt at her feet. The contraption looked even more alarming up close. "There are too many wires!"

"And not many minutes to spare," Viktor taunted. "Get to it."

The timer strapped to Helen's chest ticked as the seconds moved forward in a relentless march. They had less than fifteen minutes.

Tears ran down Helen's face as she whimpered behind the gag.

"There's a pair of wire cutters under the chair," Viktor called out. "Cutting one of them will disarm it, or so I've been assured by the Russian gentleman I paid an exorbitant sum to assemble it."

Semele found the wire cutters beneath her mother's legs. "This is insane! I have no idea what to do!"

"Because you're still trying to live in the moment instead of looking beyond it. Effect *can* precede cause. So the question is, do you survive this test or not? Do you live or not? The answer is quite simple. Don't think! Use your ability."

Semele's pulse skyrocketed. Her heart hammered in her chest so hard she thought it might give out. She was sure she was going to hyperventilate. She watched the counter tick down. . . .

13:46 . . . 13:45 . . . 13:44 . . .

"Oh my God, oh my God . . ." Free-falling into panic, she surrendered completely to its grip. All rational thought abandoned her.

She was about to die.

"Semele!" Theo's voice sounded dim, far away, and beyond her reach.

"I can't." She could barely hold the wire cutters, her hands were shaking so hard.

The timer continued: 12:59 . . . 12:58 . . . 12:57 . . .

"Yes, you can. I know you can," he said with utter conviction.

She stared at the tangle of colored wires. There were at least thirty.

With an anguished yelp, she cut the white one.

The device beeped, stopped, and then continued its countdown.

12:00 . . . 11:59 . . . 11:58 . . .

Viktor let out a strange, childlike giggle. "Oh my, that was a misstep. Please don't do that again."

The minutes belonged to him.

He's not afraid because he's already dying.

10:40 . . . 10:39 . . . 10:38 . . . 10:37 . . .

The first thought came to her swiftly, followed by the answers. *Viktor had lured her to Kairos years ago to keep her under his watchful eye. But then he had found out he had terminal cancer last year. Detected long after the jaundice set in, it had already spread from his pancreas. His impending death made him accelerate his plans. He sent Raina to New York to have a tighter grip on Mikhail. Then he put his final experiment into play. He even—* She stopped.

"My God," she whispered. "You killed Marcel too." Theo's breath caught. She closed her eyes, and as if her mind was a camera, a shutter clicked and opened up the past. Images of Viktor's life flowed through her like an electric current.

"How fascinating." Viktor leaned forward, understanding written on his face. "You can see the past as well? Well, well, this is a surprise."

Semele could only stare at him, her mind convulsing with what she now knew. "You're Nettie's . . ." She couldn't say the words, couldn't vocalize what she had seen.

"Her son?" His voice rang out in the room. "Yes. Very good." Viktor clapped. "Very good! Brava! This is so much more than what I had hoped for. You have retrocognition as well."

Semele didn't understand what that meant. She only knew what she saw.

"You are correct," he said. "Nettie was my mother. A part of my father's great experiment. He impregnated her in the hope that his child would inherit her abilities."

Semele closed her eyes, revolted, unable to look at him.

Viktor drew on the oxygen again and coughed. "Much to my father's disappointment, it turned out that Nettie's gift was carried by the X chromosome. I could never have what you have. My inability infuriated him and he despised me." He shook his head sadly. "My father died an old man with so much rage he didn't know where to put it."

Semele tried to process what she had seen of Viktor's life. In the Soviet Union, when Stalin died, paranormal studies came into the mainstream once more and research institutes cropped up all over the country. Viktor worked at an institution in Leningrad, funded by the arm of the Kremlin, studying everything from mind control and electromagnetism to telepathy and ESP. Like his father, Viktor believed reality could be controlled by psi energy. Before perestroika and the dissolution of the USSR, Viktor led some of the most ambitious psychic warfare experiments ever conducted—experiments that were still ongoing. The USSR may have dissolved, but the institutions had not. Like the race to put a man on the moon, Russian scientists were working toward being the first to control psi energy, and Viktor was at the helm. He even married a Russian medium, Natalia Burinko, to try and harness her power.

"Raina," Semele muttered, still in shock.

"My daughter. Your cousin." Viktor nodded.

5:49 . . . 5:48 . . . 5:47 . . .

He gave her a smile. "She doesn't know about you. I withheld my knowledge of your existence and the parameters for this experiment—even from my colleagues—in case I failed. My daughter only knew there was a very special manuscript I needed for one last study before I retire. She was most upset with me over your friend's death." He waved his hand in the air as if it was not a concern. "You can console each other when I take you to Moscow. I'm afraid there is laboratory work to be done—but first we must survive today."

He motioned to her mother. "I've never risked my life for my work. But what is that silly American saying of yours? 'Go big or go home'? Now you have five minutes to live."

Semele looked at the timer, unable to focus. She knelt down, spreading her hands on the ground in defeat.

Theo took several steps forward, trying to reason with Viktor. "You don't have to be like your father. Let us go."

"You know I can't do that, Theo." Viktor wagged a finger at him. "We must make sense of her power. Harness and control it. Nettie was my father's legacy never fulfilled because the war stood in his way. Semele will be mine."

Viktor paused to draw from his oxygen.

"Through her"—he gestured to Semele—"we can learn how the sixth sense functions on the quantum level. We can decipher time, and then one day transcend it—imagine that." He closed his eyes in exhaustion.

Theo saw his chance and hurried to kneel beside Semele, raising her up. "Semele. Look at me." He held her face in his hands. "You can do this. Focus on my voice."

"I'm sorry," she whispered, blinded by tears. "Go. Don't stay here."

"I'm not going anywhere. Nettie believed in you. Ionna believed in you. *I believe in you.* Look at me, dammit!"

She raised her head and tried to focus on him.

"Now breathe with me," he ordered her, taking deep breaths and forcing her to do the same. He was willing all his strength to her with every breath he took.

She stared into his eyes and saw within them the light of his unshakable belief. She breathed with him, feeling their bodies become in sync, their spirits join.

In a single inhale she saw the broad expanse of their lives—the years, the love, the joy. She saw their children. Those seeds were already planted in their future, already growing. A sense of wonder filled her. Like a key in a lock, the vision freed her. Her mind tunneled further until she was no longer in the room.

She entered a new dimension where the past and future stretched in every direction, a vast constellation of knowledge where every moment in time became one. Ionna had known she would break through. She had foretold it in the pages. Theo had read them, and he had drawn on Ionna's faith to help her get there. Semele could feel Ionna with her, their minds now connected beyond space and time. Ionna had been tasked by Wadjet to be the bridge, to connect her to a deeper antiquity. Semele saw the lives of her ancestors as clearly as Ionna had. Together they formed an unbroken chain leading her to where the Oracle of Wadjet stood waiting—her first grandmother—the world's first seer and keeper of the record. Her written words had been destroyed by time, but they still lived on in her descendents, and they always would. Wadjet's power would be carried on forever.

Semele's awareness returned to the room.

0:20 . . . 0:19 . . . 0:18 . . . 0:17 . . .

She took the cutters and cut the wire.

The clock stopped.

Theo grabbed Semele and squeezed her tight. "You did it." There were tears in his eyes as they held each other.

Viktor applauded and let out a chilling laugh. "And so they lived. What a joyous success. Truly, truly, truly!" His arms opened wide in the air with triumph, like a runner crossing the finish line.

Semele could see his eyes glistening with tears and arrogant pride. He was mad, his mind twisted like brambles.

"Now!" he clapped hands together. "Now we can move forward in the light. You made it, Semele. We did it."

Semele didn't acknowledge him. Instead she began untangling

her mother from the wires. The bomb hadn't been fully dis-armed, and only Semele knew they had three minutes before it detonated. They needed to get out.

Theo could read the panic in her eyes and rushed to help her.

Her hands fumbled with her mother's bindings. "Hurry," she whispered under her breath. "It's still going to explode."

Viktor continued talking. "It's amazing the things we do for our parents. I think Nettie and my father would be so proud. My only regret is that you removed pages from the manuscript." He looked accusingly at Theo. "I must know what Ionna thought about this little ending I'd devised. Or perhaps I should say be-ginning. Because that's what I've given you, dear girl." He gave Semele a tired smile. "Just think, maybe in a thousand years you'll be the myth. You'll be remembered as a goddess like Wad-jet, and our whole struggle to see through the fabric of reality will be ancient lore."

Semele tried hard not to listen to him as she undid the last binding. Helen fell forward. Theo caught her and helped her to stand.

Semele turned toward Viktor. "Give them to me," she com-manded, motioning to the cards and manuscript.

"I'm afraid I can't do that. These are mine. I quite earned them. Don't you agree?" He grinned.

"Please," she begged.

The cards were in his hands. Semele wanted to race across the room and rip them away. But she had run out of time.

"Semele!" Theo shouted.

"You can leave these walls but you can't escape me," Viktor said. "Our work here today is far from over, Semele." He pointed-edly quoted Ionna's words back to her. "You and I are entangled."

Semele stared at him, transfixed. He was a monster like his father, another Evanoff playing God in a laboratory.

"No, we're not," she said, shaking her head with finality.

For a split moment she saw the surprise in Viktor's eyes before she turned and ran. There would be no time for him to call Moscow, no time to reveal her identity to anyone. She had seen their futures; he had no idea his was ending.

"Run!" Semele grabbed her mother's hand and dragged her out of the room. Theo ran behind them with his arms spread wide to shield them from the blast.

They had barely made it to the street when the building exploded. The force launched them several feet forward and they hit the pavement in a broken huddle.

Semele's ears were ringing as she watched flames engulf the orphanage. She felt her body being pulled up and into the strength of Helen's arms around her. "I'm so sorry. I'm so sorry" was all she could say to her mother.

"Oh, baby. Oh, my baby," Helen cried, holding her tightly. Then she opened her arms to Theo. "Thank you," she said between sobs.

Semele closed her eyes, feeling herself wrapped in their embrace. They had made it. Viktor was gone, taking with him a nightmare that would remain forever in the past. Now Semele knew how Nettie must have felt kneeling by the river.

Time seemed to stop and hover around her as she watched the orphanage burn. Her eyes met Theo's, her heart breaking when she saw the resignation in his. Theo had known the cards and manuscript wouldn't survive. Ionna must have written it in the pages. Every ancestor who had held those cards, along with the memories Ionna had recorded, were lost forever. Semele had finally found her roots, and now she was being forced to witness their destruction. If only she had touched the cards when she'd had the chance, studied them more. She had thought she had all the time in the world—and she had also been afraid.

The wind danced and blew heat on her face, making her look away from the fire.

She saw the corner of a card peeking out from her mother's shirt pocket. Semele reached for it with shaking hands, unable to believe it.

One card had survived.

A sob caught in her throat. The physical chain between her and Ionna hadn't been completely broken. Here was one last link. When Semele held the card in her hand, her tears flowed free.

Ionna had given her *The World*.

The Lovers

When they arrived back in New York, they felt like soldiers returning from battle. Helen and Semele got their own room at the Four Seasons for several nights. They wanted to be close to Theo and to each other. Semele realized she needed to have her mother nearby. They held hands and embraced often, assuring one another that they were safe. The rift between them had begun to heal. Their love had seen to that.

Semele tried to explain everything that had happened, and only because Helen had witnessed and experienced Viktor's madness could she believe it.

Theo put in the proper calls to start the investigation on Viktor Salko and Kairos, as well as Mikhail and Raina. He discovered that Viktor was already under investigation for having ties to the Russia Mafia. Raina was missing and Mikhail had flown to St. Petersburg. Theo doubted either of them would set foot in the United States again.

Semele couldn't believe she had been working in the devil's den—Mikhail had reported directly to Viktor and must have known Viktor's intentions and tried to protect her. Cabe had lost his life because of them, and before him, her father and Marcel.

She thought of Raina.

Raina had known Viktor wanted the manuscript, but she hadn't known his whole plan. Yet she must have wondered at his obsession with Semele, even felt threatened by it.

Semele wanted to believe that Raina had nothing to do with

Cabe's death, that she was innocent. But she couldn't explain away her fury. Raina had Evanoff's and Viktor's blood in her veins. Maybe one day she would meet her cousin and know the truth.

⌣

On their second evening back, Semele and Theo were alone in Theo's suite. He pulled her close, wrapping her in his arms.

"So," she asked point-blank, "do you have your grandmother's ability?"

A gleam entered his eyes. "You're not the only one who inherited something." He had the audacity to smile.

Semele could only gape at him. "You're telling me you can see through walls?"

"It's called remote viewing," he said, as if that made it any more normal. "Basically, I can focus my mind and leave my body to travel to other places."

"What kinds of places?" Her eyebrows shot up. "How far?"

He considered the question. "Over land, pretty far. Oceans, not so much."

Oceans? A giggle welled up inside her. His mind could fly like Superman, and she could see the future and the past. Now weren't they the perfect couple?

"It's easier if I have a specific place—or person—I'm trying to connect with." He looked away, as if he was divulging an embarrassing secret. "I wanted to tell you sooner, but I couldn't find the right time."

She wondered if he had tried to "connect" with her at the château, and she realized that the day she had seen him meditating, he had actually been doing something else.

"When I was working in your father's gallery, you were watching me, weren't you?"

"Who wouldn't watch you?" He kissed the tip of her nose playfully.

All that time she had thought he was indifferent to her, when the opposite had been true. "That's how you knew the maid was in there?"

He nodded, looking pleased with himself. Semele began to get the full picture. "And do you normally sit on your bed shirtless?"

"Only when I know you're snooping around my house."

"I wasn't snooping!" She swatted his chest. "I was coming up to the library to see the *Orbis Sensualium Pictus*. Is it really an original?"

His lips found hers again. "Come to Switzerland with me and find out."

She kissed him back. "I could do that."

"The gallery and the collection are yours."

At first she didn't think she had heard him right. "But the collection's gone."

"I canceled the auction after the theft. Fritz"—he said the name with relish—"had to ship everything back."

She shook her head in amazement. "You were never planning to sell anything, were you?"

He gave her a sheepish grin. This entire time he'd been jeopardizing his collection just so she would read the manuscript.

"You realize you put priceless manuscripts at risk just by shipping them." She didn't know whether to throttle him or kiss him.

"Good thing they're back." A wicked light entered Theo's eyes. "The gallery does have my favorite table in the house."

She laughed as her hands trailed under his shirt and up his back, delighting as he shivered at her touch. "I happen to be partial to that table too."

"Semele." The way he said her name undid her.

He picked her up and carried her to the bed. They made love, holding hands, their bodies like two flames wrapping around each other. Together they were *The Lovers*, two halves made one, personified in the cards and in the stars forever.

Queen of Cups

Theo had left the manuscript's missing pages on the table in the den for her to read when she was ready.

She sat down and stared at the parchment. How was it possible to feel so much joy and sadness at the same time? Here was the last of the manuscript, the only remaining imprint of Ionna left in the world. Semele only had these few parchment leaves and one card, but at least she had something.

She picked up the surviving card—*The World*. There was a miniature painting of a naked woman dancing in the center of the world holding a wand in each hand. She traced her fingers over the paint; the Syrian artist whom Ariston had commissioned was a master.

She wiped the wetness from her cheeks and leaned forward to read the last of the manuscript. Her name was written across the top of the parchment in beautiful flowing script:

Semele

I can feel your eyes upon me as I write these last pages.

In the final days of my life, I am happy knowing these words have become our shared dream, tunneling us through the past and future so that we might meet in the middle.

Do not mourn the loss of the cards or my words. All things must return to the chasm. It is the symbols that will carry our stories, for they are the infinite doorways that can hold lifetimes.

Wadjet tasked me with teaching you. That was the riddle I had to solve. She is both of our grandmothers, and these pages are the leaves of our family tree.

The key I found in my mother's jewelry box was meant for me, passed down by ancestors who came before me. It is a key I will take to my grave. All the doors have been unlocked, and now your journey begins as mine is ending.

I will die giving birth to my daughter in a few weeks' time. I have seen her life go on without me, as I have seen my descendents walk their path to you. Ariston cried like a child when I told him, but he had to be prepared. I convinced him to abide by my wishes after I'm gone. He too had read the Oracle's scroll and knew what she had asked of me.

When I die Ariston will commission the best artist in Syria to replicate the cards using paint created with my blood. With so many years between you and me, and time waging its war to keep us apart, the truth of my body will be the only way to ensure you recognize who you are.

Now that you have accessed your power, you will need to learn to make sense of your abilities, or the visions will become as fleeting as the dreams we have in sleep. Always remember the answers come not from the rock, the teacup, the shell, or the cards. The answers come from you.

You may not believe me now, but you will become a greater seer than me. You will see farther into the future than I ever could. When the day comes, you will decide what words to leave behind. You will find your reader and you will love her as I do.

I have seen nature in its vast expanse. I have seen civilizations crumble, heard the reverberations of history as time folded and unfolded again. I have seen shooting stars rain down from heaven, watched war and destruction blacken the earth, and I have seen love revive us. I have peered through time and past its many veils to find *you*.

One of my cards, *The World,* was left behind for a reason. It is the symbol of the soul becoming conscious of the divine. Now let the world embrace you.

Author's Thanks

This story could not have been told without a childhood adventure that I must thank my parents for letting me take—a seventh grade summer school trip to France with my French teacher (and her tarot cards). Thank you, Mom and Dad, for letting me go, and to Mme Hobson, wherever you may be! Also loving thanks to Emma Ferguson for years later trying to show a very inquisitive teenage me how to read tarot.

If cards were to represent people, then my agent, Brianne Johnson, at Writers House would be *The High Priestess*. Bri, thank you for your passion for this story from the get-go, for your insights and for steering the ship yet again. My editor at Picador, Elizabeth Bruce, would have to be *The Magician*. Elizabeth, thank you for taking on this story and being such a vital partner in the creative journey—how I have loved working at your table again.

My deepest gratitude to Stephen Morrison and the talented people behind the curtain at Picador: managing editor Kolt Beringer; production team Lauren Hougen and Vincent Stanley; copyeditors Kate Davis and NaNá Stoelzle; VP of Marketing and Sales Darin Keesler; and Shannon Donnelly and Molly Fessenden in marketing; executive director of Publicity James Meader and my publicist, Isabella Alimonti; Devon Mazzone and Amber Hoover for handling subsidiary rights, assisted by Naoise McGee; interior designer Jonathan Bennett; and LeeAnn Falciani for designing the book's cover.

A very special thanks to Laura Chasen for her line edit; tarot consultant Bakara Wintner for providing invaluable insight for the story and the cards; my sister, Alexandria, and my brother Bart and his wife, Kelsi, for the brainstorming session before I began writing; and many thanks to Simon Goltsman, Julia Burke, Farah Bullara, Monika Telszewska, Sue Ebrahim, Charlotte Schillaci, Robin Wilson, Bruce Brenner, Paul O'Brien, and Nadine Nettman for the research assistance and encouragement along the way.

I read numerous nonfiction works in my research and I'd like to give a special mention to Dean Radin's book *Entangled Minds* and Michael Dummett and Ronald Decker's two books, *A Wicked Pack of Cards: Origins of the Occult Tarot* (with Thierry Depaulis) and *A History of the Occult Tarot*. They were an invaluable resource, as well as tarot scholar Mary K. Greer's website. For a full list of the selected bibliography, please visit my Web site. (Any factual errors found within these pages are my own.)

I also could not have written *The Fortune Teller* without first discovering a gem of a group, The Manuscript Society. I joined the society during my quest for research and they provided a wealth of information. Special thanks also goes to forensic specialist Gabrielle Weimer for her guidance; Mark Beaulieu for his ancient maps and logistical assistance; and Christine E. McCarthy and Raymond Clemens at the Beinecke Rare Book & Manuscript Library for graciously answering my questions.

Since publication of my first book, *The Memory Painter,* I've been filled with such gratitude to all the booksellers, librarians, reviewers, bloggers, and fellow authors who have supported me, and I am forever grateful to authors M. J. Rose, Katherine Neville, Charlie Lovett, and Anne Fortier. Many thanks to my foreign publishers; the American Booksellers Association; the FF&P and LARA chapters of RWA, the ITW Debut Program, MWA, SWFA, and the Historical Novel Society; Terry Gilman at Mysterious Galaxy Bookstore; as well as Julie Lawson Timmer, Alex Dolan, and Stacy Wise for their support. My continuing thanks to Lucy Stille, Judith Karfiol, web designers Jess Foster and Mike Ross, and JennKL Photography.

To all my friends and family, my husband and son, Kurando and Kenzo, your love and encouragement keep my world spinning. To my readers, you have my infinite thanks. I wish you all a wonderful journey on the Wheel of Life.